LET THE
Bloody
CHASE BEGIN.

Covet

BEAUTIFUL SINNER SERIES

ELENA M. REYES

SUMMARY:

I'm a sinner. A criminal.
The beast that will never let her go...

Everyone in England knows the name Casper Jameson. They know that I'm a cruel bastard with no regrets when it comes to dealing with those that cross me. They fear me; a man with no morals. Someone cold—without a weakness.
Until I see her...

She's beautiful; a delicious temptation standing across the room from me without a care. Unaware of the danger that lurks—that this man wants to consume her.

I'm going to own her every sigh.

Taste her every moan.

Drown in her pleasure.

Let the bloody chase begin.

Beautiful
SINNER

You're my ambrosia. My Heaven and Hell.

ACKNOWLEDGMENTS

Before we get to the book and its yumminess; I need to thank a few people that I adore:

C.M. Steele: Thank you: For always pushing me when I want to be lazy. For challenging me to be better. For letting me bounce ideas off you and for getting on my case when I fall behind. You're my favorite *chica* and I love you.

K.I. Lynn: My Boo. My wifey. It's crazy how we met all those years ago and the paths our lives have taken. And yet, no matter where we are or what we're doing, I know that I can always count on you to stop me from jumping off the ledge or calm me when I'm freaking out. Thank you, babes. I love you with all my heart.

Mary B. Moore: I love you and I can't thank you enough for all my British tips. You're one of the sweetest people I know, and I'm thankful to have you as a friend.

Marti Lynch: You have the patience of a saint and I love you! I thought for sure this time you'd kill me, but like always, you calm my fears and work with my crazy schedule. Thank you. THANK YOU. This book wouldn't be ready without your amazing work.

T.E. Black: YOU ARE AMAZING! Love my new covers.

Heather and Aliana: Thank you so much for coming in to Beta read this book for me. I appreciate you both so much and I'm blessed to have such amazing women on #TeamReyes. Love you to the moon and back.

Elena's Marked Girls: You guys keep me going and always give me a reason to smile. Thank you for everything. For your unconditional support and encouragement. Please know that I love you—that you mean everything to me.

Tiffany Hernandez: Girl, you came into my life like a beautifully organized tornado and I adore you so hard for it. Thank you so much for all the hard work, for keeping me on track, and stepping in without prompting. It's because of you that I'm able to focus all my energy on writing and getting things done. You ROCK!

Hubs and Kiddo: You are my heart. My entire world. Everything I do, I do it for you.

Chapter 1
CASPER

"SCREAM FOR ME," I whisper against her soft skin, licking the few beads of sweat that roll down the back of her neck. Tasting. Savoring this decadent little body that caught my bloody attention just a mere three hours ago. "Say my name, love."

My demand is met with more wetness. She's swollen; ready to be fucked like the horny little beauty she is. Like my perfect dirty fantasy.

This woman is a temptation I shouldn't imbibe tonight, but I ignore rationality and indulge. Take without concern for the state of my business or my family. With her skin against mine, I don't give a fuck about the gun shipment we lost forty-eight hours ago because of some bloke's incompetency. Because of his greed.

A reality that is dangerous. For myself. For her.

I should be ending that man as we speak, but I'm not. I should be spilling his blood as payment, but I'm here, and God himself couldn't pull me away from *Aurora*.

"Please," the beauty against me mewls, and I throb against her core. I focus on her wetness as it rolls down my girth, caressing every solid inch as I slide between soft, bare lips. Thrusting twice, I spread her slickness while my pierced head rubs against her clit from behind.

Her back is to my chest. Her body against the solid wood of my door.

She's made me break my rules.

I brought her home. For her, I've behaved like the good little boy I'm not, until the moment we stepped foot inside my manor. Now, all bets are off. Moreover, waiting to reach my bed when my hunger's near demonic is impossible.

My need is almost debilitating. It controls me.

And I'm going to make sure she feels me for days after.

This little one-off has me throbbing, beads of pre-come mixing with her slick cunt as I pull back from between her thighs. Thighs that still hold her silk panties midway down, limiting her move-ments. Her little black dress, the kind that doesn't allow for a bra, is thrown somewhere behind me along with my clothes.

In our haste, everything was ripped off almost savagely and left in tatters.

"Oh God." Another whine comes from the back of her throat, a needy little sound that travels straight down the center of my spine and settles on the tip of my length. Her hips undulate, trying to rub faster—to create the friction that I'm denying her. "Don't toy with me. I need you to...*fuck!*"

"Louder," I say with a groan, slamming inside in one fluid thrust and then pulling back slowly, just far enough so the head touches her entrance—caressing the tiny hole that clenches in search of more. "I want everyone on this street to hear whose cock you want." Pressing my lips against the back of her neck, I inhale deeply, pulling the soft scent of cherry blossoms with a hint of vanilla deep into my lungs. "Say it, sweetheart. Tell them who you're crying out for."

And I'll gift her my cock, as much as she wants it tonight, but first I want to breathe in her need for me. I'll feed off that desperation that showcases our humanity, giving in to its animalistic nature.

"If you don't move, I have a hand—" She doesn't finish, choking instead on her cry of pleasurable pain as I snap my hips forward. My strokes are relentless, almost punishing, but my sweet victim takes it with her head thrown back, meeting me thrust for thrust.

Grabbing a fistful of dark hair, I turn her head toward me and take her lips in a heated kiss. It's sloppy and hard for her to concentrate, but I don't slow down. Instead, I enjoy how lost she is to the pleasure.

It's intoxicating. Delicious.

I revel in her cries. How her fingernails dig into the wooden door. How she rises onto the tips of her toes as I hit a particular spot deep inside when I change the angle of my thrusts.

"What were you saying?" I taunt, mimicking her American accent. There's a Chicagoan lilt to her tone that I find sexy and ironic; she's from the same city I spend a couple of months in each year. *Dangerous indeed.* "You were threatening me?"

"Who the hell...*oh God!*" she cries out, a sweet sound I revel in as I hold her in place, fingers digging in to the point where I know she'll walk away with my mark. And I like the thought. More than I should.

It's frustration and want and everything we shouldn't crave, but motherfuck, it feels good. Too bloody good. Being buried balls deep as her body trembles in my hold, fighting to move and reach the orgasm she so desperately yearns for, is nothing short of nirvana.

Releasing her hair, I bring my hand down between us and smack her clit with two fingers.

Her reaction is automatic; pussy clenching and body arching against me. A harsh shiver runs down her body and into my own, causing my eyes to close.

The feel of her walls choking my cock is heaven.

The screams of pleasure are my brand of heroin.

"You are going to be nothing but trouble," I hiss from between clenched teeth, my eyes on the way her arse bounces against my thighs. It's obscene, the sight of her tight body taking everything I give her. Skin slapping against skin, I fuck her with no remorse. Without reprieve. "Such a beautiful chaos."

"Please, Casper." A gorgeous surrender. Her eyes meet mine from over her shoulder, heavy-lidded and hazy with lust. "*Fuck*, I'm so close."

She's a vocal one, and I love it. Love each sound that slips past that pouty mouth, a delicious shade of red that I've kissed off and spread down her cheek.

Aurora looks like the sweetest mess for me. Like a bad decision under the design of a priceless jewel.

Like a gem. The kind I'll covet.

"You want to come?"

"I need—"

"Me." It's a growl. An angry sound that erupts from deep within my chest and I pause my movements, keeping myself deep within her walls. "Say it. You need me to make you come."

"I do." It's low and breathy, and my balls grow heavy with those two words.

However, I need more. It's a nagging little voice in the back of my head that demands I make this right.

I need to see her.

Watch her face as she comes.

A hiss escapes me as I pull out, my hardness immediately missing her warmth, but I grit my teeth and before Aurora can protest, I flip her position. On her next breath, I have what's left of

4

her panties in my fist and I slam her back against the door with those perfect thighs around my waist.

Her sweet pussy sits just above my cock. Her juices coat the head in a soft caress.

"What are—"

"Hold on to me." That's the only warning I give her, letting go of the ruined fabric as I drop her weight, sliding back inside in one forceful thrust. One hand cradles the back of her neck, keeping our lips pressed as I maneuver her hips with the other. I'm not gentle. There's nothing soft about the way I guide her over my length.

Fast and hard. Near painful.

The only part of her touching the door is her upper back, and even then, it's almost hovering. Aurora arches, body bowing in my hold as pleasure rocks her small frame. And yet, as my assault rises into a nearly manic state, her pussy grips me tighter—almost holding me hostage.

If that's what she wants...

"Motherfuck," I grit out, slamming inside once more and then holding still. Her pussy massages my length, walls pulsing. "Shit, Gem...you're going to pull the come from me just like this." Slipping a hand between us, I ignore the use of the nickname and place my thumb over her clit, adding pressure. Just hold it there as her hips do all the work. She's wild against me, body moving, hips gyrating as she rides me in small little strokes. "That's it, love. You feel so good."

It's the most exquisite pain.

"It's never been like this," she moans out, fingernails digging into my shoulders as she uses them for leverage. Taking her pleasure from me, and while I'm a man that dominates in every facet of his life, I find this incredibly sexy. Watching her has my abs contracting —muscles coiling—as I fight the urge to take the control back. "Why?"

A question I don't have the answer to. It's never been like this for me either.

Never have I yearned to watch a woman fall apart in my arms. To drown in her pleasure.

Moreover, I'm not ready to analyze it. Not yet.

"Come for me." I massage her trembling bundle of nerves, hard little circles that cause her eyes to roll back. That won't do. Not at all. I need her pretty hazel eyes on mine. "Look at me."

At once, they do as I say. Her stare locks on mine.

I inhale her exhale, lips sweeping against hers.

"I'm so close, Casper."

"Then fall." I tap her clit with two fingers. "Give me what I want." Bringing both hands to her hips, I hold her tight and then raise her above the head. Just high enough that the swollen tip can slip inside without guidance. "Come for me."

"Need more." A tear. A plea.

"You only need what I give you." Then, because I'm an arsehole, I drop her once more. Without an ounce of care, I impale her—gift her that last push over the proverbial edge she needs. It's pleasure and pain, and the feel of her release is my sweetest torture.

"*Fuck.*" One word sums up our need perfectly. My hips piston in and out of her warmth as she comes with a scream, and a light sheen of sweat shines across her flesh. My mouth waters at the sight of her wild abandonment and I lick her chin, biting down on the soft skin as I follow her into bliss.

Her orgasm slams into me, milking my cock with each pulse of her walls. It's tight and hot. Messy. *Perfect.*

"Christ." I'm panting against her lips, kissing her slowly as spurt after spurt leaves me, mixing with her juices as I keep a slow and steady pace. My strokes keep her on the edge, riding her release until she becomes sensitive and clingy—holding onto me with her arms and legs, pulling me closer.

I almost hate how perfect she feels. Almost.

After a few minutes of trying to calm her breathing, Aurora pulls her face from mine, a now shy smile on her lips. "Wow."

I chuckle at that, pushing her matted hair back from her face. "Agreed, love. Agreed."

We don't move. Both just watch the other.

Neither give a fuck that our mess is running down my cock and probably splattering the marble floors beneath us. At this moment, nothing else matters. Not even the ringing of my mobile somewhere in the background can pull me away from her.

Those warm and sated eyes.

Those kiss-swollen lips.

That rich, dark hair that curls down the middle of her back.

And it's that kind of power that pulls the next few words from my lips.

It's without conscious thought. Without giving a shit about the consequences.

I'll deal with whatever comes...*later*.

"Spend the weekend with me?"

Chapter 2
CASPER

TWELVE HOURS AGO...

I NOTICE HER the bloody second she comes into the room. There's a shift in the air, a different kind of energy that sweeps over my over six-foot-two frame as I take in every delicate detail of her body. How she walks. How the little black dress she wears clings to each sinuous curve.

This girl commands the attention of every drunk arsehole without an ounce of effort.

From my seat, I have a view of every inch of this pub; from its entrance to the bar, to the small dance floor off to my left where bodies grind to the beat of some chart-topping artist. The place is full to the brim, and yet, she's all I see. All I can seem to focus on, taking into account every minute detail while all around me people continue to slam back pint after pint.

Each swing of her hips is a call to the animal within. A taunt.

The woman she's with stops a few tables from the one I'm occupying near the back with my men: a setup of high-top seating, and along the wall, two private booths. They greet another couple already sitting there with a small handshake, though hers is more on the distant side, the kind you give a stranger. A bit timid.

She shifts a bit—head bobbing to the music—and I follow the move, lowering my eyes to roam her small frame and liking the way her hip juts a bit to the side. Naturally coquettish, she's small but thick where it counts. Young, but legal. A beautiful little thing with the face of an angel and a body made to worship. At no more than five foot three and no older than twenty-two, she's all hips and thighs and has a gorgeous face with hazel eyes and plump, berry-colored lips.

Moreover, it's that mouth that first caught my attention.

How she throws her head back, laughing at what someone at the table says. How carefree she looks. How those lips stretch wide and her eyes close for a brief moment before meeting mine.

We hold each other's stare. Not moving.

And then that mouth parts in slow motion, her tiny pink tongue peeking out to sweep across her bottom lip, sealing her fate. At that moment, every single thought of retribution leaves my mind. My hunger morphs into something wickedly delicious.

I need that tight body on her knees.

I want her breasts encasing my thick cock as I slide between them.

I want her wetness running down my length, bathing me as those hazel orbs stay on mine.

"Sir, are you all right?" someone says from beside me, but I pay them no mind. Not when my prey turns as some bloke taps her bare shoulder. I'm out of my seat and across the room before I can register the action, but there's no ignoring the red-hot ire that burns through my veins at the sight of the pompous wanker.

I want to punch the idiot. Break the hand he touched her with, but before that can happen, he catches my eyes and pales, stumbling in his haste to get away.

Then, I'm five steps from her and pause as my rage turns into an inferno of lust. My hunger renews as the soft scent of cherry blossoms infiltrates my senses, and I bite back a groan. It's all her. The temptation and want and this lust that has me throbbing—beads of pre-come already rolling down the tip and shaft.

It's also why I take the remaining steps and bend to place my lips next to her ear. Why I revel in the way she shivers for me. "What's your name, love?"

THE NEXT MORNING I awake to her weight on my chest. To the same hunger that propelled me to take her—to manipulate this doll to my liking for hours on end—until she finally cried out in defeat.

Spent and exhausted, Aurora fell on top of me and didn't move. Not even when I placed her beside me so I could clean up, and then came back with a washcloth to wipe the evidence of my hunger from her inner thighs. Thighs that now bear perfect little marks in the shape of my fingertips, light purple and spread about—from her upper legs to those supple hips—that stand out against her lightly tanned skin.

They are the perfect reminder of the pleasure I gave her. Of what she willingly gave to me.

I also recognize that there's no sense of panic in me.

We didn't use a condom. There hadn't been anything to dispose of, and yet, I don't have a single worry about *what could be* or the *what ifs*. My mind is at ease for once. Calm.

A foreign feeling, but I'm not questioning it either as her words from last night come back to the forefront; a mumbled confession as

I pushed her against the door after slamming it closed and taking possession of her sweet mouth in a kiss. It was a promise. A plea for me not to stop.

I'm clean and on the pill. Christ...you're so...I-I haven't been with anyone in over a year since my last breakup.

And I gave in after my own reassurance of being clean. Over and over.

"Why my pub, Gem?" At my question, she lets out a cute sigh and snuggles closer, burrowing her nose into the crook of my neck. The sensation tickles, but I don't want to move her. Take away the sweet warmth of her pussy so close to my cock.

If anything, I want to bury myself deep within those walls once more. Hear her screams.

"Casper," she whimpers low in her slumber, lips skimming across my skin in an unconscious taunt. I'm hard—throbbing—as I press my length against her bare leg over my hip. It's a dangerous position for her. Too easy for me.

All I need to do is move a little lower and...

I'm interrupted by the obnoxious ringing of my mobile atop my nightstand; it's loud within the silence of the room and I worry it'll wake her up, however, she doesn't so much as stir.

Gem is definitely a heavy sleeper, I muse; a low chuckle vibrates through my chest as the device rings three times and then goes to voicemail. There's a beep that follows, a few seconds of silence, and then the blasted tone blares again, causing my amusement to cease.

The person on the other end is a persistent arsehole.

I also know why he's calling. What he's waiting on.

Life or death; it's a delicate balance that I control with a flick of a finger. With the sharp edge of my blade.

It's mine to decide—to take their last breath—and I close my eyes for just a second. Just a little longer, and those two deep breaths give me a moment to take in her softness and how at ease I feel with her near.

And with that ease comes another dose of reality:

The thought of getting rid of her hasn't crossed my mind once.

It's the opposite. Something I don't quite understand yet, but I want her here.

She's a reprieve. She's not just a fuck that I can ignore after.

Aurora is someone I want to see again. *Have again.*

My phone beeps then with an incoming text and I carefully move Gem, settling her against the space I vacate. It's selfish of me to want her here with the kind of business I run, but I'm greedy if nothing else. Hold no remorse over it. Something about this woman has caught my attention, holding it captive while making me crave more.

Of her. Of us.

Of the explosion I barely got a taste of last night. Those hours weren't enough.

Leaning over her slumbering form, I press my lips to hers while inhaling the scent of sex and cherry blossoms that still lingers on her skin. It soothes me. A seduction, and I'm more than tempted to crawl back onto the bed and part those legs so I can explore her heat once more, but I don't.

Instead, I whisper *soon* against the pillowy flesh of her mouth, nipping her bottom lip a final time before backing away. *We're not done.* And it's the bloody truth.

Naked and rock hard, I grab my phone and send off a quick text to the cock-blocker without reading his message. He will know what it means. What I expect.

Twenty. ~Jameson

Just as soon as he received it, three dots appear on my screen. However, I don't wait to read his confirmation. I'm already walking across the room and into my closet to pick out something to wear. And it takes less than three minutes to do so, grabbing a pair of denim trousers and a simple black vest without underwear.

I don't like them.

The guest bath I'll use is downstairs and as I exit the room, I pause to look over at a slumbering Gem one last time. To take in how tiny and decadent she looks. To acknowledge how her allure, the pull, is just as strong as it was last night.

Complications can be fun.

And a complication she is.

The second the door closes, there's a shift in me. Raw and ireful energy. With each step I take down the stairs—away from her temptation—I welcome the change that courses through my body.

The space between us brings back the cruel animal in me. The devil beneath the facade of a saint.

The real me.

Entering the bathroom, my eyes shift toward the large mirror and I take in my expression for a second. Gone is the smile I had for her. Gone is my relaxed state. What looks back at me is a killer.

I'm a handsome face with a cruel smile.

Green eyes that seem to glow in the lighting of this room.

Muscles that coil as I remember the two hours before noticing her:

The final report from the dock where the theft took place.

The surveillance photos of that night.

The proof of who sold the merchandise. Who bought it.

My men had forty-eight hours to gather every last bit of evidence on the betrayer and buyer. Whose name is attached. Every bloody fucking detail sits atop my desk inside the pub where I met Aurora.

"Blessed be the wicked," I tell my reflection and then walk toward the shower, turning the setting to my liking. Steam builds rather quickly within the grey and white bathroom, the water coming down from four showerheads with various pressure settings as I step inside. It cascades down my back, but I feel no relief, nothing but a craving for retribution that grows with each tick of the clock.

I don't linger as I'd like to. I don't jerk off to take the edge off my hunger for her, like I need to.

Instead, my neck stiffens further as the weight of this family finds its rightful place: back on my shoulders. I stretch it from side to side, causing a loud pop to ring throughout the shower, and yet, the tension doesn't lessen. If anything, it becomes more pronounced. Aggravated by the blatant disrespect to those I care about.

Nothing happens in London without my knowledge. Without my approval.

And yet, someone decided to play God for the day and stole from me.

It's an insult. A slap to the face. *They put an innocent in danger.*

I'm also calculating. Taking into consideration her sleeping form upstairs.

Because she will know the truth. She will run. Something inevitable, and it fucks with my already vexed mood.

"Why are you really in London, Gem?" I mutter low, making my way out of the bathroom once dressed. My manor in the Kensington area is sacred and always protected. And while it's Sunday and my staff has the day off, I have three guards and my two male boxers— outside these walls—to keep those who are curiously stupid, out.

These men will lay down their lives for me. Are loyal. Hold no qualms about shooting first.

They also know to never enter without permission, so when a knock comes as I head toward my office on the opposite end of the house, I make them wait. Family or not—my men or not—it doesn't matter.

It's a rule taken straight from my own version of the ten commandments:

In this world, I am their King.

The one responsible for their fate.

A male shadow looms through the frosted glass of the front door. "Oi, you in there, bro?" Another knock sounds, a bit harder this time, and I walk over, pulling the front door open so my guest can come inside.

"Don't make another sound," I spit out, eyes narrowing at the man who looks a lot like me, just six years younger than my thirty-two. "My office, and no deviations."

"Rough night, mate?" my cousin, Callum, jokes while raising a brow. His lips are quirked up at the corner, a shitty smirk that all the men in my family seem to have. "That pretty little thing not—"

"Don't." That's all I say, and the amusement drops from his face. In this moment I'm not family, I'm his boss. He eyes me for a second but doesn't comment. Instead, he nods and walks off in the direction of my home office, entering, while my eyes shift briefly toward another room at the top of the stairs.

Last night I gave in to her temptation and let the game of Russian Roulette take its natural course, however, today is different. I don't regret Gem, my time with her, but that must all take a back seat for now as I walk in a minute after Callum.

Even if I have to chase, she'll be my reward after.

The space is large and holds an air of old luxury that intimidates most that enter. The interior furniture is a mixture of dark and natural tones, wall-to-wall built-in bookcases to the left, and a large desk in an imported teak wood that sits center stage. The walls are painted in a deep royal blue with one white stripe at the center of each.

Rare Gothic paintings litter my walls—expensive and found throughout the black market—that depict the depraved curiosity people have with death. Demons, blood, and sexual deviancy stare back at you no matter where you sit, and it makes even the most decorated killers uncomfortable.

Then, there is a collection of weapons on display. Old and new. My favorites, and a few cruel contraptions from the medieval ages with purposes that reek of horror.

Some are loaded. Some no longer work. Some still hold a few dried drops of blood from their last kill.

And right there in the middle of it all sits someone I trust with my life. Waiting. Callum has questions, but he won't ask. Instead, he cracks his somewhat bruised knuckles.

"Did he give you that much of a fight?" I ask, tilting my head in the direction of his hands as I pause beside the chair next to his.

"Nah. That's just the consequence of fighting a spider," he says, holding two fingers together to show me its size. "Bloody thing kept running."

"What kind?" The phone in my pocket buzzes with an alert and I pull it out, swiping my finger across the screen. It's the motion-detection camera near the stairs and it shows Aurora stumbling down still half asleep, wearing my vest. Looking for me.

From the screen, I watch Gem continue down and catch glimpses of her from different angles. There are so many directions she could head, but as if pulled by an invisible string, her steps come closer across the foyer, and it's that camera with her face in my line of sight that I focus on.

"Daddy long-legs."

"Are you fucking kidding me?" I bark out a laugh to help guide Gem. Walking around the desk to take a seat, I place the phone against my computer monitor so only I can see. *That's it, sweetheart. A little bit more.* "Let me guess…you gave the wall a bunch of fives to kill it?"

"It was an instinctual reaction." No shame for his stupidity. Instead, he shrugs while stretching his hand out. "Caught the bloke on the third punch. Not that bad."

"And Otto?" Because while his story is entertaining, it's unimportant. That, and this will kill two birds with one stone. "Where's the cunt now?"

"Taking a nap near the Eye. I transferred him before coming here."

"Good." Most people don't pay attention to their surroundings, especially those that are vacationing. A tourist destination is the perfect way to mask the danger that lurks. You blend in. No one looks at you twice. No one asks questions as they imbibe the spirits you serve.

This business is overlooked on the daily as just another pub. A large two-story building with a roof-top establishment, a kitchen down below, and a hidden floor beneath where no one is allowed without my presence. And I like it that way. To hide in plain sight.

Every single one of my endeavors is the same way.

"Have you decided yet?" he asks then, pushing his hair back from his face. While mine is the same dirty blond color, his is long enough to keep in a bun. "Because what that son of a bitch did doesn't deserve your mercy."

"Is that your suggestion?" From my periphery I see a shadow loom near the still open door. There's no going back. "That he die?"

"Yes, but you know I'll follow your lead, cousin."

"I know." Reaching over, I open the top drawer to my right while looking at him to avoid the temptation of seeking her out. My favorite toys in the world lay there; two steel karambits with silver handles given to me on my sixteenth birthday by my grandfather. They're both engraved with my name on the curved, four-inch blade; a sleek and deadly design that lets me get close enough to feel the flesh give way beneath my assault.

Taking one out, I slip one finger through the circular end and the rest around the handle tightly. The weight feels good in my hold. Like an extension of me.

"Are we—"

"He pays in blood." There's a low gasp from just outside the door, so low that Callum misses it but I don't. I also don't miss how she rushes away and up my stairs to probably get dressed and then flee. That's okay, though…

I won't allow her to get far.

Not after how good she felt beneath my fingertips. How *right* we were.

She was tantalizing. Delicious. A cock-hardening manifestation of femininity that will try and slip through my fingers but won't get far.

I will chase.

We're not over.

Chapter 3
AURORA

"**W**HAT THE HELL is wrong with me?" I ask myself for the hundredth time, rushing up a stranger's staircase with my torn dress in hand—stumbling in my haste to find anything to wear and leave. To get the hell away from someone I have no business being near, much less sleeping with.

I let his smile last night lower my inhibitions. Let the feel of his fingertips skimming my arm guide me closer.

A mistake. Monumental.

Christ, I'm an idiot.

Fear and lust and desire still linger over my skin. I feel him. His touch.

And I hate how I love it. How I crave him again. How even after I heard him sentence someone to death, I want more.

Of his danger. Of how he made me come alive last night.

Of the pleasure...

But I can't. Casper Jameson is something that can never be. He's the physical embodiment of what I'll always run from.

"Get it together and focus, Aurora." His room is in my line of sight and I enter, running inside while I avoid looking at his bed, a large, king-sized monstrosity with an almost black wooden frame and headboard. It's regal. The lines are sexy, and it sits in the center of the room with soft white sheets strewn about.

It's the mess we made. Where he took me over and over again for hours on end.

Where I let him.

My thighs clench, the slight sting of pain making me look down and lift the seam of his shirt that smells just like him—woodsy with a hint of whiskey—that I found lying over a large chair in the corner of the room. It's a white Oxford that fits me like a dress, and it also made me blind to the marks he's left behind.

His fingertips. His touch.

It's more proof of my idiocy. A map of his desire.

"It's a one-night stand and nothing more." I repeat these words three times, taking in deep breaths as my heart accelerates. As my hands begin to shake. "Get in and get out."

My head whips from side to side, searching for anything else I can wear because his shirt, without panties, won't do. He tore them from me last night, leaving them unwearable. That, and I don't have the time to search them out.

I need to get far enough to call a cab before he comes up. Finds out where the hell I am.

That's when I take in an armoire on the left wall. It's large, a piece from the same line as his bed frame, and should have what I need. At least, I hope.

Walking over the sheet I let fall off my body when I went looking for him, I reach the large piece in a few steps. I'm on autopilot as I open the first two drawers and find plain undershirts. The one below has some gym clothes, and so on. Each one is full to the brim with things that don't fit my much smaller frame, and I toss everything onto the floor before noticing a pair of basketball shorts that I think will be a bit tight on him.

"These will have to do." Slipping them up my hips, I realize immediately just how wrong I am and almost laugh. Almost. They're huge, and I'm running out of time. He could come up at any minute and see the mess I'm making.

Tying the strings of the shorts as tightly as I can, I roll the waist twice and then test them by shaking my hips from side to side a few times. They fall a bit, but not enough that I will become bottomless as I walk. *Good enough.*

Next, I begin the search for my shoes. The problem with that is the heels won't work.

They'll be a hindrance. Slow me down.

"Bingo," I mutter low, opening a drawer to find socks. Lots of them. In all styles. Which makes it perfect since the kind I'll need sits atop the bunch and to the right, an old-school pair of over-the-calf socks with two black bands across the top. I put them on; they're large but perfect, warming my legs while covering me to the knees.

Sure, I look like a clown, but I'm covered and comfy. Now all I need is my...

"Crap, my purse." Last night in our rush, I tossed it somewhere behind him, not caring about the contents inside. My phone and wallet are inside, and so is the hotel's keycard and a card with the address. "I'm such an idiot."

It's also the reason why I've never had a one-night stand before. The uncertainty. The danger of an unknown person and their true intentions.

And yet you let him have you so easily. Can't deny that. The intensity as our eyes met across the room, charming green on my hazel, and then the heat that scorched my veins. The harsh lick of desire rolled down my spine as he sipped his drink, never taking his gaze from mine.

It made me weak. It made me want to take a chance.

And now here I am. Paying the price.

My breathing picks up a bit at the thought of seeing him again. Of being close to a man that is wrong for me.

The kind my mother warned me about.

Of not having an out.

"Just go downstairs and explain my family is waiting on me." It's not a lie per se. Just that our meeting was yesterday, not today, but he doesn't need to know that. It'd give me just enough time to—

A door opens and closes loudly downstairs, then nothing. No noise. No footsteps coming up the stairs.

Unconsciously, I move toward this room's entrance, turning the knob and then pulling it open just a smidge. Just enough that I see no one in the corridor or near the top of the stairs. Moreover, at that very moment, I release the breath I didn't realize I was holding in.

He's nowhere in sight and that works for me, gives me the opening I need. That maybe, just maybe, I won't see him again.

As soon as the thought crosses my mind, I feel a pang in my chest—a tiny and annoying thump that I ignore for the time being. If not forever. Deciphering what it means could be disastrous for me.

A repeating of the cycle.

Opening the door further, I tiptoe out and toward the stairs, making as little noise as possible. My heart rate accelerates, beating faster with each step closer to the top landing. Even more so when I notice a figure, tall and intimidating, near the door and to the right. Fear and excitement course through my veins, but I don't stop.

I'm on autopilot. Moving without conscious thought until I meet the eyes of the person there.

It's not him. Not even close.

This man is dressed in a black suit, his features hard and that of an older man, maybe in his late forties. His appearance is serious, and yet there's a hint of a smile that comes through as he reads the disappointed expression on my face. It's unavoidable. Can't hide it.

Confusion with a hint of regret simmers, and my heart does that stupid thump once more. I should be happy, but I'm not. I should be relieved, but instead, all I feel is used. Unimportant and stupid for making a big deal of what obviously isn't.

There stands this stranger with my purse in hand, waiting for me, while I was just another notch on his bedpost. An easy lay.

"I'm an idiot." All that worry for nothing when he wants me gone; a realization that stings and confuses me further. This is exactly what I should want. What I need.

"What was that, Miss?" he asks, voice rough as if he's a heavy smoker, while he moves closer to the bottom step. "Everything okay? Do I need to call Mr. Jameson—"

"No."

At my quick denial, he nods and holds out his hand with my belongings. "In that case, the car is ready when you are."

"The car?"

"I've been instructed to deliver you back to your hotel."

"Lead the way, then." What else can I say? I feel dismissed. Like a fool.

Luckily, the man does as I ask without further prompting, turning on his heel to open the front door where I see a sleek black sedan waiting for me. Its ignition is already on, and before I can reach for the door's handle, he's rushing to open it, letting the muted thud of the front door closing follow close behind.

A sound that reeks of finality. Of a goodbye I should want but bothers me when just a few minutes prior, I wanted to leave.

Doesn't matter anymore. It's for the best.

And it is. Casper Jameson isn't someone I need to further mix myself with.

Silence fills the inside of the car, a looming quiet that makes the voice in my head loud. Wondering. Questioning the last twelve hours and my actions.

Why did I sleep with him?

Why do I feel so restless?

My mind is a constant loop, an uncensored movie reel of our night together and then what I heard from outside his office. Moreover, there's a miniscule part of me that knew to not go home with him, and I still did.

"What's your name, love?" a deep, husky voice whispers in an English accent, lips lightly brushing the shell of my ear from behind. He's close. Close enough that the scent of whiskey with a touch of wood and spice infiltrates my senses, and I bite back my hum of approval.

It's sexy. Alluring. I also know who it is before turning around.

His heavy-lidded eyes have been following me throughout the roof-top pub for the last thirty minutes, almost since the very moment I walked in. Tempting me. Causing my nipples to tighten in anticipation.

And I've been waiting for him to make a move. To approach.

Since that first glance, I've been watching too—catching his stare every few minutes while we play a game of cat and mouse—getting lost within those hypnotic green eyes. While I appreciate just how handsome he is.

How his top lip curls to the right, a cocky little smirk that makes butterflies erupt within. How his defined and lickable jaw ticks after each sip from the glass in his hand. How his dirty blond hair flops a little over his forehead, a chaotic mess that my hands itch to pull on.

Even from where I stand, a couple of feet from him and at another small high-top table with a girl I met at the hotel today, I can tell he's tall. Muscular. A sinful surprise I wasn't expecting but want.

This man is the perfect British specimen, and I want a taste. A little of the dominating persona that stands out amongst the sea of drunk bodies all around me. There's just something about him. Something delicious. Something that calls to me.

Turning around, I look up at him from beneath long lashes. "I'm Aurora...and you?"

"Casper." He winks, picking up my hand and bringing it to his lips. Soft lips that skim across my knuckles. "And I'm your date for the evening."

At his response, I giggle. "Is that so?"

"It is."

"Miss, we're here," the driver says, snapping me back to the present. I've been so lost and inside my head that I never gave him my hotel's name or the address.

"How did you—?"

"Mr. Jameson." That's all he says before exiting the car and coming to my door behind him, an action that tells me the subject is closed. He's not divulging the how or why.

"Thanks..." I trail off, hoping he'll at the very least give me his name. He doesn't. Instead, Casper's employee gives me a nod and walks back around to his door as I watch. No more eye contact or smile, he leaves me there as he enters and then slowly pulls off the curb to merge into very busy traffic.

For a few minutes, I just stand there, still lost inside my head, when a body sidles up next to me. It's a familiar presence. Someone I know will reproach my actions even though they don't have a leg to stand on.

"You're late and you look horrible," he says after a minute, tone calm. Too calm.

Without looking over, I let out a heavy sigh. Just not in the mood. "Why are you here?"

"Because daughters shouldn't stand up their fathers."

Chapter 4
CASPER

I DON'T FOLLOW HER. It's not necessary.

Not when I send a quick text to one of my men outside the minute she rushes upstairs to get dressed. He's under strict instructions to make sure she gets to her hotel safely and then stay close by. To give me an update on her location every thirty minutes on the dot, no exceptions.

I want to know everything. The what, where, and how.

To know if she so much as coughs until I come for her once more.

Because we aren't done. Not at all.

But first, I have somewhere to be, where good little girls should never step a single foot inside.

The moment my front door closes and I see her enter the awaiting car from my security feed, I push my chair back, pocketing my phone and the two custom karambits. I walk out without another word to my cousin, knowing he has more questions, but I couldn't give a bloody fuck about them. Now isn't the time for bollocks or even a little ribbing, something that as my right hand he understands.

His footsteps follow mine out of the room, but we part ways as I head upstairs to collect something I'll need. Taking the stairs two at a time, I reach my room and find it in complete disarray with clothes—my clothing—strewn about. She's emptied every drawer of the armoire in her haste to leave. Plain vests, gym shorts, pajama bottoms, and even a few pairs of joggers are atop my bed and on the floor beneath.

However, none of that matters when I see that her little black dress lies in tatters near the furniture's bottom drawer. *Must've brought it upstairs in her rush.* The scrap of satin she calls panties are nowhere to be found, but she left with something of mine on that delectable body, a reminder of me, and for now that's enough.

"Good girl," I groan, palming my already thickening cock through the outside of my trousers as the faint scent of cherry blossoms infiltrates my senses. I'm hard for her, throbbing all over again, and want nothing more than to bring her back to my bed, but there's a more pressing matter that needs my attention.

And it's the anger, the want—that tumultuous combination that causes me to grit my teeth and walk over to a small compartment hidden behind a painting of the London skyline at night. There's a small safe there. One of the many throughout my two-story home that provides easy access to an arsenal of weapons.

This one, though, doesn't hold much outside of my favorite chrome Colt 1911 and the custom holster for my knives. Punching in a four-digit code, I grab each, and then the extra magazines ready and loaded beside them.

I'm not changing, but I do choose a pair of old combat boots for this particular meeting with Otto. He's the kind of man that will appreciate my way of handling this type of situation, the less-than-formal setting, and after lacing them tight, I walk out.

Each step toward my private parking structure next door is loud against the floors. It echoes, follows me as do the two men awaiting my orders outside. No one speaks, they just follow.

When I purchased this property, I bought the one on either side as well because I like my privacy. Because money talks, and a few extra zeros on any check will buy you anything you desire.

Once inside my garage, I point toward the two black Range Rovers while walking toward another small panel near the entrance. It's a small box with a fingerprint reader, and I place my thumb at the center. Then there's a click, and the sliding of a panel which reveals ten sets of keys.

I grab the ones to the left on the top row and press the unlock button on the fob. At once, doors open and then close.

Turning around, I notice Callum still outside while holding a hand out. "I'm guessing you're driving alone." My response is to toss him the set that belongs to the Rover where two of my men sit inside. "We'll follow, and security will be here within five minutes to replace the men coming with us."

I nod and get inside my own car, taking off toward the Eye. It's a thirty-minute drive that I cut down to fifteen, weaving in and out of traffic as drivers around me press down on their horns—glaring at me in annoyance while my car cuts them off at close range.

There's a rush of excitement that comes with the art of scaring the piss out of them, and even more so when they don't know it's me. That moment at red lights as they send curses my way—waving a fist or flicking me off—and I lower my tinted window to show my face, is priceless.

The closer we get to the touristy area, the thicker the congestion on the roads becomes. There are buses and people walking, all looking up toward the landmarks we're known for and snapping selfies.

They aren't self-aware. Ignore danger.

These wankers don't care—they ignore the fact that a man like me will run them over without an ounce of remorse for being arse-holes. And what's worse, no one will lift a finger against me. To turn me in.

Pulling into my private parking spot behind my building, I turn the ignition off and let out a perverse chuckle. I'm so close to parliament; to where all the lords of this great country hide away for hours fighting the good fight while men like me break their laws. I defy them, metaphorically flip them off, and not one will rise against me.

Callum follows, parking in the spot next to mine, and gets out a minute after, rushing to fall into step with me as I enter the kitchen's back door. Eyes lift as I make my way through, but quickly shift away when they take in my facial expression. Faces are lowered and all movement ceases; nothing can be heard outside of the sizzle of a deep fryer and the two or three pans on the burners.

I look at the manager on shift and give him a nod. No words.

His reaction is automatic, almost running to hold a finger on a nondescript button near the large walk-in coolers. It blends in with the other two there that manage the lighting and a backup fan for emergencies. Eyes on mine, he waits for me to enter my office before the fake wall begins to lower, sealing us inside.

No exit.

No entry.

It's out of sight and with soundproofing thick enough that I could blow the blasted building from below and no one would realize until it's too late.

Inside the room and behind my desk, there's a large bookcase the size of a door—a mobile bookcase that opens with the slight pulling of an old copy of Romeo and Juliet that Mum thought was funny to place there and use. Moreover, unless you know it's there, the entrance is undetectable. Clever in that hiding-in-plain-sight kind of way, and I can appreciate the subtlety.

Callum gives the book a small tug and the lock disengages, moving the wooden structure an inch or two forward, giving us a peak at the darkness behind it. A void that for most who enter is the entrance to hell, while I find the dark and morbid relaxing. A release.

My men enter first, walking down the stairs that lead to a large and open space, then they wait for me; three men with heads looking straight ahead while a low whimper meets my ears. It's a fascinating sound: fear. The way someone crumbles as reality sets in when I walk inside the room.

However, I make Otto wait. Fuck with his fragile mind the way he screwed my business.

My family's money. Took food right from their mouths.

His disloyalty, the way he took it upon himself to sell and profit from what isn't his, doesn't warrant any leniency from me. Especially after I gave him a job when his family—wife and two kids— were on the streets without a pound to their names. After I got him cleaned up. After I put them in a home that same night and made sure his family was taken care of while his training down at the pier began.

He earned more than most because of the women in his life.

None of that seems to matter, though, when greed becomes a prominent driver in a person's life. They don't think. Don't process that shit could go wrong and you will find yourself staring at the end of a murderer's knife.

Once again, I crack my neck, shaking my head from side to side as another pulsing energy begins to flow through my system. It's a heady concoction. Almost as delicious as Aurora's pussy.

Placing my holster, knives, phone, and gun down atop my desk, I shake my arms out, loosening my limbs. The room is cool, and yet I'm a raging inferno as the moment begins to settle. As I let my need for blood to spill take over.

Rationality and compassion have no place inside this meeting.

I pull my vest over my head and then fold the cotton fabric, leaving it beside my gun. A gun I won't be taking with me. This sentencing will be more of an intimate affair. Hands on.

To the victor goes the spoils.

"Please." It comes from the floor below, a yell of desperation that pulls a smile to my face. "Mr. Jameson, I'll work the debt off...do anything you need me to. Just don't..." a broken sob follows and I've yet to make an entrance "...my daughters and wife need me."

I don't answer.

I don't utter a single word as I put my holster on, securing the leather strap down each side of my chest, and then pick up each karambit. In the low lighting, the steel gleams, a sharp contrast to every single item within the space. It's weight feels good in my hand, like an extension of me, but I don't plan to use them yet.

No. I'm nothing if not fair.

Placing one in each holster, I turn and walk toward the stairs, taking them down to the all-dark room. My men await orders. Await my decision with their heads straight ahead while the traitor squirms under the scrutiny.

The man in question, *Otto*, is kneeling on the cold concrete floor. His shadow shakes and a chain rattles with each move. But louder than anything else is his breathing—harsh intakes of air that seem to choke him as his lungs close up and panic sets in.

"Lights," I say, and someone flips the switch a second later. Everyone in this room knows the rules except my guest, and they quietly take position, blocking the stairs behind me. Only one way in and one way out. "Look at me, Otto."

His eyes, which have remained on the floor, meet mine and they are a horrified blue on my light green ones. They're terrified— almost accepting of his fate—but a small speckle of hope still peeks through. One which I hold no qualms about stomping out.

He thinks I have a soft side when it comes to his daughters because of their young ages.

It's almost sad. Almost.

Otto doesn't say anything as I tower above him, bare chested—the black ink on my skin bold against my flesh—and with a smirk on my lips. Not as I take in his near naked and bruised form. Not even as I wrinkle my nose in disgust at his stench; a combination of sweat and piss hits my nostrils.

My eyes leave him, and I take in the small tray beside his body with an empty plate and cup. There's a tiny piece of tomato and lettuce on the all-white dish and a crumb here or there. It's evidence to just how far my mercy goes; he's been fed, the room is at a cool temperature, and the leash around his neck has enough leeway that he can move about a bit.

I've become the bloody saint of all demons.

"You've disappointed me."

Chapter 5
CASPER

"MR. JAMESON, I—"

"Silence." Taking a step back, I look over my shoulder toward Callum, who comes forward. He takes my place as I walk over to the wall on the left, stretching out my limbs with my back to Otto. The sound of his restraints meeting the hard concrete floor come a second later followed by the grunts of pain as he tries to stand.

"Am I being forgiven?" the wanker asks, a slight tremble in his tone.

"Mr. Jameson has granted you the privilege of fighting for your life. You'll have—"

"I said I was sorry. That I swear to pay off every single quid...*fuck*!" I turn my head slightly at his yell, barely catching the movement of Callum's strike and then him resuming his stance.

"Interrupt me again and the boss won't begrudge me a few minutes of fun. Understood?" There's a moment of silence, then an almost too-low-to-hear whimper that my cousin lets slide. "Good. Now, as I was saying..." footsteps move about, almost pacing "...you will have ten minutes to either knock out or subdue Mr. Jameson and then walk out a free man. No repercussions or debts. A clean slate."

"May I ask—"

"You will have your choice of weapon from those we provide. Choose wisely, Otto, because you get one choice."

"Guns?"

Callum chuckles. "No guns are allowed."

"Unless he manages to make it upstairs and takes my Colt from the desk." Turning to face them, I lean back on the brick wall with my knee slightly bent. Both men look at me with different expressions on their faces: one amusement and the other palpable fear. They also watch me as I pull out a knife and run my finger down the blade, slicing my thumb. It's a nice little cut—deep enough that blood drips down my hand and onto my wrist, showing the ungrateful arsehole just how sharp this blade is. "It's the only way to make sure I don't change my mind."

Otto looks at Callum, who just shrugs. "His rules, mate."

"Is there any other—"

"No." As I say this, Jeffrey, a guard, walks toward a small area behind the stairs and pulls out a cart. He brings it toward us, stopping before Otto, and lifts the sheet covering the few items it holds: an assortment of knives, a pair of brass knuckles, a baseball bat, and crowbar. "Pick."

"I...please...can't we—"

"Choose, or I'll do so for you. You have ten seconds." I snarl, lip curling over my teeth while my hand clenches around the silver handle as I slip my thumb within the circular hole at the end. For now, I'll only use one. That's all I'll need.

His hand trembles as he reaches out toward the assortment I've provided. They hover over the crowbar for a second, fingers almost skimming the iron, but then changes his mind at the last moment. For some reason, Otto picks up the aluminum bat, weighing it in his hands, and then takes a step back.

"Is that your choice?" At my question, Otto nods and my men retake their place by the stairs. The cart goes with them, and a harsh pounding begins to fill the room. It's an abrasive beat. An angry guitar riff that clears my head—flows through me as I give him my back. "The first strike is yours—make it count—there won't be another chance out of here."

I take three steps forward and close my eyes. In that moment the room stills, and I focus on the movement inside the room. How Otto lets out a long shuddering breath and then lets out a heavy grunt while rising the bat above his head, holding it there as his fear wages against the need to survive.

It's a natural reaction. We all have the need to protect ourselves at all cost. To kill if it means we get to head home and be the same useless bastard we were the day prior.

Because this isn't about his family. His wife and kids.

Not in the least.

His gambling addiction is his downfall. The reason he's in this room and minutes from death. He's lost money—owes someone that wanted my shipment as repayment—and he agreed with a little compensation on top. Stupidity overruled common sense.

Like now; if he were smarter, he'd keep his noises down to a minimum. He wouldn't shift his weight from foot to foot, dragging his feet on the cold concrete and kicking the chain that was his leash.

He also wouldn't take so long to make a decision. To strike.

But then again, I expect this. It's why I'm good at what I do.

Over the years, since I was a young bloke, my father taught me to rely on more than just what's in front of me. To pay attention. To focus.

It doesn't matter if you're inside a packed stadium, the mind has a way to block out distractions. To pick apart movement and keep track of a threat. Use that. Hone it.

Kill without mercy, kid.

That's why when his arm lowers, bringing the aluminum bat with it, I duck out of the way, letting it barely graze my shoulder as I shift. I follow his action with a counter of my own, turning with my karambit's blade open and in his direction while lowering toward my target. The cut is across the back of his knee—I feel every second in slow motion as the knife slices through flesh and ligaments—leaving an almost surgically precise line while his upper body follows the movement of a missed swing. It's a bloody thing of beauty how he falls.

How the blood rushes out through the open wound.

How he cries out in pain, unable to stand.

How his eyes snap to mine, full of horror.

I'm behind him with my hand in his hair and yanking his head back before the scum can even think to try and crawl away. His life's essence seeps from the deep wound, pooling around him and staining my boots—boots that I use to stomp down on his left ankle. Once. Twice. I don't stop.

Not until I hear the bone crack. Not until it's broken and at an awkward angle.

"Please!"

"Please what, arsehole?" I sneer, ready to end the dumb fuck. He owes me for much more than a missing shipment. For stealing from me. "Tell me why I should let you go?"

His eyes, wide and full of panic, settle on mine. "It was a mistake…it'll never happen again, Mr. Jameson. Just please. My kids."

His kids. His kids.

Bending at the waist, I place my lips near his ear and bring my blade to his left nipple, digging the tip in. "Did you stop when you smacked Melinda around? When you beat her in front of the girls?"

"I've never—"

"What about when you walked out on them two weeks ago to fuck a whore?"

"That's not—"

"Liar." In one swift move, I slice down, leaving a deep wound in the exact same place he kicked her a few weeks ago. It's not lost on him either as he chokes on his mistake. It's another rule of mine he broke: we take care of our family. "What was the first thing I told you after taking you in? After giving you the help you asked for?"

"To never...fuck!" My blade slips lower, opening the area over his ribs. I can feel each one. It's almost like playing a xylophone. "No more. I can't take any more."

"You'll take what I give you." To punctuate my point, I turn the curved tip of my karambit and follow the path to his belly button. With a slow cut, I take my time parting his flesh and then embedding the four-inch blade within.

I let him bleed while his body fights to coil into itself—to move away from my hold.

And because I'm a generous bloke, I release his head after a few minutes and remove my blade. "Don't move." His reply comes in the form of a whimper and then a nod; his body's sweating profusely. "Callum?"

"Yes, Boss?"

"Bring our guest a glass of water."

"Of course." Behind me there's movement, the footsteps of more than one man as things are put into place. Jeffrey brings a file with him as Callum offers my guest a drink. Both are put in his line of sight—given to him—yet he doesn't move.

"It's rude to not take what's being offered," I say, taking the file from Jeffrey while giving him a nod. Silently, he moves away and retakes his place while my cousin and I watch the crying cunt. "Take it."

"Casper, I—"

Callum strikes him, a closed-fist punch to the face that snaps Otto's head to the side. "He's Mr. Jameson to you."

"Relax," I say, tossing the file on the floor in front of him. Its contents spill out: photos, a bank statement, and the deed to a new home. They show a life he will never live with those he claims to love. Their future. Their security. Their peace. "Hurts, doesn't it?"

"What's this?" Otto eyes the picture of his wife and kids, his loss of blood making it hard to move. To raise his hand. "Where's my wife?"

"Safe." In the first picture his wife and girls are smiling, sitting out on the back porch while eating ice cream. In the next, she's taking them to a new school. A private and very expensive one. "Building a better life."

"They need me." It comes out low as his body sways a bit.

Walking behind him, I yank his head back once more and force his eyes to mine. I want to be the last thing he sees. I am his end. "No. They don't." With that I bring my karambit to his neck and slice his throat clean from one side to the other. Blood splutters and stains my skin, while Otto chokes on his last breath. Releasing my hold, I let his lifeless form buckle and hit the ground while I take the glass of water from Callum. I pour a bit onto my hand over his body to wash the blood off. "Did he show up?"

"Yes." He chuckles and passes me a small towel. "We have eyes on them as they talk near the hotel's elevator bank. I'll forward you the pictures now."

"Good." Taking the cotton, I clean off as much as I can. "I expected as much."

"Is that why you didn't ask him about Boston? About the sale?"

"It's not necessary when I already have what I need." Stepping over the dead, I walk to the stairs as my men move to the side. "Clean it up and burn the body."

"Yes, sir," they say in unison as I take the stairs up with Callum following close behind. I know he has questions. "Spit it out."

"Did you know about—?"

"Doesn't matter to me."

"It's a problem, cousin."

I nod, a cocky smirk on my lips. "This problem is mine."

Chapter 6
AURORA

"THAT'S FUNNY COMING from an absent father."

"You know it wasn't like that. I had no choice—"

"There's always a choice. We just weren't yours," I spit out, clenching my hands into tight fists as I turn, leaving him alone in front of the hotel's entrance.

"For the love of God, Aurora." It's a hiss, low and heavy with a warning I ignore from behind me. His footsteps match mine, entering the almost-empty lobby a second or two after, and following close as I make a beeline for the elevator bank. "We need to talk. Where were you last night? Who dropped you off?"

What he fails to understand—accept—is that I'm not in the mood for this. That I'm not a little girl he can control. That I just don't have it in me to explain *why* his predicament means nothing to me.

Especially while I'm riding a rollercoaster of emotions that I've yet to understand.

My mind is still on him.

His scent surrounds me.

How it bothers me that he just sent me away without another word.

Casper Jameson.

"None of your concern. And no, we don't need to talk," I throw over my shoulder. Besides, these conversations always lead back down the same hurtful path: he abandoned us. We meant nothing to him when push came to shove. "You made your decision a long time ago, Matteo. Leave me out of your future endeavors."

"Don't call me that. I'm your father and—"

"You didn't raise me. Don't give yourself a title you haven't earned." I'm but a step or two from the *up* button, and just as I lift a hand to press it, I'm whirled around to face him. The eyes that bore into me are the same shade as mine. My father's hold isn't threatening or hard, but his expression is full of anger mixed with regret, a sadness that makes my brows furrow and chest clench.

It also causes me to look away, surveying the room to make sure we aren't attracting attention. That, and to compose myself. To not show him that I care.

Because I've never seen this man be anything but the hardcore criminal he is: the head of the biggest mob in Boston with connections all across the US and South America, Brazil being his biggest suppliers.

That, or the cocky and shrewd real estate mogul.

But with him, there's never an in-between. Criminal or unscrupulous businessman.

Matteo Cancio is known for being a cruel and egotistical man with no patience, and yet, right now, he looks almost defeated. Almost hurt by my rejection.

"Will you ever forgive me? Your mother did before she—"

"How's Samantha, by the way?" I cut him off, eyes snapping to his and narrowing at a man I barely know. My heart hardens all over again at his almost statement. At his reminder of what I lost. "Does she know you're here and visiting your bastard child? That you're offering me something that belongs to her son?"

He flinches at my words but regains his composure quickly. "You know we're divorced, Roe. And more importantly, it belongs to my firstborn…you."

"How quickly I've come to matter in the last few months. How easily you find me now that you want something from me."

"Why are we fighting?" he says, his fingers flexing on my arm as if he's afraid the moment he lets go, I'll bolt. "Aurora, I flew all the way out here because you promised to hear me out. You skipped dinner yesterday, and I sent you a message saying I'd be here at one."

"When did I confirm this?" I raise a brow.

At least he has the decency to look away. "I waited in the lobby hoping to catch you."

"So, you're stalking me?"

"It's not stalking when you agreed to hear me out," he counters, nose flaring a bit in his annoyance. I also know he hates this, that he finds the begging beneath him and believes I should just fall into line, but it's not happening. I'm not afraid of him. "And I've never done that to you. It's the one promise I made to your mother and kept."

"Again, no." I snort, the sound not attractive in the least as I ignore his last statement. His words hold no value to me. Not after years of being let down. This man is an unbelievable manipulator and nothing else. The poster child for *give an inch and they'll take a mile* kind of personality. "That's not how our conversation went at all, *Father*. I mentioned a vacation in Europe, and you decided to crash and make this about my duties as your child."

"I love you, Aurora. Please believe that if nothing else."

"Liar." As soon as I turned twenty-one, his call came. He thinks now is the perfect time to create some kind of bull-crap bond after years of missing visits, important dates, and remembering that I existed all around. Our time together over the years has always been few and far between, his attention always on my mother's life and never on me. I'm the forgotten one he now needs. "And quit avoiding my question. Samantha?"

Releasing his hold, he takes a step back and runs an agitated hand through his hair. "You know we're divorced."

"Because she cheated."

"Because we both made mistakes. Horrible ones." His cell phone rings somewhere on him, but he chooses to ignore it. A first for him. "With her, it was never about love."

"And yet you married her anyways," I sneer, my disdain for him and his actions clear to see. "This is your bed, and you will lie in it."

"Roe, I—"

"Don't. No excuses." An older couple comes near us then, and I move to the side with a smile on my face. "Good morning."

"Morning," they say in unison, looking between my father and me, noticing the tension—but choosing smartly not to comment. They mind their business while waiting for the elevator and then they enter, letting the doors close while avoiding our stares.

"As you can see, this isn't the best place for this type of conversation..." he tilts his head now in the direction of a crowd of what looks to be tourists that are gathering nearby "...why don't we go to lunch after you clean up, instead? I'll wait for you here and—"

"No." I take in a deep breath and let it out slowly, giving myself an extra minute to gather my thoughts. To come up with a better way to tell him to leave and never come back that doesn't use my favorite four-letter word. "Listen, Dad...I'm trying here. Really trying to keep my composure, but your insistence is making this very difficult.

I already told you, I'm not interested. My answer hasn't changed. It's the same as when we spoke in Chicago and Boston. You chose a marriage of convenience over my mother's love. Over being my father. I owe you nothing."

As the last word slips past my lips, a man I've seen once, when I agreed to visit my father's Boston office three months ago, reaches us while holding a phone out. He's tall and handsome, but in that generic sort of way with dark hair and brown eyes in a black suit and shiny shoes. Too put together. Nothing about him is as effortless as the man I spent last night with.

The man I vow to forget. To leave behind as a memory of my night in London.

My father takes the cell phone, covering the receiver. "Who is it, Dominic? I asked not to be interrupted."

"It's Lucas, sir." For a brief second the man's eyes shift toward me, and I don't like it. His stare. I don't know why he rubs me wrong and I shift from foot to foot, something my father doesn't take notice of.

Instead, at the mention of his ten-year-old son's name, Matteo Cancio smiles. It's the kind a loving father makes. The kind I've never seen directed at me. "Thank you." Then, like I've watched him do all my life, he holds a finger up and walks away without another word.

Because he just expects me to wait. To be here while he leaves me with someone I don't know—who makes me uncomfortable—while he attends to his real life.

The one I'm not privy to. The one I want no part in.

If I wasn't good enough as a child, then as an adult, I just don't care. *I'm done with him.*

Giving him my back, I take the few steps between myself and the elevator button, pressing the small circle. It lights up and a whirling sound follows as the elevator comes down. "Tell him I said no."

"Mr. Cancio didn't say you could leave." Dominic is much closer than I anticipate, and as I turn around to tell him exactly what his boss can go do, I bump into his much taller frame. I stumble, almost tripping on his foot, but his tight hold on my arm keeps me upright. "You'll wait here until he returns."

"Let go."

"Learn your place," he spits out, eyeing my clothes with disdain and a hint of something else that I can't quite identify. His proximity makes me uncomfortable. "You also look like trash. A man in his position can't be seen with a—"

"A what?" I snap, trying to yank my arm out of his grip. Thank God the group from before has left and the couple near the sitting area is oblivious to us. "Leave a mark, and it's your head."

"I'm his second-in-command. Well above a whore."

"So, you think his daughter is a whore?" How the hell does his right hand not know who I am? How much of a secret have I been kept from everyone?

"His daughter? Cancio has a daughter?" The shock is evident and all the answer I need. I've been kept a dirty secret, a thought that hurts, but I can't focus on that now. Not when his reaction causes his grip to loosen just as a ding rings clear from behind me.

"Yes. He does." Eyes on him, I step back, one foot after the other until I'm inside the car and pressing my floor's number. And it's as the doors begin to close that he realizes his mistake, stretching a hand out to keep them open. However, before he can come inside, I'm holding the taser my mother gave me years ago. It's small— almost untraceable—and does the job, forcing him away from the doors he stops from closing.

"Motherfuck," he hisses, shaking his left hand.

"Touch me again, and I'll show you just how much his daughter I am."

THE SECOND I'm back inside my room, the walls cave in. My emotions overflow in rivulets of hurt down my cheek, and no matter how much I wipe them away, another tear follows its path.

I'm angry and overwhelmed—choking on confusion and physical exhaustion. On my regret and need. On a push and pull that makes no sense, and no matter how badly I want to let go—fall apart at yet another reminder of how little I mean to Matteo—there's another, more prominent desire: to flee. To get far away from this city and the last twenty-four hours.

Away from the memory of someone who's just like my father. A criminal.

With that thought in mind, I stumble toward the hotel's closet and pull out my luggage; a midsize piece that I'll gladly tote through any train station or airport in order to escape and forget. To not seek him out—demand an apology—by going back to the pub where I met him.

Rushing into the bathroom, I stop at the vanity to collect my things when my eyes glance up. "*Christ*, I'm a mess." My dark waves are a tangled disaster from Casper's fingers, from the way he wrapped the long strands around his fist and tugged. A memory that causes my nipples to harden and rub against the soft fabric of his shirt. The sensation pulls a low moan from me as yet another tear falls, its track creating a charcoal-colored line down my cheek and toward my kiss-swollen lips. Lips that tingle as if he were kissing me. "Out of everyone I could've slept with, why him?"

Casper represents everything I loathe, and yet a sick part of me wants another night. To feel as alive as I did under his fingertips. *How can I want his touch after hearing him sentence a man to death?*

After what happened downstairs? Seeing my father should deter me. I shouldn't be flip-flopping from one extreme to the next within the same breath.

One second I want to punch a wall and then cry. Then, the very next, I want to find Casper and smack him for making me feel this unstable.

"Get in the shower," I tell myself, forcing my fingers to come up and undo each button of his dress shirt. It's torturous and slow, but I manage to peel it off while watching through the mirror and cataloguing each small bite he left behind.

On my breast. On my collarbones.

Then, when I lower his shorts, the purplish fingerprints stand out on my hips. Yet another reminder of my stupidity.

Closing my eyes, I count to ten and reopen them. Then I do it again. And again.

Each time I look at my reflection, I let go of a little guilt and forgive myself for being human.

"I won't see him again. I won't repeat my mother's mistake." Pulling his socks off, I step into the shower and turn the faucet to as hot as I can stand it. I'm in a rush to put this all behind me, to wash him from my skin. Lather, rinse, and repeat; I let what's left of his touch flow down the drain in a rain of vanilla suds before stepping out and drying off.

And it's after brushing my teeth and collecting his clothes from the floor that my phone begins to ring. It's a ringtone I know. A ringtone I have no plans to answer.

Instead, I bring everything in my hands to the bed and dump it beside my open luggage. I never really unpacked, and it's a blessing as I pull out a pair of yoga pants and tank top from the very top, then my underwear from a separate small pocket attached to the lid.

I'm dressed before the ping of a text comes three minutes later.

I have my toiletries in hand as the next message comes in.

Five in total, and I don't reply to any.

My focus is on packing up, closing the luggage, and slipping my feet into a pair of trainers for the long trip ahead. This change in plans will put me in Ibiza a few days early, but the extra cost will be worth it. Money isn't an issue thanks to my inheritance, and this is an expense I can justify without thinking twice.

My mother would approve of this change in plans and so would my best friend, Aliana. She's holding down the fort back home, and I'd like to think she'd slap me for letting a man get to me this way. For not using my better judgement. *Or she'll cheer me on for getting some.*

That last thought isn't helping, and I block out everything around me, tunneling my focus on getting the hell out of this place.

I can't run the risk of seeing Casper again.

I don't want to be anywhere near my father.

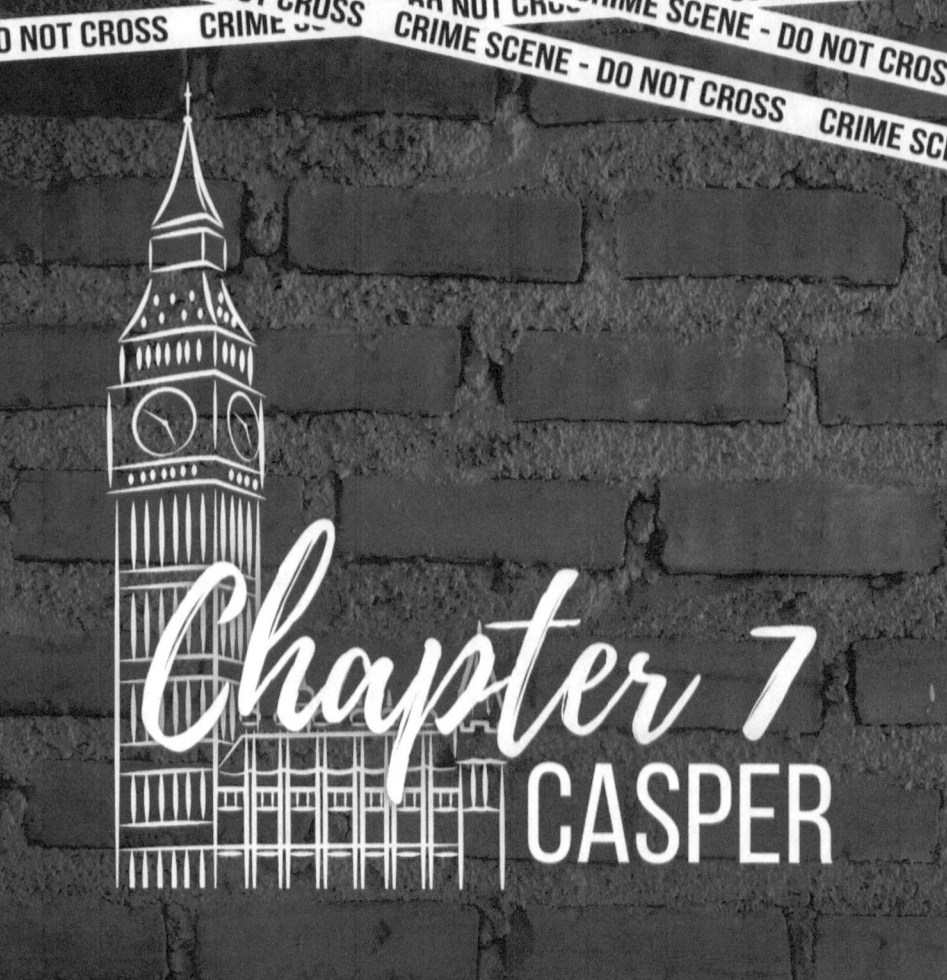

Chapter 7
CASPER

I'VE BEEN WATCHING her since my arrival in Ibiza two days ago.

Just watching. Cataloguing her mannerisms. Taking in every bloody detail without the outside world interrupting the voyeur-like tendencies that have risen since my meeting Gem.

She's become my own personal show. This sad little doll who hides her pain from the world and I want to make smile again.

Because I see her. What she hides.

Aurora knows what I am because I'll never hide that, but I'm also not the one she's truly running from. Her past is dictating her future, and that won't bloody work with me.

After she left London, I took forty-eight hours to do my homework while one of my men tailed her. While he made sure she was safe and not being followed, I confirmed my suspicions on her ties with Matteo Cancio; a father/daughter relationship with no real bond.

The video feed I procured through the manager was enlightening to say the least. As they spoke in the hotel's lobby near the elevator bank, there was a coldness—clear unfamiliarity between the two. Her body language showed discomfort and distrust, while his was nothing but frustration. No warmth. No clear connection.

Then, there's the lack of his involvement in her life.

She's his firstborn. His heir. And yet, Aurora Conte doesn't carry his last name. She doesn't so much as have a security detail.

Her father has the same resources I have—knows where she is—but chooses to leave her unprotected. Not so much as a location tracker was found on her phone by my hacker, Ezra, after breaking into the device.

Why?

It's an arsehole move, but useful as I took over the position and put a man on her I trust. Alexander is ruthless and very much committed to his husband. He has eyes for no one but him and understands what I'm capable of. Knows that I won't hesitate to end him and his spouse if so much as a hair on her head is touched.

I'm protective of her.

The second my private flight touched down on Spanish soil, I sent my man back home with a message for Callum. We still have visitors in London, and I want him to follow their every move—to make sure Matteo doesn't change his mind and comes after Aurora.

That, and to pinpoint the location of my guns.

Because they're still inside the country. No container has left the port or has been transferred since the theft. No manifesto for export has been reported by my employee at the docks, either.

They've gone ghost, and I want them found.

My phone buzzes atop the small beachside table then and I look down, reading the quick message from Callum.

> Flight booked for tomorrow back to the States.
> Ten in the morn. ~Callum

I pick up the phone to reply but stop when movement from the pool catches my attention.

"Christ," I groan low, taking in her delicious curves as she exits the pool, and then as she walks toward the lounger she's occupying. Aurora is a vision; drops of water skimming down her body as the sun kisses her skin—the light-golden tone making her look like a goddess. She's temptation and heat and the definition of femininity while crawling onto the beach chair and then lying face down.

Her arse—the bottom curve with just the hint of my bruise—is on display as those tiny black bottoms ride up a tiny bit, molding onto those plump cheeks that make my mouth water.

She's a pleasurable puzzle I crave. A drug I will indulge in soon.

My mobile buzzes again in my hand and I look down.

> B.O.L. for a container to Massachusetts just went
> through. Code? ~Callum

> Registered Name? ~Casper

Three tiny dots appear on my screen while he types.

> It's to Cancio. ~Callum

> Code to proceed? ~Callum

Bringing the two fingers' worth of whiskey to my lips, I take a sip while considering my options. It'd be so easy to take back what's mine with quick retribution, but something doesn't quite add up in this equation. It reeks of a bloody rat.

His actions back at the hotel don't add up with just how alone she is. How unprotected.

This bothers me. Nags at me.

She needs me. A truth I'm coming to accept with each tick of the clock. With the way my eyes always stray to hers.

I don't hesitate on my reply, fingers flying over the screen.

Green. ~Casper

His reply is immediate.

Are you sure? ~Callum

I smell something foul. ~Casper

Then I'll find the source. ~Callum

With that, I pocket the small device and stand, throwing a heated glare at the arsehole serving drinks behind the hotel's bar. The bandage over his nose should've been enough of a deterrent—my visit and then the broken bone—to keep his bodged-up mug from looking in her direction, however, he seems to need a reminder.

The bloke doesn't see me approach and neither do the people milling about. They're all too busy watching a group of women letting loose and dancing, stumbling as their inebriated state becomes evident.

The moment the blonde trips into the pool, most rush to the edge in order to help or get a closer view of the hot mess, and I move closer. As her mates yell and the lifeguard dives in, I stop right in front of him.

His eyes widen. He pales. "Sir, I—"

"Not a sound," I warn, and before the crowd dissipates, I grab him by the hair and slam his face down against the stone edge of his bar top. At once, a gash appears on his forehead and blood spills from the cut, while his scream is muffled by the cries of panicking women. He's pathetic, afraid, and I laugh—a sinister little chuckle that makes him tremble. "Don't so much as breathe in her direction, lad. I'm watching."

With those parting words, I pat his cheek and walk away. I have plans. A surprise.

Before the end of the night, Gem will know the lengths I'll always go to find her.

To have her.

How I want more of us.

For her, I've become a stalker. The lion in our private game of chase.

UP UNTIL A FEW DAYS AGO, I had not slept with a woman in months, and she'd been a true one-off catered by the private club in Chicago's Lake Forest. They know of my appetite. Of my rules. Of what I demand.

Anonymity.

No names. No conversation. And my cock wrapped tight above all else.

Those encounters were few and far between; once or twice during my four-month stay in Illinois each year because I don't do relationships. I don't trust easily. I don't want a woman who hangs off my arm or spreads her thighs at night so she can spend millions on some bullshit that only impresses the snobby arseholes that frequent elite establishments.

The easy type that see a man in my position as nothing more than a bank account.

Moreover, with my job—lifestyle—I couldn't afford that kind of a distraction.

However, the day I met this woman, something within my rationality changed. Made me want more.

A thought cemented by the hardening of my cock as I watch her in that tiny towel fresh out of the shower. Walking toward me. Toward the darkened corner of the room I sit in, unbeknownst to her.

Aurora pushes her hair over her left shoulder with a delicate hand, stretching her neck as drops of water disappear beneath the fabric of her towel. Tantalizing. Mouthwatering.

I want to follow the path of those rivulets with my tongue.

"Fuck, Gem." It's a low groan. A hungry warning.

"Casper," she says, and it's a bit breathy. No screaming or even a hint of shock in her expression. Instead, those beautiful eyes meet mine and they're full of curiosity and want. With the same cheeky fire of that night a few days back.

"I'm here, love."

At the term of endearment, she swallows hard while goose bumps rise across her flushing skin. "I knew I wasn't going crazy. There's this insane pull and I...*Christ*...by the pool...I kept looking, trying to find you but couldn't. Yet I knew. I knew you were here."

"Good." I push the small button on the lamp atop a table beside me. It illuminates the room, a soft glow that makes her look almost ethereal.

Like my perfect wet dream.

"It's insane and makes absolutely no sense." Aurora shakes her head then, those wet tendrils moving across her collarbone. "Why did I sense you near? How is that even possible?"

Standing, I take the few steps between us slowly, almost predatory, stopping when there's only an inch of space between her almost naked body and mine. "I'll never be too far." Slowly, I bring a hand up and cup her face, reveling in how she nuzzles my palm without conscious thought. How she rubs her thighs together, a slow movement I don't call attention to. "But you know that already. Don't you, Gem?"

"Do I?" She pulls back a bit but lets the tip of my thumb rest against her bottom lip. An action that is followed by the quick swipe of her pink, soft tongue across my skin—by the warmth of her breath as a pant escapes.

"Careful." My voice is rough, exposing my undeniable yearning. How close I am to taking those lips and then her body.

"Sorry?" The way she phrases it like a question shows she's anything but.

"Not your fault I find you dangerous."

Her eyes widen and a rosy tint dances across her cheeks. "Me? Dangerous?"

"Completely." With that, I let my hand drop and take a few steps back. I have plans and won't ruin them by giving in to the temptation so soon. "Now, how about you get dressed and join me for dinner. We have reservations for eight."

"We do? When did that happen?" Gem is trying hard to fight back a smile, but I notice the twitch in her upper lip immediately. This girl is crazy, beautiful, and not denying my request.

"While you were having lunch."

"And if I say no?"

"You won't."

"How do you know that?"

"Because, Gem—"

"Why do you keep calling me that?" Fuck, that mouth. That sass. How she questions everything makes me hard. Has me throbbing. More so when she arches her defined brow and places a hand on her hip, waiting, demanding an answer.

Reminds me of an angry kitten. Cute and with claws.

Three steps forward and I have her heat caressing my skin, her scent—soft and feminine—infiltrating my senses. She consumes me, and yet, I'm also aware of every little thing. Notice how the flush on her cheeks travels down her neck and over the top of her breasts. How her lips part, a sweet little pant escaping her mouth as I bring my face closer.

I want to kiss those lips. To taste her again, but not yet.

"What are you doing?" It leaves her on a shaky whisper.

"Nothing at all." Turning my face, I trail my lips up from her cheek to her ear, releasing a rough exhale there that makes my Gem shake. To make this little noise from the back of her throat that causes my cock to jerk hard within the confines of my trousers, beads of pre-come rolling down the sensitive skin. I can feel each one. How they coat my piercing and then the fabric of my trousers. "Be ready by eight and I'll tell you."

"Tell me what?" Aurora arches her neck to give me better access.

"Why you're my Gem." Then, because I can't help myself, I nip the skin she's offering. A bite just shy of pain and that will leave my small mark. "Eight on the dot."

"Eight." It's a moan. A plea for another.

"Yes," I hum and stand up to my full height, towering over her small frame with a smirk. Loving the dazed look in her eyes, the quick rise and fall of her chest. How I affect her. "See you in an hour, love."

"Okay."

Leaving is hard, but I do so without another word.

I'll give her the next sixty minutes to prepare for me. To get her thoughts in order, but that's it.

I'm ready for her to meet me as I am.

The devil behind the eyes of a saint.

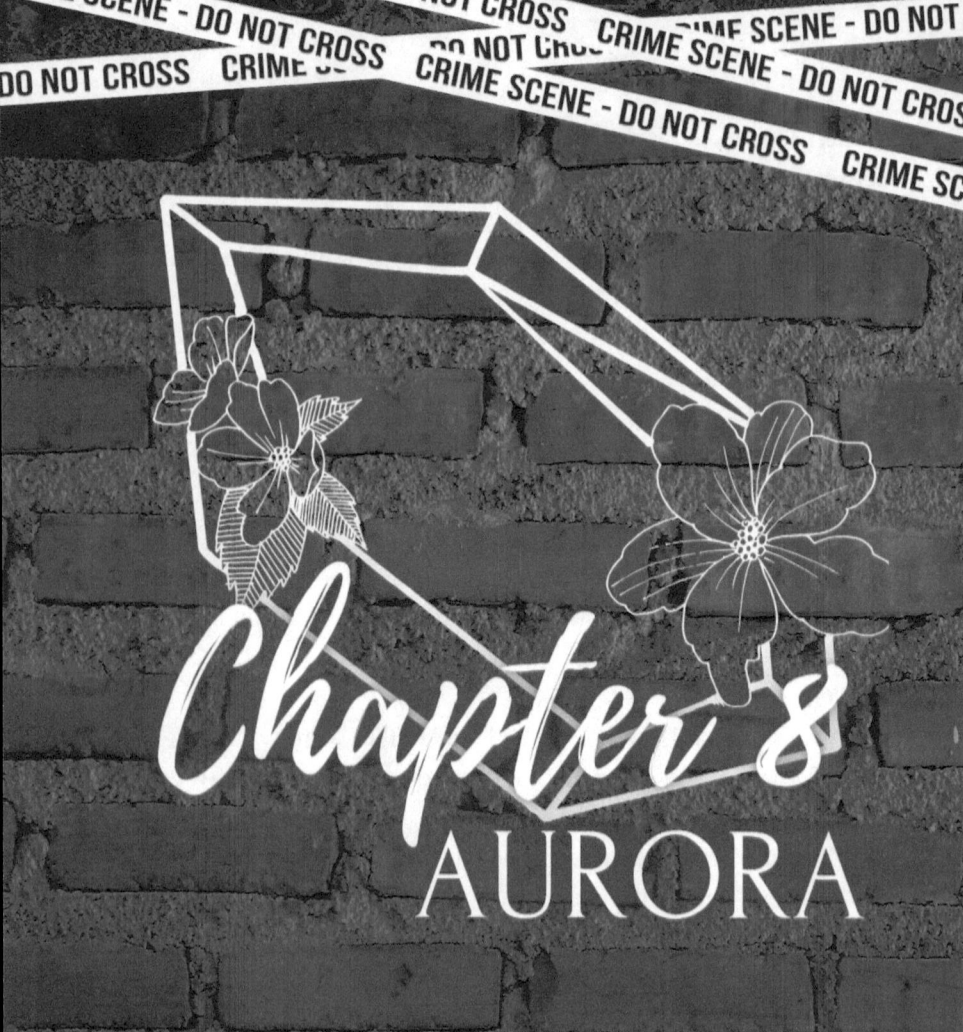

Chapter 8

AURORA

T HE SECOND HE walks out, I let out the breath I'd been holding. I'm shivering and my legs feel weak. I'm confused and angry and feel elated all at once.

I've been expecting him. It's why I didn't scream. Why I let him get close and then convince me to attend this dinner.

This effect he has on me isn't fair, and he uses it to his advantage. He gets under my skin, and I forget the reasons why *we—I—* shouldn't.

Like his similarities to my father. What I heard inside his office. How he had his employee see me out.

That last one stings the most, which is hypocritical since I was already looking for a way out. I know this. Admit it. However, the mind is a torturous bitch, and mine seems to hate me since I woke up in his bed. It won't let me rest, agree with the rational side of me.

He's nothing but bad news wrapped up in a handsome package. A beautiful disaster.

This man has heartbreak written all over him, and I'm going to be damaged goods after he leaves. Because all men do that in the end. They come and conquer and then disappear into the night with nothing but the occasional smoke signal left in their wake if you're lucky.

I don't want that life. His kind of life. The kind my father gave my mother and me.

And what's worse, I have a feeling he knows more than he lets on. That he sees more than I want him to.

"Why didn't I just tell him to go?" I ask myself aloud, but the answer is pretty obvious. Even with all those strikes against him, I want Casper. Want him near. Desire his lustful wrath.

There's something about him that pulls me in; I wasn't lying when I told him this. Just like I'm aware of his presence, that dominating force that takes over any room and makes you take notice:

Of him.

Of just how dangerous he is.

That night at the club, I felt it. Let it consume me.

Let him take over my senses—rationality—and I followed his lead. With him, I lowered my inhibitions and let the almost painful need that bloomed at his touch dictate my actions.

I slept with him without a condom.

I begged for more.

I became a needy whore without an ounce of shame.

My thighs clench at the memory of his rough hands, and I place my palm on the door to hold myself up, leaning my forehead against the cool metal for a second. "Why is he here?"

Another question with a simple answer: me.

For two days now I've felt him near, could smell that lingering scent of wood and spice in the air around me. Haunting me. Making me doubt my sanity as I looked around but couldn't find his handsome face.

And even as he evaded my eyes, I knew.

In a sick way, I felt nothing but relief when he spoke from the darkened corner of my room. I like that he came for me. More than I should, and it brings forth a tumultuous mixture of emotions that I'm not ready to decipher.

"Maybe I am going insane?" Damn him, I'm yo-yoing again. Going from one emotional extreme to the next as I did back at his home. It's making me unstable. Agreeable. Too curious for my own damn good. "Or maybe I'm just an idiot when it comes to him."

Not a question. My actions prove as much.

My curiosity will be my downfall, and I'm walking straight toward it.

Turning, I head toward the closet in the room and grab a little taupe-colored faux wrap dress that I bought in London during my afternoon outing. It's sexy, comfortable, and fits me like a glove. Then, I peruse my shoes and grab a pair of nude, embellished-buckle heels and the pearl drop earrings inside of a small case with my jewelry.

Normally, I don't wear anything outside of a bracelet with a large charm my mom gave me when I turned sixteen, but today calls for something extra. At the very least, I want the man to suffer. To want what I'm not going to give him.

I've become certifiable. Playing with the devil.

It thrills and scares me all in the same breath. Makes me feel guilty but alive.

This combustible attraction pushes me to seek out answers to questions I shouldn't have but can't deny.

Once I have everything in my hand, I walk back out and cast a glance at the hotel alarm clock, realizing I only have forty minutes left to get ready. "I need something with lace," I mumble under my breath, mentally checking through what I have with me. I never took my lingerie out of my luggage, choosing instead to leave the suitcase inside the small sitting area and above the coffee table there. The lid is closed but not zipped, and I flip it open to the small compartment. I know what I'm looking for: a black and lace pair of boy shorts and a bralette in the same material.

The bra doesn't do much in the lifting department, but mine are perky and this just gives my nipples an extra barrier of protection against his charm.

With everything laid out atop the bed, I drop the towel and get dressed. Everything fits me just right, and as I walk to the bathroom to do my makeup and hair, I decide to go the natural route. Just a bit of mascara, my winged liner, and a hint of gloss on my full lips.

Then, I leave my hair to air dry. Grabbing the mousse atop the counter, I dispense a healthy amount and work it through my hair, scrunching the raw waves and giving them an extra bit of bounce. It's the perfect complement to the atmosphere; the sea salt in the air and the waves crashing upon on the shore.

Besides, if he pisses me off, I can go from date night to a club like this. *Keep telling yourself that.*

Ignoring my inner thoughts, I open the faucet to wash my hands, when there's a knock. Three simple raps against the metal door and my thighs clench—heart trying to beat out of my chest as my panties dampen.

I know it's him. Casper.

It's that same crazy electricity that flows through my system when he's near.

Another knock follows a few seconds after, and I give myself one last look in the mirror. "Just dinner, Roe. Behave and don't lose yourself."

Easier said than done, because the moment I open that door a few seconds later, I know it's a lost cause. Every single cell in my body comes alive, and I thrum with excitement. With that dangerous edge of fire I'm currently playing with.

I'm going to burn for this.

He's going to ruin me.

"You look motherfucking delicious, Gem."

"So, tell me a bit about yourself?" he asks from beside me just as I lift my forkful of saffron rice to my lips. "Where are you from? Tell me about your family."

Putting the utensil back on my plate, I take a moment to sip from my wine glass instead—trying to find the right way to phrase my answer without explaining just who my father is. How similar they are.

Because my mother wouldn't be a hard or long topic; I don't speak of her in detail. It's not necessary, more so after saying a certain four-letter word that makes others uncomfortable.

However, Matteo Cancio is another beast. One he will grill me on. Ask me questions I don't have answers to.

These men don't have a reason to know about each other. They should never meet; Casper's in the UK and my father in Boston.

There should be no business ties. These two worlds should never collide.

Besides, it's not like I'll be seeing Casper after this. *You hate liars.*

"You're saying my accent doesn't give me away?" I say instead, changing the subject while waving my right hand in the air. My eyes are on his, watching, and I catch the moment a hint of amusement flashes through his eyes. As if he's privy to what I'm doing. "What?"

You're hiding something yourself, hypocrite.

"What's *what*?" he counters, taking a sip from his own glass, savoring the full-bodied red he chose to accompany his steak. Watching him swallow is a sinful experience—the way his throat bobs is sexy, and he knows this. The curl at the corner of his top lip tells me just how aware he is of his appeal. "Be more specific, Gem."

"Fine," I huff, finding my opening. The perfect way to avoid. "How about you tell me about the nickname? What does it mean?"

"So tit for tat."

"More like I want answers, and you owe me." I lift a bitch brow, while on the inside I'm relieved he's following. That I won't have to lie.

"How'd you figure that, love?" There's something in his tone that I can't quite decipher. His posture is completely at ease while a boyish grin spreads across full lips. Lips that I want to taste. Remember how good they felt against my own.

Focus, Roe. Don't let him jumble our conviction.

Taking in a deep breath, I let it out slowly while squaring my shoulders. I won't be dissuaded. "Because you sent me away the morning after via your employee without a goodbye. Because you followed me here—imposed yourself on my vacation—without me ever sharing my location. Because you were inside of my hotel room, waiting, as I took a shower without my giving you a key." I tick each point off with my fingers, mimicking his posture, my voice at an even decibel. "What are you looking for?"

"You." A simple answer that causes goose bumps to rise on my skin. "I'm here because of you."

I let out a small huff. "Explain, Casper. I deserve more than that."

The waiter comes around then, pulling my attention away. "How's the food? Is there anything else I can get you?"

"No," we reply in unison, remaining quiet until the man is out of earshot. A minute or two passes and I'm beginning to get frustrated, the silence more than awkward.

"Ask me." Casper's low words pull my eyes back to his warm green ones. My breath catches inside my throat; the softness in them isn't something I'm expecting, and my traitorous heart thumps harshly within my chest. "Ask me again why I am here."

"Tell me." My own response is a whisper. Almost afraid to hear his response.

To face what his words could mean.

Sitting forward, he extends his left hand toward me, palm facing upwards. Long fingers wiggle while the handsome devil raises a brow; it's an invitation. A welcoming gesture that I can't turn down.

I place mine atop his and a current—this inexplicable feeling begins to flow through my limbs. It's heady. Pulling me in closer by this inexplicable and invisible force.

"That's why. Right there." His thumb runs across my wrist, over my pulse point that thumps wildly beneath his fingertip. "There's something about you, Aurora Conte, that pulls me in. That I can't get out of my head." His hand grips my wrist then and tugs me over, enough so that I'm but a few inches from his face. Tasting his every exhale. "That same desire is what put me on a plane to Ibiza so I could steal another kiss."

"I don't—"

Casper shakes his head, telling me he isn't finished, and I close my lips. "Want to know why I call you Gem." It's not a question and yet, I still nod. Waiting with bated breath for another confession. "You're my Gem because you're trouble under the disguise of a priceless jewel. Rare and hidden, but once found, they come attached to a heavy price tag. A life of servitude."

"What are you trying to say?" Because I need more clarification. To understand.

His fingers intertwine with mine and tug, causing our lips to meet. At once, that spark of desire and life and warmth reignites, seeping into every single cell in my body. Making me move closer. Moan as he sweeps his mouth over mine, once, twice, and then parts his lips, letting me taste him as he releases a rough exhale.

"What I'm saying, love, is that we'll be fucked in this together."

Chapter 9
CASPER

"SO, THIS IS ME," Aurora says as we stop in front of her room door an hour later. She's a tiny bit tipsy, smiling and fucking adorable while looking up at me.

We've done nothing but talk, eat, and drink—laugh—all night. Just being. Something I don't have the luxury to do, but with her seem to effortlessly fall into.

I've also held back from kissing those sweet lips again for the sake of showing I *can* be a gentleman if I so choose. To show her that I'm not just after what's between her thighs, that torturous heat that I can feel through the fabric of my trousers. That I want to drown in.

I'm here for more than that.

I'm here to get to know all of her. Figure out why I can't stay away.

Just a taste. Just one and I'll leave.

"Are you sure, love?" I close the gap between us, pushing her against the solid metal, one hand on her hip while the other is flat on the door beside her head. "What if it's mine?"

"You're not staying here." It's a matter-of-fact response that pulls a small chuckle from me. "I would know."

"If you say so."

"I do." Then, her brows furrow while nimble fingers dig into her small clutch, bringing the keycard up to her face. "Says room 916...that's mine?"

"Then I guess it is."

"Told you." The look she gives me is full of sass and fire—of a playfulness that makes my length twitch against her lower abdomen.

Motherfuck, she's beautiful. Adorably erotic in these tiny bouts of softness that come forth when her guard is down. And I like her like this, relaxed and without the purse in her lips or the stiffness in her posture.

Right now, she's languid against me. Melting into me.

Without realizing, her body seeks mine. My warmth. My touch.

While her shoulders are pressed against the door, those hips are slightly pushing forward. Small gyrations against my cock that cause me to grit my teeth.

"Behave."

"Why?"

Instead of answering, I bring the hand at her hip up, skimming up the center of her chest and pause at her throat. Aurora swallows hard and my fingers stretch out over the expanse, tightening just a bit to see her reaction.

It's automatic. Sensual.

Those hazel eyes close and lips part, my name slipping past those lips on a sacred moan. "Casper."

That sound breaks me, and before she can take her next inhale, I slam my lips to hers. I pin her body against that door, tilting her head back as I devour her natural sweetness. It shakes me and pulls an almost animalistic growl from deep within my chest as I part her lips, caressing my tongue with hers as I take more.

As she lets me. As I dominate the kiss.

And fuck me if she isn't a responsive little thing.

Her clutch meets the floor and those small fingers embed themselves in my hair, tugging at the ends to pull me closer. "I shouldn't want this, but I do," she mewls, a low kittenish sound that settles on the swollen head of my cock and I thrust against her. It's pleasurable pain. It's a guttural need.

It brings rationality back and I slow down our kiss to a few soft pecks. Because while I want her—fucking crave her—I want her to trust me. To beg me. To call on me.

Stepping back, I bend down and pick up her small purse and the phone that slipped out. I don't look at her as I do this, nor do I ask her for permission while entering my phone number into the device.

"What are...why?" Aurora huffs, frustration and want ringing clear through her words.

"I'll see you in the morning."

Gem snatches her belongings from my hand, eyes narrowed. "I'm not a toy."

"And I'm just a man," I counter, loving how her eyes immediately shift to the bulge in my trousers. "A hard-as-fuck man."

"Then why—"

Placing a finger over her lips, I shake my head. "Because I'm trying to be more than the arsehole you think I am."

At once, whatever rebuttal she had evaporates and the soft girl from a bit ago returns. "Okay." There's a hint of a blush on her cheeks that makes my mouth water, even more so when she turns, fumbling with the card and its slot. Her hands are shaking, breathing a bit labored.

On the third try, the light turns green and her hand turns the handle, pushing the door wide open. Her right foot moves, entering the threshold, and I press myself one last time against her back, pushing her soft tresses over one shoulder so I can lay a tiny kiss below her ear.

"If you need me, I'm right next door. Sweet dreams, Gem."

HER BODY CALLS to mine like a siren's song.

An unrelenting tune set out to destroy the last of my mental stability. Not that there's ever been much there; I'm a proud arsehole without an ounce of shame. Without remorse.

Being a criminal is second nature.

Taking a life is as easy as breathing.

And yet, with her, I'm different. Hard as fuck but relaxed. Enjoying myself without the itch—the need to get my hands dirty.

Like now.

I should be in London and putting a bullet between her old man's eyes. Killing the three men he brought with him, especially the one with a wandering eye. Eyes that continuously strayed toward my Gem.

I saw it in the video and pictures while she argued with her father. His interest was plain to see. The dumb cunt wanted a taste of her forbidden fruits.

I'll be taking care of him myself when the time comes.

Pacing the length of the room, I stretch my neck, trying to control the insatiable hunger Aurora creates. My need is growing. Each time the clocks ticks signaling the passing of another minute, I'm wound tighter, hands clenching as I try to behave. To not seek her out.

So, I pace again. Then once more.

There's nothing but a wall separating me from her temptation. Nothing but a door with a lock that I have the key for.

It would be so easy...

"Fuck," I grit through my teeth, palming my thick cock through the thin cotton of my lounge pants. The material is soft, sliding down my length with each jerk of my hands and leaving behind a wet spot right below the waistband.

Another firm stroke and the bulbous tip slips out, meeting the cold air and pulling a hiss from me. Hot and cold, it feels good— bobbing on its own accord—and I lower the bottoms over my hips.

It slaps against my lower abdomen and I take hold, wrapping my fingers tight around the smooth shaft. Pumping my wrist one, twice, I swipe my thumb over the head and piercing, flicking the metal.

A shock of pleasure runs down my spine and it's mediocre at best. Moreover, I'm afraid everything after Aurora will fit that profile.

That nothing but her pussy will ever be enough.

Tightening my fist, I close my eyes and focus on the scent of cherry blossoms that still lingers from when she clung to me. How good that tight little body felt against mine. The warmth between her thighs as she gyrated—

My mobile pings with an incoming text and my muscles clench. Needing. Wanting.

Another text.

"Lord, please give me strength." Opening my eyes, I walk over to the nightstand and grab my phone with my unoccupied hand. My thumb swipes across the screen and what meets my eyes is the devil's temptation.

It's my redemption and cross.

Gem is lying down with a sweet little smirk on her lips while wearing my white Oxford, the same one the little thief took when running from my home. The first three buttons are undone, giving me a small peak of her breasts, while those hazel eyes dare me to come. To take.

And I will.

Fuck it.

She wants to play with fire. So be it, but on my terms.

I told her all she had to do was ask. To tell me what she wanted, and I'd be there.

But this picture was a dare, not a plea.

Giving my dick three harsh strokes, I remove my hold and pull the lounge pants up. There's a decent-sized sitting area in this room and I walk toward it, taking a bloody seat at the center of the couch. I'm throbbing, needing to come, but I ignore the pain and set an alarm instead.

Her punishment will be the desperation that builds as I make her wait.

My reward will be her screams of pleasure as I mark her soft skin with my come.

TWO HOURS later I'm pushing the hotel's keycard into the scanner and slipping inside her room, keeping my movements as quiet as possible while Gem sleeps. She's unaware and at my mercy.

The room is dark except for a small sliver of moonlight coming in from the large window to the left of the bed; it takes me a minute or two, but my eyes adjust, and I take in her curves. Aurora is face down and semi-covered with a half thrown blanket over her hips and my long sleeves to keep her warm.

Her lower body, though, from that bottom curve where arse meets thigh, is bare. Looks soft. Ready for me.

And I'm hard for her—throbbing as I leak pre-come down my shaft; the drops roll over my piercing before marking my pajama bottoms. It's proof of my desire. My weakness for her.

For her, I've become a gluttonous bastard willing to live in hell in order to enjoy this slice of heaven.

Poor girl has no idea of the devil's trap she's fallen into.

My feet carry me closer and I stop at the edge of the bed, lowering my pajama bottoms before placing a knee on the mattress. It dips beneath the weight, but she doesn't wake up. Instead, a light sigh escapes her pouty lips and she lifts a leg higher.

Unconsciously opening herself to me. An invitation I accept by climbing up and kneeling just over her dainty feet while fisting my length, stroking twice. Harsh strokes that cause another pearl-like bead to pool at the tip and then fall, this time right over the arch of her foot.

Motherfuck, the sight is sinful, the heat coming from her skin maddening.

I can almost taste her sweetness in the air all around me.

"Fucking perfection." And she is. Those words hit me in the gut the second they pass through my lips, and I accept their weight.

From the moment I laid my eyes on her face, I've become an addict. Wanting more. Needing her closer. It's something that makes absolutely no sense, but I'm not fighting either.

It just is. We just are.

Moreover, it's this pull that has me crawling over her sensuous body with a throbbing cock and pressing my mouth to the corner of those pouty lips. The act startles her awake, but I just peck them again. "It's me," I whisper, nuzzling her cheek before giving her chin a small nip.

At the sound of my voice, her body loses its rigidity. "Casper, what...*oh!*"

My body covers hers, thick cock pressing against her arse. "You pulled the wrong lion's tail, Gem."

"You left me hanging." Subconsciously, she pushes back. Back arching as she gyrates beneath me. No fear. No pushing me away. "I waited for you."

"I know." Placing an elbow beside her head, I put most of my weight on it while using the other hand to trail down her body. Softly. Slowly. Barely there caresses as I make my way toward the bottom edge of my shirt that has ridden up. The end sits halfway over her arse, but it's not enough. I want her bare from head to toe. Pinned beneath me. Writhing for me.

Fisting the material, I lower my lips to her ear and groan. Release a harsh exhale over the fragrant flesh of her neck as I push it up higher, not stopping until the expanse of her back is against my front. "Little girls that taunt deserve to be left wanting."

The simple contact burns me. Sears me from the outside in as she moans low from the back of her throat. "No games. I *need—*"

"Tell me." It's a rough grunt, my hips thrusting against her bare cheeks.

Aurora turns her head then, hazel eyes locking on mine from over her shoulder. "I want you."

Three words that promise nirvana. Gift me her submission.

"Lift up a bit." She does as I ask without another prompt, giving me just enough space to slip a hand between her and the mattress. There are two buttons which hold the top in place, and I undo those quickly, parting the material before pulling it off and tossing it aside. She's not wearing panties and I don't hesitate to cup her pussy, spreading her wetness with the tips of two fingers.

I follow the length of her slit, just slightly adding pressure on each pass and on her next whimper, I bury them deep.

"Oh God," Gem releases a tiny moan then, walls clenching as she tries to pull me in deeper. Her hips undulate against my hand and I pump them in and out a few times, slowly dragging my fingers against her walls before pulling out and replacing them with my dick.

The bulbous tip runs from her folds to clit, and then back again. Once. Twice. And on the third slide, I slam in to the hilt, causing her to choke on a scream.

"There's my girl." A warm rush of wetness coats me on the second stroke and I groan, holding still for a second to enjoy the tight squeeze. How her walls flutter around me. "This beautiful little pussy missed me."

Not a question. I know she missed my touch; her photo proved as much. Aurora wanted to test me—push me to act without her admitting our truth.

Together we're an exquisite explosion. An unavoidable catastrophe we will morph into a beautiful beginning.

"That feels...so...*more*," she whimpers, bucking back against me as she rises up on all fours. That sinful body never stops moving, though.

Working herself on and off my length, Gem motherfucking rides my cock, hard. Her arse bounces. Her wetness coats my inner thighs and balls.

Balls that grow heavier each time she clenches.

Pleasure rips through my limbs as the perverse sound of her wetness becomes the soundtrack of this moment.

My eyes roll back and my hands grab her hips, fingers digging in as I retake control. Pulling out, I don't allow her to move. I don't allow her take what she needs.

"Don't move," I hiss out, gritting my teeth when my piercing grazes her entrance. A harsh shiver rushes down my spine and my muscles lock down.

I'm close. So close.

But not without her. She'll always come first.

With my knee, I spread her legs further apart, forcing her body low to the mattress with mine following. From head to toe, we were one.

And through it all she never stops looking back at me. Those hypnotic eyes on mine. Those parted lips moaning my name.

But that's not what breaks me. What annihilates the last shred of my control is the slow glide of her tongue across her bottom lip before she closes her eyes and mouths the word *fuck me.*

That's it. I'm done.

I'm not letting her go.

A truth that has me slamming back in to the hilt on my next breath. It clouds my senses and I lose myself in her. In her touch. In her scent.

In the way she arches against my hold to match my strokes, pushing that round arse back. No matter how hard I take her—fuck the imprint of my cock into her walls—Aurora stays with me. Matches my every thrust with a gyration of her own.

"Casper, please...I need you—"

"You have me." Fisting her hair, I force her head back and eyes toward the headboard. The deep arch changes the angle—it's deeper —and I bring my lips to the area just below her ear. Kissing. Nipping. Licking a path down to her neck where I nuzzle the lightly sweaty skin. "*Motherfuck*, you have me."

And it's as the last word passes through my lips that she clamps down, body seizing as her orgasm hits. I don't stop. Instead, my strokes become almost punishing with how out of control she has me. Seeing her come undone is my ultimate high, and my own release follows hers two strokes later.

"Christ, you're tight. So fucking good." It's messy; I spill every last drop inside and don't pull out—rope after hot rope mixing with her juices and dripping onto the sheets below. The entire room smells of us, and it's a heady scent that I've come to crave. Need.

As we lay there trying to regain our breathing, silence fills the room. Her slick body writhes as the aftershocks of her orgasm begin to subside.

Neither of us say a word, and the more she relaxes, I do too. We can talk tomorrow. For now, I let the slow rise and fall of her chest lull me into a semi-conscious state.

She feels too good. Like *home*.

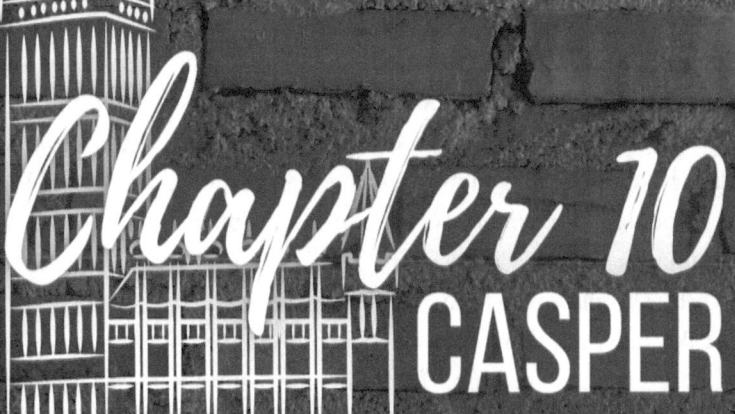

Chapter 10
CASPER

"**W**HY IS SAYING NO to him so hard?" Aurora whispers from her position on my chest with a leg thrown over my waist, breath skimming across my skin for the fourth time. It's been like this for the last thirty minutes or so while I pretend to sleep. While I lie completely still with my arm thrown over my face, covering my expression while ignoring the twitch of my cock. How much I want her again. How we're both naked. "Handsome asshole." Christ, it's hard to hold in my smile at that, but I do. More so when a huff follows a few seconds later. "Why me?"

Her questions don't upset me; I expect them. If anything, I'm amused by her reactions.

Find her cute.

I'm becoming a total wanker for this woman.

A realization that doesn't bother me. Not one bit.

I'll always be the same depraved arsehole, but with an exception now. Gem *is* the exception.

My wrath will never reach her. She'll never be buried beneath the weight of my darkness.

She shifts her position again, hand sweeping across my left pec where a large tattoo of a Cerberus sits in all black with eyes in white, giving it a sharp contrast. It's bold and depicts who I am deep down; a man not afraid to shed blood for the well-being of my family. Her tiny fingers caress the skin over the head at the center, softly, an action I doubt she's even aware of making while watching me. Waiting. Looking for some sort of magical bloody answer to her dilemma.

Why she can't resist me. Why she gave in again.

Like now, another annoyed grumble escapes her while she tilts her pelvis against my hip. Tempting me with her bare sex on my skin. Making my mouth water as her wetness seeps into my skin.

Tight, wet heat.

"Need help with that, love?" I say, my tone husky as my hands skim down to grab her thigh before she can pull away.

Something she tries a second later as she jumps in place. "Shit!"

"Easy, tiger." Green eyes meet shocked hazel ones as I tighten my hold, placing her thigh right over my hard length. Throbbing against her.

"What is wrong with you?" Her stare hardens and the arm that a second ago was flailing comes down over my abdomen where the Jameson name is in Old English across my flesh. The slap had some strength to it and I grunt, loving the sting of pain as her leg rubs my cock. Then, her eyes turn to slits, lips pursing. "How long have you been awake and listening?"

"Not long," I lie, keeping my face neutral. "How long have you been awake?"

Her expression morphs, mimicking mine. "Not long."

"Is that so?"

"It is."

"Little girls shouldn't lie."

"This girl learned a long time ago that wolves are never truthful." Those words stop my reply. The teasing joke sitting on the tip of my tongue disintegrates as I take in the flash of sadness that crosses her eyes—*I see her*:

How her brows furrow for a brief second.

How her lips purse.

How those hazel eyes lose their brightness and she looks past me to avoid any questions.

And while this all unfolds, I digest what those words could possibly mean with a father like Matteo Cancio in her life. What she would have witnessed growing up. Been a part of.

"What the fuck did that arsehole do?" Those words are out of my mouth before I can stop them, dripping with venom. Because I'll kill him without a second thought if Matteo is the cause of her pain. I'd kill anyone for her.

A truth I accept with honor.

The more I'm with her, feeling those soft curves melt against my flesh, I accept it. This.

She's precious, like a jewel. Moreover, I protect what's mine. And she is just that, even if she fails to recognize it.

"Who?" Gem tenses in my arms, her voice low but steady. Those eyes won't look at me, though, not even when she places her hand atop of mine on her thigh and taps it twice. "And loosen the grip a bit, buddy."

"Sorry." A word I've never said to anyone but my mum.

"It's okay."

I relax my fingers but don't let go. Instead, I massage her leg in slow, comforting circles, up and down, until she loses the hard posture. Once she relaxes, I bring my lips to the back of her head and kiss the crown. "What did he do to you?"

"Who…" she stops, swallowing hard when my hand trails a little higher on her thigh "…who are you—"

"Whoever the wolf was that broke your trust."

Hazel orbs snap to mine, head shaking. "It's not what you think."

"Then tell me." Simple as. I know most of their story, but some things can only be shared by those involved.

"Why don't we get up and—"

"I'm not letting you hide from me." Slipping out from beneath her, I sit up against the headboard and then pull her with me. Closer. Skin to skin. She doesn't complain as I situate us, her back to my chest while her arse sits between my parted legs. Nor when my hand traverses slowly up to her hip, giving the flesh there a soft squeeze. "Talk to me. Let me in."

"Why should I?" Gem says this so low I almost don't hear her.

"Because I'm not him."

"But that's where you're wrong. You couldn't be more like my father if you tried." Aurora mutters a very low *fuck* after her confession. Her confirmation.

"Explain." Pressing my lips against her temple, I lay a tiny kiss there while taking her scent into my lungs, soothing us both. Her anxiousness and my need for her. Now isn't the time to do anything but this; I need her walls down. I'll confirm her suspicions, but I'm not him and won't pay for those broken plates. "What does your father have to do with me?"

"Everything." Aurora takes in a deep breath and then lets it out at a very slow pace. Almost as if she's extending the silent moment after admitting such a heavy truth. And I let her. Let her gather her thoughts and say the words we both know are coming. "All the men in your industry are the same."

"Industry?"

"Participants in illegal activities."

"I don't agree with your earlier statement."

"Of course you wouldn't. Men in your—"

"You mean criminals."

"Just like that…what the hell!"

I lift her like a rag-doll and position her to straddle my thighs, her sweet pussy but a few inches from my cock. "Better?"

"I'm not a toy."

"You're adorable, love."

"And you're unbelievable," Aurora says incredulously, ignoring the compliment while crossing her arms over her chest. Her well-defined brow is arched and lips thinned, trying to look mad when we both know she isn't. If anything, she hates how easily I've gotten under her skin. "You aren't even going to try to deny it?"

"Should I?"

"How high in the ranks?"

"I'm the head of the Jameson Syndicate."

"Christ." She closes her eyes and throws her head back, muttering something unintelligible to herself.

"Share with the class, Gem."

"Why me?" That question isn't directed at me, and I don't reply. Instead, I just wait. Leave her to reconcile the truth with what she already knows. "But then again, I knew it. I heard you sentence that man to death while your men listened. You sent me home with an employee that looked more like a hired hit man than a driver."

And yet, she remains with her perky arse perched on my thighs. Straddling the devil reborn.

While talking to herself, Aurora turned her face from mine, but I rectify this with the tips of two fingers. "Eyes on me always. I don't like it when you look away."

"Why are you doing this?"

"Why are you fighting this?" Now, our mouths hover and her lips slacken, that tiny pink tongue coming out to wet the bottom one as I come a little closer.

She looks down at my lip and then up again. "We shouldn't."

Not that we won't. No real conviction behind the words.

For a minute or two I hold her stare, and then when a small whimper slips past her lips, I slant my mouth over hers, kissing her deeply while the arguing girl in my lap succumbs to my touch. Moving closer. Matching my hunger.

Tiny fingers embed themselves in my hair and pull, eliciting a deep grunt from me as she presses her core against my cock, wetness coating my taut skin. It's a move I welcome and reciprocate with a hard bite to her lower lip that I soothe with my tongue.

I swallow her moans.

I can feel each drop of her juices as it rolls down my shaft and onto my balls.

Moreover, she's proving my point. She might hate what I do, but wants this. Me.

Slowing the kiss, I peck her lips twice more and pull back. "Are you going to run again?"

"Yes, run." The lost look on her face is comical and I chuckle, loving how easily she gets lost in us. It's natural. Alluring. "If you do, Gem, I'll follow. Remember that. I'll always be but a few steps behind."

Something about those words resonates with her, but they also cause her to frown, an action that causes my heart to clench. I can literally feel her sadness, and it's the most intoxicating yet confusing thing.

Why do I feel so connected to her?

"Please don't make promises you won't keep."

"I'm a man of my word." Bringing a hand up, I cup her face and rub my thumb across her cheek. "Can you try and believe that?"

She shrugs. "Promises are broken every day."

"Who let you down?"

"I've seen this story in the past, you know." Aurora closes her eyes then, a sad and wistful smile on her lips. It's the most unguarded expression I've seen on her. "My mother met my father when she was eighteen and fell head over heels in love with his bigger-than-life persona. A few years older than her and charming, the man was in Chicago for college—her freshman year to his third—and they became inseparable. It was a whirlwind romance, the kind where she claimed to have been swept off her feet and made to feel like a princess. Almost two years later, that same love resulted in me." My sweet girl pauses to reach for the sheet bunched up by my hip, pulling it over her shoulders.

"Are you cold?" I ask, rubbing her hip beneath the fabric with my free hand. "Need me to turn up the temperature?"

"No, and a little." Gem nods. She leans forward, pressing her forehead against mine. The move covers us both and causes my hand on her face to fall. I want to protest, love the feel of her skin beneath my fingertips in any capacity, but the private cocoon brings a level of comfort in her body, so I choose to remain quiet. "Now, back to my story on why we are completely wrong. Why this will end in disaster."

"That's bullshit and you know it, love. You can feel it."

"As I was saying." My mouth opens, the rebuttal sitting on the tip of my tongue, but she shakes her head. "You asked me to let you in, and now I'm saying to just listen."

"Okay."

"Thank you." Her wild brown tresses move across her skin as she situates herself a little down my lap and away from my cock. For this conversation it's better this way, even if I miss her soft warmth immediately. So, I focus on the long strands as they sweep over her shoulder and the top of her perky right breast, on how they move with her every inhale.

After a minute, I push them back, letting my hand linger on the back of her neck. Massaging the tense muscles there until she releases a sigh. "Go on, Gem."

"Sadly for her, his love came with an expiration date," Gem whispers and I stop all movement, keeping my hand where it is as I take in the painful lilt to her tone. The small shake in her limbs. "His engagement to another woman three years after I was born broke my mother. Annihilated her trust in men while he just moved back to

Boston and assumed his role. She had no notice. No knowledge of the plans my grandfather had for his prodigal son—the same man that didn't even know I existed until I was five and a knock came to our door."

"Your father is a cunt, Aurora," I say, keeping my voice soft. "End of. No real man does that."

My girl sits back then, taking my face between her hands, while the expression in her eyes begs me to understand. "He walked away because *the family* came first. Not us. Not his child. The business demanded, and he gave in always." Two fat tears roll down her cheeks and I quickly wipe them away with my free hand, watching as her bottom lip trembles. "So, you see, I know all about what's expected from a man like you."

"The blood on my hands, or the type of man you think I am?"

"I'm the daughter of a mob boss, Casper, and I'd be a hypocrite to judge you for what I'll never crucify my father for. However, I do hate that he left us. That he chose the business above us, when we would've proudly stood at his side."

I nod in understanding. "Did he provide for you at all?"

"My mother came from a pretty well-off family, and whatever money he gave her each month, she put away in a savings account for me." Even her shrug is listless. The hurt and exhaustion this topic brings is palpable. "But when it mattered, when I needed him the most, he was never there. I know the disappointment and heartache that follows, Casper—I saw it every day—and I refuse to follow down that same rabbit hole. It's why we can't be anything more than these last few days. I won't repeat their history."

"I'm not him."

"You have the potential to be worse." That's the rubbish she's fighting to believe, but I won't allow it. This woman, beautiful and a bit heartbroken, has a hold on me that refuses to budge no matter how hard she pushes. Fight this. Us. "Until the very end, she waited for him."

Past tense. And while I know there's more to it—her mother's story—I'll wait for her to come share on her own, confirming what I already know. I also don't need to ask for clarification on something that if you read between the lines is clear to see.

"I'm not walking away, Aurora. Can't." Needing her closer, I grip the back of her neck and guide her lips to mine until they're almost touching. "All I want is the chance to show you. Let me in, gorgeous. Get to know me before placing me in a category I don't belong in."

"We don't even live in the same country, for God's sake." It's a weak rebuttal at best, and we both know it. One that I don't answer to, and her sigh of defeat a few minutes later is an admission of that same truth if nothing else. "Just don't hurt me. I don't think I can handle any more disappointment, Casper."

"I don't think I ever could." At my words, her body falls against mine and I wrap my arms around her much smaller frame. This is her giving an inch, and it's enough for now.

Even if she doesn't realize it yet, Aurora has already let me in.

Slowly. Effortlessly.

I'll show her who I am, too.

I might be a bastard. An unapologetic arsehole.

But I'm not a liar.

Chapter 11
AURORA

THE NEXT TIME I awake, I'm alone in bed.

There's a cover thrown over my body and the scent of fresh coffee lingering in the air—that, and the low hum of his voice coming from the room's balcony. There's a gravely timbre to it. A low and dangerous thrum that's both hypnotizing and scary.

He's not yelling. However, the angry cadence makes me sit up, throw my legs over the edge of the mattress, and stand up. The need to be closer becomes overwhelming the more alert I become.

"Why can't I fight this pull," I whisper under my breath, reaching over to grab the same bedsheet to cover up my nakedness. Before it's secure around my torso, I'm walking closer to where he is. Each step makes my body ache for his touch. Each inhale bonds my DNA with his scent.

I've lost my ever-loving mind.

Coming to a stop just before the partially-open sliding glass door, I admire his form. This view gives me the perfect view of his other persona. Casper's but a few feet from me and facing the Mediterranean Sea, wearing a pair of pajama bottoms and nothing else, hair disheveled, but the danger radiating off his skin sears me.

I can feel it.

This almost choking presence that makes goose bumps appear on my skin.

The corded muscles in his back are tense and the hand not holding onto his cell phone is gripping the veranda tight, almost choking the metal frame.

This is not the man I fell asleep against just a few hours ago.

This is not the charismatic devil who made me question my logic.

No, this man is ire personified. Angry and every bit the reason I ran.

And yet you still want him.

"How the hell did this happen?" he snarls, stretching his neck from side to side. "Where was she?" *She? There's a she?* "I don't give a bloody fuck that it was mid-morning and on West End near Burberry, Callum." There's another pause as the other person speaks, but Casper only seems to become more agitated. His chest expands with each breath, a rapid succession that worries me. "Why was she alone? Where were her bodyguards?"

"Who is she?" I mumble under my breath, too low for him to hear as my mind goes straight for the worst-case explanation. There's a woman in his life that means a lot. That's important enough for his reaction to be so severe.

It stings. Literally takes the breath from my lungs, and tears spring to my eyes.

This is why we—

"Dad, where's—" The sudden crack in Casper's voice stops me from completing that thought. I'm frozen in my spot, watching as his mood flips once more. How his head drops a bit while listening to his father's account of whatever happened. "And where's Mum now? Who's attending her?" Moreover, I feel like an asshole. Like utter crap for thinking the worst when something is wrong with his mother. "Is she...don't lie to me." There's another pause. "Okay."

His posture is different, the shift exposing his concern and fear. Seeing him like this hurts me. Reminds me of days when I was in his same position.

And it's that concern that brings me outside, stopping just behind him. His head tilts to the side, letting me know he heard me, but he doesn't look back.

However, the moment I wrap my arms around his midsection, he exhales. It's rough. "Tell Callum to...yeah...thanks. See you soon." The second he hangs up, Casper's turning around and pulling us chest to chest. His lips are on my temple, breathing me in while I hug him tight. "I have to—"

"I know."

"This isn't what I had in mind for today." He pulls back a bit after a few minutes, causing me to look up. "There's been an accident with my mum and—"

I silence him by placing a finger over his lips. "No need for an explanation, and more so when it comes to your mom. I understand and don't hold it against you...I was the same with my own."

"You keep speaking in past tense."

I give him a sad smile. "That's because she died a little over two years ago." *And still hurts just the same.*

"I'm so sorry, love."

"Thank you."

His phone pings three times in his right hand, one after the other, and he nods. "That should be my flight info."

"Then don't let me keep you." I take a step back, but his own hold doesn't let me get far. "Go on. It's okay."

Bringing his hand to my face, he sweeps his fingers across my cheek in a soft caress before cupping it. "This isn't the end of our time together, Gem."

"Focus on your mother, Casper." I'm shaking my head, trying to keep my own emotions in check. To not let him see that this sudden goodbye hurts. Because it does. To me, this is it. "I'll be fine."

"Look at me."

"You're going to be late."

"I own the fucking plane and they can very well wait. Look at me, Gem." Reluctantly, I let him tip my face up. Our eyes meet, and I can't hold back the small gasp that escapes. Nor can I stop myself from moving closer, pressing my chest once again to his.

"Please don't make this any harder."

"I'll come for you, sweet girl. Expect my call." Then his lips are on mine, kissing me with so much passion I can't think straight. Can't understand anything past the feel of his mouth against mine and the taste of him on my tongue. It's quick and fast and desperate. Sexy. It also breaks me into a million and one pieces.

Pieces that I doubt will ever be put back together correctly because as Casper walks toward the door and exits, two truths smack me in the face.

I'll never be the same.

There's no place like home.

Without a second thought, I rush back into the room and make a dash for my phone on the nightstand. There's a lump in my throat that shouldn't be there; I shouldn't be emotional when it's for the best that he left.

And yet, my eyes prick with tears as I dial my best friend's number—hands shaking so much that I almost drop the device while waiting for her to pick up. There's this sudden need in me to run and hide and lick my wounds, which is absurd, but I can't stop the loneliness from creeping in.

"Come on," I grit out with the phone cradled between my neck and ear. The closet is but a few feet away and I walk inside with purpose, pulling things down from the hangers without a care if they rip; it's all inconsequential at this point.

There's a click from the other end after the fourth ring, and Aliana sounds out of breath. "Yolo! How's the vacation going?"

I swallow hard, pushing my emotions back so she doesn't ask too many questions. "It's going."

"What's wrong?" she asks, her tone holding alarm. "Because that doesn't sound like you're having fun on this European escape. Are you hurt?"

If only she knew the truth.

Physically? No. But emotionally I am a mess for reasons that don't compute.

To be honest, nothing does at the moment.

Even after telling Casper all the reasons we shouldn't.

After he assured me we should.

I'm lost. Inexplicably and without a doubt confused about what is wrong and right. My path in life has been set for years, but his arrival has shaken that. Made me want something I've never craved before. Not like this.

He's wrong for me, but I forget all of that when I'm in his arms. And it's that belonging that I chase.

It's idiotic, I know, but I can't control it either.

"I'm sick with the plague," I lie, sniffling at the end from fighting back tears. From choking back my truth. "For days I've been feeling off and today it hit me full force. I'm miserable."

"Did you see a doctor? Did you eat something bad?" Her concern guts me. I hate liars and now because of *him*, I am one.

"No, but I am going to be booking my flight back home. This vacation has been the worst."

"Are you sure? Maybe you'll feel better tomorrow and can enjoy the view?"

"Between this and my father's visit in London, I'm done. I want to go home."

"He showed up? Seriously?"

"As a heart attack."

"Fucker," she hisses, and I can see her in my head rolling her eyes. "He won't give up."

"No, he won't." Grabbing a pair of cotton hipsters and a sports bra, I drop the blanket and put her on speakerphone while putting them on. The more we talk, the more I begin to relax—shows me how much I needed my friend these last few days. *Christ, it's only been a few days.* "But that's not as much of a surprise to me as my stubbornness is to him. I won't budge, and he hates it."

"Like mother, like daughter." She laughs, and I can't help but smile.

"Proud of it too." Then, there's an old pair of jeans I brought with me in case I'd do a walking tour of some sort and wanted the comfort. Those I shimmy into and pair them with a vintage concert tee from my New Kids On The Block obsession phase. "Besides, why should I play nice? I owe him no loyalty and have no desire to play the puppet."

"You're okay with the family entrepreneurship?"

"Are you with yours?" I counter, because she's the only person who can understand where I stand—on a slightly smaller scale but still gets the shift. Shady politicians run in her family, while mine is the crime boss funding campaigns to push certain agendas.

"Touché." There's the sound of a doorbell from her end. "About time."

"Food?"

"You know it."

After a few seconds of silence, I let out a long and tired sigh. "I'm coming home, Ali. I need to be home."

"Are you sure there's nothing else bothering you?"

"No." *Yes.*

"Then just come home." No judgment or further inquiry, even though the small huff on her end tells me she isn't buying my excuse entirely. "Send me your flight info and I'll pick you up."

"Thank you."

"I got you, boo."

Chapter 12

CASPER

"I'M SO SORRY, BROTHER."

I hear the words, but I'm not quite understanding them. There's a haze that creates fogginess, then the rapid beating of my heart—a thundering war drum inside my chest—that makes it near impossible for me to digest Callum's words.

What he's saying to me can't be right.

There's no fucking way that...

"Son, can you hear me?" Dad's face comes into focus then. He's leaning down to get a good look into my eyes, and it's his red-rimmed ones that slam me back to reality within the hospital's

waiting room. In that instant, sounds and light rush back to the forefront as I watch his own emotions burst forth. A man that for most of
his life has been stoic is breaking apart at the seams. "I know this is
hard, Casper. Fuck, this is hard, but I need you here with me. "

He. Needs. Me.

He. Needs. Me.

"Who?" That's all I say as I look away from a man I admire but
would love nothing more than to give a bunch of fives to in that
moment. One or two solid punches to the mouth would help this
growing need for violence that's slowly consuming me. This pain is
eating away at my rationality like a disease.

Had he been with her instead of staying back to talk shit with my
uncle.

Had he insisted she take more than one guard.

Had he, my mum...

Motherfuck.

I can't say it. Can't think it.

"Casper, we have someone in custody. The sack of shit claimed
to have information on her—"

I'm out of my chair and in his face before Callum can blink.
"Don't finish that sentence."

"Cousin, I know this is painful."

"You know fuck all at the moment," I seethe, chest heaving as
my vision becomes hazy. The anger and hurt and pure venom
flowing through my veins makes it hard to understand anything, and
yet the words he said to me upon arriving continue to play on a
constant loop.

"Aunt Penelope died on the operating table."

Those seven words broke something inside of me that will never
be repaired. No one ever wants to think of a parent dying. Of the
pain it will bring.

Then, with that sadness comes a regret that I'm not ready to deal
with; she will never meet my Gem. A beautiful girl that I walked out
on without looking back because the sadness in her eyes made it

difficult to do so. She herself has been in my position. Dealt with this all on her own because her bloody cunt of a father forgot how to be a real man.

Because real men don't abandon their families.

Because real men don't skive on their responsibilities.

Because a real man takes care of those he considers his.

I stretch my neck from side to side. "Where is he?"

"Beneath the pub."

"Good." Turning my head slightly, I look at my father. "I'll have everything taken care—"

"We planned for this, son. Your mum..." He pauses to clear his throat as a single tear rolls down his cheek. I know this is hard for him. She was his everything for over forty years and I'm fighting to remember that. "Y-your mum and I planned for this when you two were boys. Granted, I thought I'd always go first, so I took care of everything to make it easy for her. She picked the flowers and location while I put together the rest."

"That's not what I'm talking about." My voice is terse, and Callum gives me a look that screams *not now*, but I can't control it, nor do I want to. My emotions are high, a battle between ire and sorrow that's suffocating me.

There's nothing I can do to fix this, but at the least, I'll avenge her. My beautiful mum didn't deserve her lot. Didn't deserve to have a bunch of delinquent arseholes as family.

I'll gut the son of a bitch that did this. He and anyone else involved are dead men walking.

"Let's take a walk, mate." Callum puts himself between us, and I didn't realize I'd moved. "We don't need to be fighting. Family first."

"I left for less than four motherfucking days," I yell out, fist pounding my chest hard enough that the sound in the room makes a passing nurse jump. "Four days, and my mum, bro. My mum..." I trail off, unable to finish.

"Casper," Dad says then, the tone in his voice one I haven't heard in a while. Not since he was *boss,* and I look back at him through narrowed eyes.

"Yes."

"Find him and bring him to me."

"You can have the scraps when I'm done." With that I walk out, pausing just long enough to squeeze his shoulder on the way out. I'm angry. Fucking furious, but I love him, and past the tumultuous emotions swirling within, this isn't his fault.

He won't feel my fury, but the rest of the world won't be so lucky.

THE PUB IS empty when Callum and I arrive.

It's quiet, the streets almost empty, and the night holds an edge of eeriness that mimics my mood at the moment. Even the few people walking to their cars or entering another eatery are quiet and with their heads down.

No one makes eye contact. No one so much as breathes in my direction.

Closing my eyes, I take a moment to help my mind settle. To focus on what's important: the death of an enemy.

"Jeffrey is the only person inside," my right-hand says, and I open one eye to meet Callum's. "How do you want to handle this? We can wait outside if you like?"

"Just you and me." I shift my Glock to behind my waistband so the arse doesn't see it upon my entering. Not yet. They can become intimate after a friendly chat.

"Send him home?"

"No. He can clean up afterward." The back door is just a few feet from me, and with each step I take closer, my muscles tighten and hands begin to clench and unclench. Death is close.

I can feel it all around me; a heady sensation overtakes my senses whenever I take a life.

Because while the man below didn't plan or pull the trigger, he helped by not coming to me.

The door is unlocked when I turn the handle, and my foot has not fully crossed the threshold when a scream rents the air. It's masculine and reeks of fear, making goose bumps appear on my skin.

All doors and the divider are open inside the dark kitchen. Moreover, I follow the sound without pausing. Don't need to.

Step after step, I make my way through my office and then down the staircase that leads to my playground. The lighting is soft and music even plays in the background, a song all football fans know by memory as a war cry for their team.

And there in the center of it all is a man around my age that I've never seen before mouthing what I think is a prayer. It's the same lip movement over and over, and it causes my glare to deepen while I take in the rest of him.

His hands are bound above him to a small metal pipe and his chest is bare, bruises and a few deep cuts littering his upper torso. Lower, I take in the streaks of blood that meet at the center of his chest and then flow as one down to his lower abdomen, staining his beige trousers.

The red liquid is dry, and his skin looks pallid. A bit sickly.

"My condolences, boss," Jeffrey say lowly from the prisoner's left, and the man's eyes snap to mine. It's obvious he knows who I am. They widen at the sight of me, his fear growing the closer to him I get.

I give my man a nod in appreciation for his words. "Wait outside and close the door behind you."

"Of course. I'll await orders." His footsteps are loud inside the room as he exits, but more deafening is the harsh breathing of the arsehole tied up in my prison. He's fighting against his restraints, pulling hard enough that blood appears at his wrist as he breaks the skin there.

Bloody idiot.

Callum takes his place behind him while I stop a few inches from his face. Eyes on his. "Name?"

"This is a mistake, sir. I don't—" He doesn't finish as my hand across his face silences him, snapping his head back and jostling his entire body as it sways.

"Answer the question and nothing else," I say, my tone even. I'm watching him, cataloging his reactions to make sure the idiot doesn't pass out from fear before I get what I need. Because fight or flight is quite an interesting thing. Causes reactions in people that they simply can't control, and escaping into your own mind is one of them. "Name, mate. If I have to ask you again, it will hurt."

"Andre Gellar."

"And where are you from, Andre Gellar?" Because his accent is American. Callum meets my eye from behind him and I nod for him to proceed, beginning to push the buttons of my long-sleeved vest through their respective holes. One by one they become undone and Andre watches, sometimes flinching if I make a certain rapid movement with my hand. He does so again when I take it off and toss it somewhere behind me. Still no answer. "Last warning. Where the fuck are you from?"

"New Jersey."

"Where in Jersey?"

"Patterson."

I crack my knuckles. "And what exactly is a man from New Jersey doing in London?"

"Just on vacation. I swear to you that...*please*!" he cries out through a split lip, blood rushing to the new cut after my strike. "This is a mistake."

"The mistake was running your mouth and claiming you set up the hit on my mum." His mouth opens to deny this, but before he gets a single word out, I bring my closed fist forward and clock him in the nose. The sound of it breaking, bone crushing behind the hit, only ignites the fury I have within.

I don't stop after one punch. I land one after another as a red haze overtakes my senses, using his face as a punching bag without feeling the stress on my knuckles. If anything, I want to feel that kind of pain—to forget for just a few minutes that because of this cunt and whoever is working with him, I lost the most important woman in my life.

Another bare-knuckle strike lands across the bridge of his nose and the skin gives way, opening to form a gash that bleeds profusely, splattering across my hands and bare chest.

"No more." It leaves him on a nasal whimper, and I stop for half a second to admire the damage. "I'll tell you anything you want to know."

"All right." I stretch my hand out, head tilting to the side as I appraise that sack of shit. "Talk."

"Mr. Jameson, I'm just an errand boy."

"Gathered as much. Talk." Turning away from him, I walk toward the back and grab a folding chair, bringing it with me to sit in front of his bloodied form. My eyes connect with Callum as I do, and he moves into position with a large plastic bag in his hand behind him. "Amuse me."

"My job was simply to deliver payment to the man hired to make the hit." Andre swallows hard, trying to see what Callum has in his hand from the corner of his eye. "He was supposed to kill a male member of your family, not your mother. It was a mistake."

"I want names," I grit out. Now isn't the time to fully lose control, at least until I get the information I need to proceed—to unleash my wrath on those who crossed me and mine.

"I've never met the man hired by my boss—" His airflow is cut off by the plastic bag closed over his head. At once, his body thrashes as breathing becomes difficult with the lack of oxygen. The expression on Andre's face is of pure terror a second before the material becomes foggy.

Callum removes the bag. "Tell us the truth."

Andre is gasping, face red and eyes a bit bloodshot. "I swear on my—"

I pull my gun from the waistband of my trousers and cock it, holding it up in his line of sight. "Let's try this again, Mr. Gellar. Who pulled the trigger?"

"Before making the delivery, I'd never seen the man before."

"I'm beginning to lose my bloody patience here, mate. You have three minutes to give me the name of your boss and the hired help." Still no answer; the arsehole is too busy watching the Glock in my hand. To help him along, I fire a warning shot to his kneecap. "Clock is ticking."

"Motherfuck!" he yells out, body trying to fold into itself as the rush of pain hits his nervous system.

"Names." This man has got to be the most incompetent man I've ever encountered. Bullet hole in his leg, battered face, and my cousin behind him ready to suffocate his arse, and still he doesn't speak up. Instead, he whimpers, a pathetic little sound that grates my nerves on a level that leaves me with little choice. "Again, Callum."

"Of course, boss." Callum places the bag once more, this time tightening the plastic so it molds to his facial features as he sucks in a desperate breath. "I loathe liars," my cousin seethes next to Andre's head, finally letting his own emotions out as he pulls the bag off a minute later. My mum was like his own. Probably more so since Aunt Miriam lives to travel and pretend that what funds her expensive lifestyle isn't drug and gun money. "Give up those names or it's your life."

"All I know..." he coughs, bloodied spit dribbling down his chin "...is that the guy lives on and off on a Caribbean island and takes on jobs like these as a hobby." Andre takes another pause, and I raise a brow. There isn't much time left in my countdown.

"Carry on, bloke. Today is not the day to test me."

"Please. I have a wife and kid on the way."

"No, you don't," Callum interjects, yanking his head back, exposing his neck. "When Jeffrey picked you up and offered you cheap pussy to strike a conversation, you told him you were newly divorced and desperate for an easy fuck."

Andre flinches when I use the barrel of the gun to scratch my chin. "His name is Mauricio Hernandez and he was paid $500,000 in cash to do it."

"And who the fuck do you work for?"

"He lives in New Jersey but is looking to take over the state of Massachu—" Andre doesn't get to finish as I put a single bullet between his eyes. That's all I needed to know.

Chapter 13
CASPER

THERE'S SIX OF US carrying my mum's casket down the row of the cemetery where she's being laid to rest. We own the entire area where the family's mausoleum is—toward the back end away from others—and the surrounding graves; about thirty of them outside of ours.

My grandfather bought them just in case someone who works for the family needed one, an example we continue to follow:

A Jameson always takes care of their own.

And we will. My mum's guard who died protecting her, who took six bullets while trying to save her, will also be buried here in a private ceremony for his family. He will receive full honors, and they will be under our care for the rest of their lives. My care.

It's also that sense of loyalty that brought so many here today to pay their last respects. It's why everyone, including a few of the wives, are carrying and not concealing it. With our family being well known in the UK, many are out to see for themselves—to catch a glimpse of us in our private moment of grief. Magazines, international newspapers, and even social media bloggers turned conspiracy theorists are out to feature this story.

They have no respect.

Especially this one son of a bitch I'm seconds away from putting a bullet in the body of: a particular reporter for the largest network news station. He's cocky and pushing the boundaries; he's continuously getting closer with his phone out and recording our walk.

My father is at the front with mum's brother and I'm at the back, eyes on the man who just took another step.

"Leave it, brother. I have it," Malcolm Asher, a business associate and long-time friend, says from beside me. His voice is low so only I hear, and I flick my eyes toward him for a second, giving him a small nod that he understands. We're cut from the same cloth. Trust each other. "Ignore him until later. Javier will keep the man entertained for a few hours."

At the mention of Javier, his right-hand, I notice the reporter's gone. Not a single trace of him left behind, nor is there any commotion from the bystanders dissecting our every move.

Either way, I don't question it.

Know better than most that people have one-track minds and easily miss the obvious. A person could get stabbed in the middle of a concert surrounded by large bodies of strangers and not a single person will remember seeing the attack. It's why corrupt governments get away with so much.

Distract the mind and kill without repercussions.

We walk a few steps further and reach the open mausoleum, a tall Victorian building that houses our grandparents and now will have my mum. Everyone halts their steps and the employees help us put her down gently into a lift of some sort that will help them place her safely within.

And the moment we do, the skies open and a light sprinkling of rain begins to feed the earth. Her favorite flower, large pink peonies, are in full bloom, and I walk over to the nearest growth and pluck a single one as the priest begins to talk. I tune him out. I tune everyone out; my focus is on her.

My memory of her baking cookies after my football games.

The look on her face when I graduated from secondary school and then got my acceptance to Oxford.

The first time I killed a man, an arsehole that tried to rob me, and she helped me wash his blood from my favorite coat.

Mum was always there. Always.

My throat bobs harshly as I swallow back my emotions. This hurts. My anger and guilt are a heady combination, but showing any weakness is forbidden.

Not in public. Not until I avenge her death.

"Your mum would've loved these," my father says, coming to a stop beside me a few seconds later. He's been a pillar of calm these last few days, but the tremble in his hand as he reaches for a flower speaks volumes. "Thank you."

"Thank me when I bring you the head of her killer."

He gives me a barely perceptible nod. "Are you heading back to the US?"

"Soon."

"We need to talk."

"We will, but not for a few days." At my response his mouth opens, but when I look over at him, the rebuttal dies. I don't know what he sees in my eyes—grief or regret—but his backing down helps.

Right now I'm not okay.

I'm a ticking time bomb.

"...*let us pray.*" The priest's words meet my ears and I turn around, taking in how every head bows. How they all begin to recite their own plea to God above for her soul and our solace.

I don't join them.

Instead, I walk over to her casket and place the peony atop, hand lingering. My eyes close and my chest feels tight. My entire body shakes with the painful rage I have to swallow.

This is goodbye for now.

"I love you, Mum," I whisper, lightly tapping the coffin. "And I promise this will not go without punishment. I'll bathe the street with their blood in your name."

I'VE BEEN BIDING my time. Waiting.

Settling my affairs for when the time comes, and I decide on a change of scenery.

I'm also letting those playing this game move the chess pieces into the position I want.

They think I'm clueless. That I've given up as not a single attempt to find the hitman has been made.

That is, until now.

Something, the piece of shit inside of an abandoned warehouse in West Hendon Broadway, once used by union workers as their head-quarters, doesn't know. The lights are on and I can hear the heavy thrum of a guitar throughout, but no security outside.

My eyes shift once more to my informant. "Are you sure?"

"Yeah." He's tweaking a bit; jerky little movements show how badly he's feigning for a hit, and yet his only request is that I pay his mum's hospital bills. "Bert was given the guns three days ago as payment for getting Mauricio out of the country. They led him out through the Chunnel to Paris where he later took a flight back to Guatemala."

"Guatemala?" I say, looking over at Callum who's raising a brow. That's Central America, not the Caribbean, but close. Close enough that he could jump back and forth with ease while withholding just where he lives.

Smart little cunt.

He's also a dead arsehole.

"That's what Bert told someone on the phone a few days ago." Tilting his head to the side, he nods to himself. All the while, his fingernails are tearing into his forearms and leaving deep welts in their wake. "I was emptying the trash in Bert's office when it happened, and no one looks at the tweaker as a threat, so he carried on as if I wasn't there. The plan was to take out your father or uncle, an older male, but they were just as happy with it being your mum. They wanted to hurt you, hurt your business, while a larger play is being made. You're a pawn in a bigger game, Mr. Jameson, and it all leads back to Boston."

"Why are you putting yourself in harm's way?" Callum asks, but I know the answer. I know because this man could've asked me for money and drugs and a plethora of shit, but he didn't. He wants his mum taken care of.

He loves his mum.

He understands they are not to be touched, and doing so is crossing a line there's no coming back from.

"Because I may be an arsehole, but what they did was wrong. Mums are sacred."

"Thank you," I say and reach out to stop him from tearing off more skin. "Now go back to the car and wait there. I'll take care of the rest."

He nods and walks off back in the direction he led us without another word, and I turn around. Look back at the building. Watching for movement.

"You trust him?" Callum steps up beside me, checking the magazine in his Glock.

"I do." *His loyalty just bought him a second chance at life. One, I'll make sure he succeeds at.*

"Then so do I."

Pulling out my own weapon, I raise a hand and then point in two separate directions. My men, six in total, know what to do and disburse without a verbal command. Two of them will take their position at the back of this building, and the other four will guard the sides. Two men at each possible exit while Callum and I walk in.

Literally step right inside the building while the wankers inside are too high to notice.

There are tables littered with old needles and cheap liquor. Bodies; a group of five men and two women are naked—taking turns fucking in each available hole—while flying high as a kite. Moreover, in the middle of that group of grunting animals is the man I came to pay a visit to.

Bert Holmes is a nobody trying to play the role of a top dog. A petty dealer at best.

I've let his business slide with the agreement that I take fifteen percent clean off the top and he stays in his lane. This deviation—betrayal—will cost him his life.

"Everyone with a pussy between their legs has one minute to get the fuck out." At the sound of my voice all within freeze, shocked expressions traversing their features before the scrambling begins.

One man to his left reaches for his trouser pocket, but before he can pull anything out, I shoot him in the head. A clean entry and exit wound near the center of his skull leaves blood and fragments of what looks to be his brain on the woman closest to his dead body. Her screams follow; she's struck with fear and doesn't move while the other woman runs out naked without looking back.

"Miss, you have thirty seconds before I do the same to you." I smile down at her, pointing my gun at the man behind her when he makes a sudden move. My finger on the trigger twitches, his fingers skim over the butt of his gun on the floor, and I shoot. Once. Twice. Three bullets into his chest and he bleeds out at her feet. "Ten seconds."

"Please, I'm just here to entertain—"

"Get the fuck out," I snarl, walking forward, taking her by the arm and then pulling her to her feet in one swift move. That's when rationality hits and fight becomes the predominant behavior. She's thrashing in my hold as I all but drag her toward the door. Yelling at me. Begging. I ignore it all.

"Make a single move, arsehole, and I'll shoot," Callum hisses, stepping forward only to plant his foot on another guard's head. From the corner of my eye, I see his head snap back but don't pause my steps.

"I won't tell anyone." The woman is in tears and still not recognizing my chivalry. Not realizing she's a few feet outside the door. "Don't kill me."

Looking down at her tear-stained face, I lower my voice so only she hears. "Leave and don't look back. Don't so much as think of this night again. Agreed?"

"Yes."

"Good." Taking off my button-down, I give it to her and stay in an undervest. "Now, go."

"Thank you." When she takes off a second later, I head back inside and lock the door behind me, taking in the sudden change in the large and dirty room's dynamic.

My men are now inside and standing around the still-alive men on their knees with Bert at the end. All heads are bowed, and some are shaking. Their fear is palpable. The bloodied bodies of their friends with vacant eyes lay before them as a reminder of what is to come.

"Good evening, gentlemen," I say, coming to a stop before the first one, another nobody that falls to the ground as I empty the rest of my magazine into his body. "Let's try this again...shall we?" Coming to a stop beside the next man, I pull out a second magazine from my back pocket, I change it out and then cock it, all the while pointing the barrel at his head. As I do this, the putrid scent of urine hits my nostrils and I tsk in disgust. "*Good evening, gentlemen.*"

"Evening," the three of them mumble, voices shaking.

"Good job." It's patronizing, more so when I pat the pissing lad's head. "You can follow orders."

"Casper, what is—"

Callum backhands Bert with the handle of his gun, shutting him up and breaking his large nose and two front teeth in the process. "Speak when spoken to."

"Today is not the day to test me, Holmes." My eyes shift to Jeffrey for a split second. "Find them and bring them here."

"Right away, sir." He takes three of my men with him and they walk toward the back, directly toward the unlit section where I know his office is. Their footsteps are loud, more so as they move items out of their way—boxes, a few tarps, and then there's the subtle sound of a click.

One by one, lights come on. Each dingy fixture illuminates my belongings.

My guns. My property.

Jeffrey removes another tarp and finds a rolling container with wrapped bricks inside. He picks one up, weighing the contents in his hand, and then walks back over, leaving the other three to catalog what is there.

I've brought a large semi with me and they already have instructions to load and leave, which they do silently as one of my employees exits the building. The sound of a large engine follows, the headlights shining our way as he parks it and then they begin the retrieval process.

"Watch them," I command, and those three fuckwits do at once, shaking from their kneeling positions. For almost half an hour all that is heard is the sound of items being moved—wooden crates scraping against the floor and out the back loading area. One by one they disappear while Jeffrey stands beside me with a gift for my troubles. "Rubbish or worth it?"

He tears a corner of the wrapping off and tastes it. "It's very cheap quality."

I nod. Expecting as much. "Callum, please help Mr. Holmes to a chair."

"Oi, you heard him." Callum presses the trigger, shooting the pompous arse in the thigh. "Get up."

"This is all a misunderstanding. We can come to—" Bert shuts the fuck up, gritting his teeth after I shoot his other leg. He forces himself to a standing position, wincing as pain radiates throughout his body and blood runs down both limbs. Taking a step forward and then another, he doesn't stop until he's standing right in front of the chair my cousin pulled out for him.

"Do you need an invitation?" Callum waves a hand in the air, the same one with the loaded gun and finger on the trigger.

"I'm sorry." No, he's not. He's just fucked and knows it.

"Silence." The two still on the floor whimper at my barely contained snarl and I shift my attention toward the employee standing behind them. "They so much as move a muscle or cough, shoot them. A bullet for each minute twitch and sound."

"Yes, boss."

"Now, let's have a little chat, old friend." Jeffrey and Callum have moved a table in front of Bert and have added a chair for me, which I take, turning it around and straddling it backward. "How have you been?"

"Casper...this can be fixed." He's sweating profusely, body trembling from either the blood loss or nakedness, as I stare him down. His hands are up in a gesture of surrender, not that it means shit to me, but the longer I glare, the more nervous he becomes. "I didn't have anything to do with your mum...I swear."

"You swear?" Placing the gun down on the table, I pull one of my karambits out from my right pocket and flip open the blade. Its blade glimmers in the low lighting. "Is that right?"

"Yes, I—"

"I want your hands flat on the table."

"Okay." Bert does as I ask, palms face down, but he eyes the knife with distrust. And he should. "Casper, I can help you find the man responsible. I-I didn't...*fuck!*" His scream rings loud inside the warehouse, the echo bouncing off the walls as I embed the blade straight through the center of his hand and down between his middle finger and pointer, tearing the flesh in two.

"Your words mean fuck all to me." Bringing the bloody knife up, I wipe it on my vest before tearing the cocaine brick right down the center. A little bit of the white powder falls to the table and some on my trousers as I push it across to him. "However, you will be helping me. Talk."

"Are you going to kill me?"

"Are you going to talk?"

"Casper, I've been loyal to you and the Jameson family." Before I can reach across and snap his fat neck, Callum slams his face down into the powder. He holds him there, forcing Bert to pull the substance deep into his lungs as he fights to catch his breath. "Please!" He coughs, hands pushing against the cheap wooden table, the mangled fingers failing to grasp the edge.

After a minute, Callum pulls him back. "Ready to talk?"

"All I know is what I was paid for." He coughs, gagging while his pupils dilate. His speech is also becoming fast, chest heaving rapidly as the high begins to ascend. "Mauricio lives in Guatemala, but that information stayed between Nico Savino and me, as a precaution."

"Who's Nico Savino?"

"He wants Boston and now the daughter." Bert wipes his brow, only managing to smear blood across his face. "You're just the catalyst for that to happen."

"How am I involved in this?"

"You rejected his sister a year ago in Chicago during a visit. Does the name Antonella ring a bell?"

"No. It doesn't."

"She bloody remembers you, mate, and so does he. They wanted an in here—an alliance—to destroy Cancio." Bert suddenly shoots up from his chair, the pain from his wounds now nonexistent. "Is it hot in here? I'm sweating bullets."

"Why didn't you come to me when they approached you?"

"They offered me your position; I'd be an idiot not to accept."

"So you let an innocent woman die...my mother...and all because of your greed." Not a question, and he knows this. Sees the murderous rage that I am fighting to keep under control until I get what I need. He's a nobody in a long chain of bodies that will bleed for her death.

"I'm truly sorry for that." Bloodshot eyes meet mine, and in them, I see euphoria mixed with a hint of death lingering in the background. "Your mum wasn't something I was made aware of until after, Casper. She wasn't supposed to die."

"You're just as guilty."

He ignores the last part, fanning his face suddenly. "Christ, my heart feels like it's going to beat right out of my fucking chest. Can you turn on the fan?" Then, like the piece-of-shit lowlife he is, he walks over and does another small line and then smiles at me as if we're best mates.

Stupid bastard.

With him so close, I can't stop myself. Don't want to. Without blinking, I stand and reach out quickly with my blade open, slicing across his face. From orb to chin, I open a deep gash.

However, he doesn't so much as notice the deep cut or the profuse amount of blood falling now down his face. It's a testament to what a person can do or withstand while under the influence of a narcotic.

"Sit," I grit out, waving at Jeffrey to help the idiot. Which he does, pushing him down hard enough that one of the chair's legs break from under his weight, and it's a domino effect if I ever saw one.

His body falls forward, tipping the table as they both crash to the floor; the blow hits the dirty concrete below a second before his face follows. His inhale is deep and so is his groan. They both pull more into his system and he begins to seize, body shaking as breathing begins to get difficult.

I don't help him. Instead, I kneel beside him to pick up my fallen gun—a barrel that I use to place at the back of his head while placing my lips near his ear. "Never betray your master."

There are choking sounds coming from him, thrashing and jerky movements. Using the back of his head, I push the tip of my Glock deep into his skull as I stand.

Then, after a few minutes, all movements stop. His breathing is slow, almost nonexistent, and we all stand there watching as he gets closer and closer to an overdose with each deep inhale.

There's no regret in me when it comes, either.

Fuck him. Fuck them all.

I have the information I need and a girl to look out for. That I need to get in contact with.

And while I haven't been in Chicago in the physical sense, I still have eyes on her. Eyes that give me a report of her day every single bloody night that I'm away. She's protected. Will always be as long as I have breath in my body, and if this Nico wants her, he'll have to kill me himself.

Gem is mine.

Chapter 14
AURORA

"**M**OMMY, WHAT'S WRONG?" I ask, pausing at her doorway on my way to my own room. She's sitting in her little nook, what looks to be a letter in hand, and crying. It's not the kind of sobbing that attracts attention. No. This is silent and choking; her eyes are closed while tears fall, ruining her always-impeccable makeup.

I've seen her upset before, but never like this. This feels different. Like whatever is in her hands will cut deep. Has cut deep.

"Baby girl, I need you to give me a few minutes," she manages between uneven breaths, not looking at me. But I don't listen.

Instead, I drop my book-bag on the ground and enter, not stopping until I'm right in front of her. She's shaking and my ten-year-old heart hurts, a feeling coming over me that I've never experienced before.

It's worry and fear and I know it has to do with Dad. He's the only one that makes her cry. "Is Dad okay?" I ask first, needing to know more than anything because while he's not the best father, I do love him. Wish he was here and not in Boston. "Just tell me. I'm a big girl and c-can handle it."

Whatever she hears in my voice makes her tearful eyes snap to mine, her expression morphing into one of tenderness. "He's alive and without a single scratch." There's a hint of bitterness in her tone, but I don't say anything and nod. "But we do need to talk, Roe. How about you go and change and meet me downstairs in twenty or—"

"Now, please."

"Aurora, I said—"

"Mom, you're starting to freak me out. Please."

"Okay. Okay." Standing from her seat, she gives me a sad smile, wiping under eyes with the pads of her fingers. "Give me two minutes. Drop off your book-bag and come back."

I nod, turning to walk out of the room, but before taking a single step, I turn around and hug her. Wrap my arms tightly around her midsection. "I love you, Mom. You know that, right?"

"Of course, baby. And I love you."

"Always and forever?"

"To the moon and back." Mom kisses my forehead then and pulls my arms from around her, squeezing my hands before letting them go. That haunting expression on her face is almost gone, but not quite. It's like a Band-Aid on a wound; covers the cut but doesn't make it go away. It's there hurting beneath the surface. "Now, go. I'll be here waiting."

"Be right back." I leave her there and almost make it to the door when she speaks again, making me pause.

"When you grow up, Aurora, I need you to find a man that will love you completely. Solely." It's a whisper full of so much emotion that I'm hit with another wave of hurt. I don't know if she wants a reply, but I still nod my head so she knows I'm listening. That I understand her. *"Your happiness to him must come first, and you'll live to do the same for him. Never settle, baby girl. Never. No man that causes you a moment of pain due to selfishness is worth the heartache. You deserve the world. Never to be an afterthought."*

I awake with a start, my body breaking out in a cold sweat as it's done every single time this memory re-emerges in the shape of a dream for the last few weeks. Ever since coming back home to Chicago a month ago—since my time with *him*—I've been off-kilter and can't shake these mental pictures.

I'm unfocused and questioning things.

My beliefs and life choices.

What led me to where I am now.

Because I remember that day to the very last second when I finally fell asleep:

The news that broke my heart. The tears that followed from both of us. The acceptance that I would never have a family—a real one— where my father lived with us and we were happy together.

Because just a few weeks after my eleventh birthday, Matteo Cancio and his wife announced the birth of their first child, a son, through a magazine article. The Bostonian businessman, as they were more than likely paid to portray him, was ecstatic about the arrival and looked so in love while holding the days-old infant.

It was an exclusive he gave this publication in exchange for good press. To help sway the way people saw him before his insider trading case of all things.

He's an asshole, but smart. He has never been caught or convicted of a single crime.

That day as I read the article, I lost a bit of my innocence, too. Every single word was a stab to the heart, and more so because he didn't tell me himself. No. I had to find out as a stranger would.

All of my hopes for a better relationship died, and so did the way I viewed my father.

Grabbing my cell from the nightstand, I look at the time while ignoring the four missed calls and sigh. "Great, it's almost six," I grumble, knowing that it'll be nearly impossible for me to fall back to sleep and with my alarm set for seven, I push the covers off. I'm tired and don't want to but throw my legs over the edge anyways. Grudgingly, I stumble a bit and manage to keep myself upright, walking into the en suite bath while hissing as the bright lights come on when the sensor picks up my movement.

My reflection in the mirror shows my displeasure. The bags under my eyes from lack of sleep show how unhealthy this all is.

And even though that dream makes me relive a hard memory, I know that its resurfacing has everything to do with a certain British man whose presence I can't evade while awake or asleep.

This same man has yet to contact me.

To so much as send a text message to assuage my thoughts.

Because I still hear his promises when I close my eyes. I remember how those hypnotic green eyes watched me from between my thighs while bringing me to orgasm.

I want him but despise the very thought on the same breath, more so as each day passes without a single call.

"What the hell is wrong with me?" I ask my reflection while taking my tank top off and then panties, hating how my eyes lower to the places on my torso where his marks are fading. The imprint of his fingertips on my skin is almost nonexistent and I miss them. I miss how alive he made me feel. "I can't be with someone like my father. A liar."

And it's with that thought that I walk over to the shower and turn the faucet, letting the water heat up before stepping in. It feels good on my body and for a second or ten, I just stand there while the warm water soothes my tired limbs before lathering. Something that I quickly realize is a mistake.

Not now. This needs to be an in-and-out situation.

My hands over my body, slippery from the suds—a woodsy scent that reminds me of him—makes my nipples harden into stiff, throbbing peaks. It's been a month since I felt the delicious ache Casper leaves behind and I'm needy. Aching as the image of his handsome face haunts me.

I hate how much I want him again. How easily I would give myself to him.

How if I slip a hand between the juncture of my thighs, I'll find my pussy slick and not from the water.

"*Christ*, I need help." And I'm also now in a rush because the temptation to touch myself—to come—is near maddening. Each inhale dares me to do it. To let my mind wander back to those hours where he took me over and over again, exhausting my body while leaving me afloat on a blissful cloud. "Wash, rinse, and out," I chant while doing so, fighting with myself when all I want is to give in—and I almost do, but the phone pinging on my countertop stops me.

Turning the handle, I shut the water off and step out, grabbing my towel off the rack before walking over. My hand touches the screen without picking it up, a quick swipe that nearly sends me stumbling back.

I miss the sweetness of your pussy on my tongue.
~Casper

How your walls choke my cock when you come.
~Casper

I'll be seeing you soon, Gem. ~Casper

Three quick texts that scare and excite me more than they should. They have me on edge and breathing hard. Thinking. Craving. Swallowing hard.

No. No. No, damnit. I need to get my mind off him and forget. I need to move on and thank my lucky stars that I didn't get in any deeper. I return the favor, ignore him like he has me for these last thirty days.

If only my heart would listen to my head.

"So you've been a bit distant lately?" Aliana asks as we walk out of the women's shelter I inherited and run. It's late, easily almost eight at night, and I'm dead on my feet. "What gives?"

I can't help but be irritated by her question each time she asks, even though it's not her fault. To be honest, it's no one's, but I just haven't been myself since coming home.

Between the dreams, my father's insistence, and thoughts of Casper, I'm fried. Beyond exhausted, and she sees this. My best friend since middle school knows me, is worried, and I just don't have a way to explain the craziness my life has become since my trip to London.

So, like the hot mess I've become, I evade. Take a moment of silence to just look around the front grounds of the Conte House while ignoring the *tap tap tapping* of her foot.

This place was my mother's. Her dream that I continue to carry on and make thrive while doing so.

Sure, I could've gone to school to become a doctor or lawyer, but that was never my passion. This is. And after graduating high school at seventeen, I immersed myself—worked with her every single day until she couldn't—in order to take over.

Hell, this has been my second home since the age of fourteen when it opened; I've worked in every department. From helping in the kitchens to CEO and everything in between, I've done them all and with pride. It's my way of honoring her memory.

To keep her dream of helping women get out of toxic environments—to leave the men that broke them down—alive.

This place keeps me close to her memory. Every successful case helps to fill the void that her death left behind.

Aliana clears her throat. "Quit Ignoring me."

I let out a tired sigh. "I'm fine. Just really tired—"

"Finish that sentence and I'll kick you," she deadpans, pulling on my arm so we stop at the end of the sidewalk that leads to the parking lot. "Look at me."

"What?" Turing my head, I find her brown eyes narrowed, searching my face for the answer as to why I'm so distracted. A little lost. Although I'm sure it's pretty clear to see that I have a problem named Casper Jameson that follows me around. Like a ghost. Like a life-altering realization, nagging at me from the back of my mind.

"Talk to me."

Out of all the words she could say, why those? The same ones he used back in Ibiza between rounds of mind-blowing sex. When he caught me with my walls down and I was most vulnerable. Open to him.

"Maybe I'm just hungry and in need of a strong margarita?"

Releasing my arm, she pulls out her phone. "Uber? I'll treat while you spill?"

"There's nothing to..." I trail off as my own phone goes off, and it's a text from him. His special ringtone. Then, because I have no control when it comes to this man, there's an automatic pull at my lips. They curl at the right, a cheesy grin, while her eyes get an evil glint to them. "Don't."

"Aren't you going to look?"

"Nope."

"Why?" She reaches for the device in my hand, but I pull back before she can snatch it. "I knew it!"

"Stop. It's nothing." My attempt at nonchalance is met with a laugh. "I'm serious. It was a one-time thing that—"

"You had a one-night stand?"

"It was more than one night."

"You hoochie!" *Christ, the decibel of her voice is loud.* "Who and where? Are you dating him? Do I know the dude?" My eyes shift around us, hoping no one heard, but I'm not so lucky when two volunteers a row down in the parking lot look our way. They wave, but the one to the left adds his version of a flirty grin to it. "Poor guy. He's going to be so sad when he realizes you're taken."

I shrug with a grimace. "Lawrence just isn't my type."

"No one has been since that douche bag, who shall not be named, that you dumped months ago." Ali raises both hands in a "praise the lord" gesture and I laugh.

"You're so extra, babes."

"And you're so not getting out of this." My shoulders drop, causing her to giggle and clap. She won and she knows this.

"Fine. Just hurry up and call for a car." *I'm going to need alcohol courage for this. A lot of it.*

"Yay! I can't wait to..." I don't hear the rest of her excited speech as my eyes stray toward the cell I'm unconsciously holding up. My right index finger swipes across the screen without my permission and I read his words. A gasp gets caught in my throat and my skin prickles with excitement.

With a need so palpable, a harsh shiver runs down my spine.

I need you. ~Casper

Chapter 15
AURORA

"**O**H MY GOD," Ali says for the sixth time since I began my story, vibrating in her seat inside our favorite Mexican restaurant. Just those three words. Nothing else. It's almost like she's a scratched CD, which would be funny if it wasn't due to my stupidity. "I'm shook."

Yup, she is definitely cheering me on. Why did I hope for anything different?

"Can we drop it?"

"We most certainly will not," she counters while wagging her brows. "Now, tell me..."

"For the love of all things holy, Aliana. What now?"

"Was he huge? Cause I'm living vicariously through you at the moment." Her lips purse in an exaggerated pout as I choke on the remaining drink in my glass. "I haven't had a single date in months."

"I'm not discussing that," I hissed through clenched teeth before faking a smile for the older couple a few tables away. "And can you tone it down a bit, chick? You're drawing attention."

"Why are you being so overprotective if it meant nothing?" Aliana grabs our shared pitcher of margarita and pours us another drink before bringing the glass to her lips and taking a healthy sip. "This is some pure hot epicness and I'm happy for you."

"And you're a dork."

"We came to that conclusion back in junior high, babes. Remember when I did the Macarena—danced my heart out for the talent show and won the creative award?" She waves me off, but her eyes are analyzing my expression. The woman is like a dog sniffing out a juicy piece of meat. "Now, tell me the truth. How did he make you feel?"

I laugh, remembering her trying to guilt-trip me into performing with her. "Still not answering—"

"Is this seat taken?" a voice says from behind me and I stiffen, my entire body tensing. The anger I experience is instant and so are my biting words. "What are you doing here?"

"You and I both know the answer to that, Aurora." He pulls the chair out from beside me and sits, waving over some random waiter to take his drink order. The server doesn't hesitate, most in the country knowing who he is, and making him wait like a normal person is a no go. "Scotch on the rocks," he says before the man can ask.

"Right away, sir." Then he hurries off to do his bidding while I sit in my chair quietly seething.

"Leave."

"You left me no choice." His eyes shift to my companion and smiles. "Hello, Ali. How are you, sweetheart?"

"I'm good, Mr. Cancio." She looks at me with a *what do we do* expression. "Working hard and taking some business classes at night."

"That's wonderful to hear." My father nods to himself as the waiter drops off his drink. "And you, dear? Still running the women's shelter?"

"You know the answer to that."

"I do," he muses and brings the glass to his lips, taking a slow sip and then savoring the amber liquid. "Which is why I am here with an offer."

"Maybe I should go?" Aliana says, shifting uncomfortably in her seat. "Or do you need—"

"There's a car waiting to take you home, Miss Rubens. I appreciate your understanding."

Her eyes meet mine and I nod. "Yeah. I'll see you tomorrow."

"Okay. Goodnight, sir." Her smile is a bit forced, but he doesn't seem to notice. That, or he doesn't care.

"Goodnight."

Pushing her chair back, she stands and grabs her purse. "Want me to pick up breakfast tomorrow on my way in?" In other words, our conversation isn't over.

"At nine in my office."

"Love you, boo."

"Love you, too," I say and then she's gone, leaving me alone with *him*. A him I turn to stare at with impassiveness. "Talk."

"Why are you avoiding me, Roe?" The tinge of annoyance makes me bristle, but before I can respond, Matteo holds a hand up. "And don't give me the crap about my absence or the business; you've never ignored my calls before. We've never gone so long without so much as a hello."

"May I speak?" At his nod, I snort. "That was rhetorical."

"Can we please cut the attitude?"

"Can you stop stalking me?"

"I'm not stalking you. Not in the way you think."

"Then how?" I demand, pushing my mostly empty chimichanga plate forward. "Because popping up at random places I'm visiting constitutes as that. You *are* having me followed."

"I'm not."

"Lie to me again and I'll—"

"You might not believe this, but I do know you." Sitting forward, he places both elbows on the table. While his stance is relaxed, I know he's uncomfortable. That talking about his feelings isn't something he enjoys. "I know the kind of books you like to read, that you hate to exercise but love to swim and that Mexican food is a weakness of yours. Just like your mother, Roe...this place was a favorite of hers."

Those words pierce me. They soften the stiffness in my posture, and I slump in my seat. "So you randomly picked this place because we like tacos?"

"No." The smile he gives me is sad. As if he's remembering something. "I chose this place because every Wednesday you two would have dinner here without fail."

"How would you even know that?" Because Christ, since when does he care?

"Believe it or not, Bianca and I spoke every Friday night to share our week. This meal was always the highlight of it...you were always at the top of her priorities."

"She was an amazing mother and I never doubted her love for me."

He nods, a sad smile on his face. "I'm sorry for making you believe that I didn't care, Roe. I also know that the failure of our relationship does fall at my feet, kid, but I'm trying. At least give me that. Trust that I do care."

"So you keep saying, but actions...or better yet, years of your inaction have proven the *opposite*." Matteo opens his mouth to argue, but I hold a hand up. "Which begs the question: why are you here now? You're not retiring at the moment, and by the time you do, you'll have Lucas to take over. If he's your pride and joy, why not mold him for the position?"

"You're right, I'm not retiring just yet, but...and here's the *but* you're missing; I'd like to within a year. I want you in my life, Roe. Want to give you the place I should've years ago as my firstborn and heir." He reaches across the table and takes my hand in his, giving it a squeeze. "And while the rejection hurts, I know it's my fault. I did this to our relationship."

Those words bring tears to my eyes that I refuse to let fall, and I choke them back. "I don't know what you want me to say or do, Dad."

"I know." Releasing my hand, he sits back and picks up his drink, taking a hearty sip. "Which is why I have a proposition for you."

Mimicking his pose, I take a sip of my margarita. "A proposition?"

"Yes."

"Go on." I'm curious if nothing else.

"How would you feel about coming to Boston for a few days next month." The word *no* is on the tip of my tongue and he notices this, shaking his head. "Before you shoot me down, hear me out."

"Okay."

"I'd like for you to come down and meet some people...see the business, and not just go by what you have in your head. There's more to our name than the illicit side of things, Roe. Just give me a chance to show you that."

"It's a complete package. One doesn't go without the other."

"It does, but all I'm asking for is a few days of your time."

"And if I say no?" I raise a brow in challenge.

He gives me a grimace. "I'm really hoping you don't."

"Why that face?"

"I have one more proposition if all else fails, and I know you won't like it."

"Then don't ask me."

"Just come to Boston with an open mind."

"Give me a few weeks and I will." This has the word mistake written all over it, and yet I don't turn him down like I should. "However, I need you to keep one thing in mind…"

"What's that?"

"I make no promises."

———

THE NIGHT AIR is a bit chilly as I exit the restaurant, leaving my father inside to settle the tab since he insisted on paying. I've already ordered an Uber to come and pick me up, much to his annoyance, but tonight isn't the night to push. I've acquiesced, made a promise to come and see him—spend time with a man that I still really don't know.

Checking the app, I realize that the driver is still a good eight minutes away and sigh. "Hurry up, dude. All I want is my bed and—"

"How are you, Miss Cancio?"

I know who it is before I turn my face, not at all shocked to find him lurking. He looks the type. The kind that is always waiting and biding his time to strike.

Dominic reminds me of a snake in the grass, and I hate how immediately uneasy I feel with him.

"It's Conte."

"Excuse me?" His expression shows a perplexing look that I'm not buying.

"I'm sure you've done your homework by now." Looking back at the restaurant's entrance, I'm hoping for my father's appearance. "Right-hand men are usually more on their game than what you showed in London. The same mistake wouldn't be made twice."

Dominic pushes off the wall, gait slow as he comes closer. "You're right. I'll give you that."

"Then why pretend?" I ask, raising a brow, holding my position because I'll never show just how uncomfortable he makes me feel.

"I'm just trying to make conversation, Aurora." Dominic raises both hands in a showing of peace, stopping a few feet from me. Close enough that the harsh scent of his aftershave tickles my nose. "Our last encounter was unpleasant and that's my fault—something I owe you an apology for, if you give me the chance to."

"Go on."

"Okay." At my quick response, he smiles, and it does nothing to soften his features. "I'm very sorry about what happened back in London between us a month ago and would like to make amends. That's not me, and my shitty day shouldn't have been taken out on you."

"Thank you." He seems sincere, and I'll take it with a grain of salt. Still don't trust him, but I'll play nice for now. At the very least, make it less unpleasant when I eventually see him in Boston. "I appreciate that."

"I'd also like to invite you out for a few drinks tomorrow. To get to know each other a little better."

"That sounds a lot like a date."

He shrugs, that grin turning into a smirk. "I would like it to be."

Not happening, buddy. "I'm sorry, but I'm seeing someone."

"Who?" he says, an accusatory tinge to his tone that has no place being there. That, and I don't miss the flash of anger on his face.

It's quick, but I saw it. Don't like it either; he has no place to feel any kind of way when it comes to my persona.

"That's none of your—" I'm interrupted by the ringing of my cell and I look down, noticing right away that the area code is foreign and at once, a smile tugs at my lips. Excitement fills my belly because it has to be him. No one but him has my number that doesn't live here. "I need to take this."

"I see."

"Have a good night."

"You too, Miss Conte." The emphasis on my last name makes me look up, but I still swipe a finger across the screen, accepting the call. "We should be seeing each other again, and very soon."

I don't answer. Don't have time to, either.

My Uber pulls up then and just as I reach for the car door, Dominic opens it for me in a show of chivalry that doesn't come off as genuine. It's the one thing I've been blessed to inherit from my father; I can spot bullshit a mile away.

And he reeks of it.

Before stepping into the car, I give my father's employee a nod while bringing the phone to my ear. "Hey," I say, and then close the car door without acknowledging him again. There's something not right there and the next time I see Matteo, we will be discussing it. *I just hope he listens and doesn't brush me off.* "It's been a while, Mr. Jameson."

"Too fucking long, Gem."

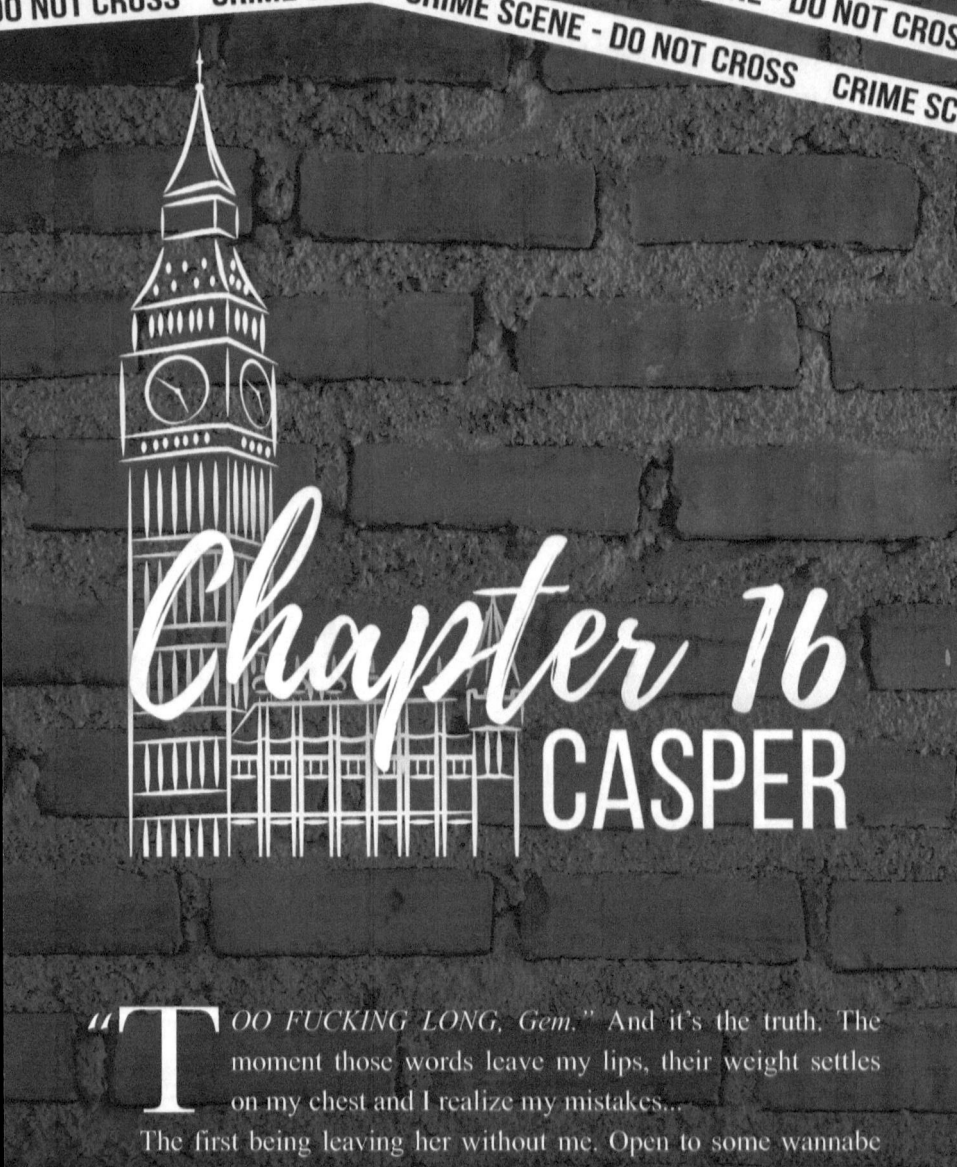

Chapter 16
CASPER

"**T**OO FUCKING LONG, Gem.*" And it's the truth. The moment those words leave my lips, their weight settles on my chest and I realize my mistakes...

The first being leaving her without me. Open to some wannabe cunt sniffing around what doesn't belong to him. Her bodyguard, Alexander, lets me know about my little friend Dominic. Of him asking her out on a date, and even though I'm not physically there to break his face, I interrupt. Made sure to call where he could see her expression at my call. The smile on her face that he sends me a picture of.

Then, there's another area I bodged up; I didn't call. Didn't communicate like I should've after leaving her so abruptly, and if anyone would have understood, it's her. My Gem would've been there for me.

I'm an arse.

A car horn sounds in the distance before she releases a sigh, yet I feel no animosity. "Where have you been? It's been weeks, and I was worried about you."

"I'm sorry, love, but—"

"But what? Talk to me...wait...give me two secs." She pulls the mobile from her ear to answer someone, telling them to turn left at the end of the road. *Where is she?* Then it hits me. It's Wednesday, and that's Mexican night with Aliana. Something they don't deviate from. "Sorry, Uber driver took a wrong turn."

"It's all right." A chuckle escapes me at her adorableness, the first in a while. This shyness that seeps through when her guard is down. "Are you heading home?"

"Don't change the subject on me, Mr. Jameson, but yes I am. Now, let me in." Her throwing those words back at me, the teasing tinge in her tone, and the fact there's been no recrimination—no distrust—cements what I've known since the moment my eyes landed on her in my pub.

She's special and not like the rest. That Gem was meant for me.

So, I give in. Taking the top off my half-full bottle of whiskey, I take a sip before placing the container back on the center console. "My mum passed away a few hours after I left you in Ibiza, Aurora." From her end there's a soft gasp and then heavy breathing, the kind one makes when emotions choke you—when tears form at the corner of your eyes. Listening to her, I let out a heavy breath of my own, sitting back while staring at my childhood home. Taking in the guards on duty as they make their rounds while pretending to ignore me. "A hired assassin took her from us, and...and it's why I left straight for the hospital after my cousin delivered the news. It's why I've been gone and uncommunicative."

"*Christ*, Casper. I'm so—"

"I know, sweet girl." The tears in her voice gut me and I rub a hand over my chest. This weird connection we have, even thousands of miles away, is palpable. It lets me sense her emotions as if they're mine. Clearing my throat, I grab my drink and take another sip, focusing on the slight burn it leaves behind instead. "You're too perfect to be anything but, and while I appreciate it, right now I just need you. For a few minutes, I need nothing but you."

"You have me." It's low and soft and soothes a part of me that's both in pain and restless. That wants to bring back the bloody bastard I killed earlier tonight just to watch the life drain from his body again, a drop of blood or inhale of coke at a time. "Can you stay on the phone for a few minutes?"

"I can."

"Can we FaceTime where you are?"

"We can."

"Good, now hush. Just don't hang up." Then, there's some rustling and the jingling of keys. A car door opens then closes, there's a muffled goodbye, and she's back. Her breathing is a soothing balm as I roll down my windows and light up a cigarette, pulling the earthy smoke deep into my lungs and then release it slowly. We do this for a few minutes, just being, and I enjoy the silence by taking a few deep drags and then toss it out the window, ignoring the man that picks it up and then returns to his post. And I'm still looking his way when she lets out a snort. A cute one. "I don't know why I'm nervous all of a sudden. You've seen me naked."

I know this is hard for her. It's easy to see the pain Aurora tries to hide whenever her mother is mentioned—when she revisits the memories, and yet, the small joke is made for my benefit. To ease my tension.

I'm falling helplessly for her. Without an ounce of struggle or restraint.

"And I think about it—you—constantly."

"Accept, perv," she says, and I close my eyes to picture that decadent blush of hers. "I'm waiting."

"So impatient, little girl," I chastise and then do. Pulling the device from my ear, I press the FaceTime button on the mobile. A click. A few seconds. A beautiful face staring back at me. Her expression is soft, and those expressive hazel eyes are full of unshed tears she's refusing to let drop. She looks exhausted but happy. Unguarded and peaceful. "Hi."

"Hello, love." Her smile is blinding at the term of endearment, a sweet little curl of her lips, and I can't stop myself from swiping a finger across the screen. From wishing she was here so I could taste that berry-colored mouth. "Let me see you."

"Naked?" At her words my cock twitches, an automatic response.

"No, but if you're offering..." I trail off, raising a brow suggestively. And while I'd love nothing more, now isn't the time. It'd be a cruel punishment for the two of us. "But seriously, Gem. Just pull the phone back and let me see my girl."

"Your girl?" she questions but is already placing the device somewhere that holds it up and allows her to stand back, giving me a full view of her beautiful body in a pair of painted-on denim trousers and a sky-blue vest with her company logo on it. The top is tight and has a few splatters of paint—accentuating her larger-than-a-handful breasts—while the denim trousers have a few bleach stains on them, the kind strategically placed by the designer with rips at the knees.

Comfortable yet sexy. But then again, the woman could wear an old potato sack and I'd still find her attractive. A cock-throbbing fantasy.

"Yes. Mine." Bringing my hand to my chin, I rub my thumb across my bottom lip a few times. "Rough day at the women's home, love?"

"Why do you say...wait. How do you know where I work?"

"Own, Gem," I correct. "You own the place."

"Fine. Own it." She huffs, pulling her long hair down from the high ponytail she had it in. It tumbles down her shoulders, the waves with curls at the ends framing her face. "I never told you anything about where I work, Casper. Did you pull a file on me?"

"Had it waiting for me at my desk the second I left you at the hotel."

"No shame, huh?"

"None when it comes to you." I'm not going to deny or lie to her.

Tilting her head to the side, she purses her lips. "That should really piss me off."

"And yet it doesn't." Not a question, but a statement. "A part of you likes the fact I'm obsessed with every minute detail. Infatuated with you."

"I will neither confirm nor deny that." Aurora shimmies out of her trousers, letting them drop to the ground while giving me a peak of a light purple pair of cotton panties. They're molded like a second skin, outlining the perfect little pussy my mouth waters for.

At the sight, my cock gives a harsh jerk within the confines of my trousers, beads of pre-come rolling down the tip. "You don't need to."

"What else do you have in that magical file on me?" A yawn escapes her then, and I shift my eyes to the clock on my dash. It's late, and I feel a little guilty for keeping her. I'm used to being awake at this time—it's well past three in the morning here and I'm six hours ahead. "Is the math test I failed my senior year in there, too? Or what about the time I got suspended for punching a kid in the year below mine for trying to touch my ass?"

"Give me his name."

"My father threatened him personally when he found out." Gem rolls her eyes, but you can tell she finds it amusing. "He made him pee his pants while his father watched, and then apologized for him being a creeper."

"So he kissed arse, then?"

"Absolutely. Now, about that file..."

"That's a topic to be discussed later. When you're more awake." She pouts, looking at me with this sassy little expression that I want to kiss off her face. "How about I put you to bed instead?"

"How?"

"Take me to your room and lay me on the bed beside you." My father is standing at the door looking toward my car, probably wondering why I haven't come inside, but I ignore him. He's been having trouble sleeping since mum passed, and I find myself stopping by every other night to make sure he's okay. Tonight, though, he called me later than normal and can wait a little while longer. "I'll keep you company until you fall asleep."

"You'd do that?"

"Pretty girl, I'm starting to realize that there isn't much I wouldn't do for you."

"SOMETHING YOU WANT to tell me, son?" my father asks the very second I take a seat across from him in the living room. His features are hard and lips thinned; the sign of an impending reproach. Not that I've gotten many over the years, but the few I did were memorable.

"Spit it out." Because quite frankly I don't have time for whatever stupidity he wants to impart. How he wants to act like he has an active role—his old one—in our organization. "I'm tired and have no interest in playing a game or going around in circles. You have something to say, just say it. What did you ask me to come over for?"

He sits back and regards me, something that in my early teens intimidated me. "You know I still have some pull of my own, Casper. That I know about—"

"I'd be very careful in choosing your next words, Dad. Don't start something with me you won't win."

"I'm not the enemy here."

"And she is?" I hiss out, gritting my teeth in order to not say something that will cut deep. My anger toward him hasn't waned completely. It's there, festering, and made worse by his audacity to look into Aurora. And while I understand the circumstances, I still hold him partially responsible too.

"Her arsehole father—"

"Did not kill Mum." At the finality in my tone, his mouth snaps shut. "There's a family trying to overthrow Matteo Cancio and keep her as a prize. Something that I'll never allow to happen."

"How are we involved, then?" There's less hostility to his tone, but the stone-cold expression is still very present. His narrowed eyes are pleading with me to make him understand. To make it easier. "Why did I just bury my w-wife?"

And it's at that very moment, as his voice cracks, that my anger toward him evaporates. It's just gone. Seeing him break, the tears that spill forth and then the tremble of his hand as he rushes to wipe them away, are proof that he's living with a pang of guilt that's crippling him. Choking him.

"I'm going to need you to listen very carefully. Can you do that?"

"I think it's best if I head to bed. I'll see you in the morning."

"No. You need to stop and listen." Sitting forward, I let my hands hang between my parted thighs, eyes on his. "It's not your fault."

"I should've been there."

"It's not your fault."

"I see it in your eyes, son. I let you both down and—"

"It's not your bloody fault," I all but snarl, slamming a hand atop the vintage coffee table my mum spent hours restoring during one of her phases. "There are two fucking cunts responsible and I have their names. *I* will go to the ends of the earth if I have to in order to bring you their heads. They did this and will pay with blood. You have my word."

He nods but holds a hand up. "I want to be there."

"Done."

"Thank you." His head tilts a bit then, and this time the way he's watching me is different. "Is she worth going to war for? Because we both know it will head that way if you step in to protect."

She's more than that. "Aurora is mine."

Chapter 17
CASPER

I T'S BEEN WEEKS, and nothing on the whereabouts of Mauricio. Not a fucking sign of the son of a bitch has been found. He's gone deep into hiding, and now I have another matter to take care of at the moment. Aside from not seeing my Gem since Ibiza, I now have a monetary transaction being investigated by the United States government.

They made a move to seize the wire, to tack it onto Asher Holdings as a launder attempt—to expose him for what we all know he is. The man is an arsehole with brass balls unafraid to do what he does best: move money for criminal organizations, without fear.

I make it, and he *cleans* it.

However, what was supposed to be a simple transaction has been compromised by two very stupid individuals. One by greed, and the other by trying to impress a useless cunt below him.

He let his ego talk for him, and that's a big *no no* in this business.

You see, hear, and know of nothing. You don't talk. You don't try to make moves outside of your lane or it will cost you.

Pulling out my mobile, I send a quick text to Gem.

> Morning, beautiful. Any plans today? ~Casper

My plan is to surprise her later. To fuck my beautiful Gem like the perfect obsession she's become.

> Hey! How's it going? ~Gem

> And my plans are the following today: nothing, couch, junk food, and Netflix. ~Gem

> Sounds amazing, love. Rest as much as you can today...Skype later? ~Casper

She's typing just as I hear a man scream from the inside and I chuckle. *Bastard is having fun.*

> We can most definitely sexy Skype later today. 😉 Around 8 p.m. my time? ~Gem

Fuck, she's perfect. My perfect.

> It's a date. ~Casper

I reply back to keep up the charade. Let her think I'm far away... it'll be much sweeter that way.

Pocketing the device, I refocus on the issue that brought me back to Chicago without my letting Aurora know. It's why on a late

Sunday morning I find myself opening a large metal door with enough force that it bounces off the wall, and the resounding bang that follows causes a woman to cry out.

Jeffrey and Callum are with me—leaving the three other men outside—walking just a few paces behind and with the hoods of their black sweatshirts over their heads. The hallway is long, but there at the end is my friend kneeling in front of a man—while a few close by are on their knees.

The concrete is already stained with someone's blood.

"Good morning," Malcolm says, standing up to greet me, extending his hand out while the woman whimpers again. Something that isn't the norm; we don't harm women this way. We have more civilized ways to make them cooperate. *What did you do to find yourself in this mess?* "How are you, my friend?"

"Could be better, mate." I grip his hand in mine and then pull him into a hug. "Thank you for the *help* at the funeral with the reporter. My father and I are very appreciative." My whisper is met with a barely perceptible nod. Just enough of a movement to let me know he heard. We don't know what happened to the man, nor do we care, but he was never seen again. Pulling back, I pat his shoulder twice. "Bloody traffic here always gets me in a mood."

"You're a native, Casper. You should be used to it by now."

"Semi native, thank you very much." The motherfucker just laughs, rolling his eyes as someone groans from behind us. Malcolm Asher's crazy matches mine, and it's one of the reasons we work so well together. With global operations, he provides certain money management services that a family like mine requires.

He sets them up. He watches over them.

Strip clubs.

Launderettes.

Car washes.

All businesses that deposit large quantities of cash day in and out. It's almost like recycling in a sense; the dirty and unusable goes in and the clean and untraceable comes out.

"Four months a year is enough to qualify."

"Fuck you, and never." At my reply he laughs, slapping my back. The men around us chuckle, but just as soon it all dies down, the seriousness resettling in. "Now, how are we going to fix this, Malcolm? Cause we have a lot of money being held up by—"

"I have it all," he interrupts while I raise a brow in question, not understanding what's going on, especially after our last phone conversation where he asked me to be here today. "Before the feds got ahold of it or put a pause on the transaction, I froze everything. Moved the capital offshore, and my guys did what they needed to do to make everything disappear."

"So we're good, then?" *Why am I here?*

"No. Not in the least." Malcolm tilts his head toward two men I've never seen before. I take in both his hostility and how they cower under his glower. "We won't be okay until I make an example out of this asshole and his family."

"Who are they?"

"The orchestrators." At once, I pull my Colt out and point it at the younger of the two males as my ire resurfaces to the forefront. This cunt set my operations back and that's un unforgivable offense, but before I can shoot, Malcolm pushes my hand down. "They are mine, Casper. All three."

"Then why tell me, arsehole?" I hiss, shrugging his hand off. "This delay is costing me a shipment coming in tomorrow night. With the heat on my operations, the weapons supplier isn't feeling comfortable."

"Because I want them to watch you leave this warehouse with every single *ounce* of their merch." As the last word leaves him, I notice the few men attending to barrels upon barrels of bricks wrapped in plastic. "The coke and electronics are yours to do with as you please. Dump them in the river for all I care, but they won't make a fucking cent in profit."

"Apology accepted, bloke." Walking over to one of the containers, I pull out one of my karambits, a smaller version of my two back home, and rip open one of the packages. With the blade's tip, I take a small amount and taste it. Nod to myself as I realize the quality at once: Columbian pure white. "I'll take it all."

"Done." Malcolm looks down at the younger male with a smirk. "Load it up. Three trucks are outside waiting, and Casper's men will drive them away."

"Understood." Javier whistles and within minutes, everything is gone. As if it was never here.

"Thank you, Malcolm. I know my business is always safe with you…"

"But?"

Walking back over to my friend, my eyes shift between the men with covered faces and the three on the floor in front of them. How pallid the older man looks. The blood he's lost on the floor. "How will we make sure this never happens again?"

"Like this," Malcolm says, and Carmelo comes forward then, a box in his hands. "Go on. Open it."

"If it's a bloody snake, you arse, I'll shoot you."

"Open it." He laughs and so does Callum behind me. They know how much I despise reptiles. I'm an equal opportunity hater when it comes to them—a weakness those closest to me find hilarious. Me, not so much.

Opening the box, I look back him. "What the pissing hell is this?"

"Two tongues. One for each man that played a part in this."

"Michael?"

"Knows to never betray his family again. Losing *his* was his penance."

"He's family…no?"

"Then he should know better. They all do now."

"And the other?"

"Belonged to Phillip Mitchell. A low-level criminal that he…" Malcolm points toward the younger male "…paid to try and extort me. His idiocy cost him his life."

"Thank you." Because I do appreciate the gesture. Tossing the box containing the two appendages toward the crying woman, I hold in a laugh when she scrambles back with a shriek when it lands near her leg. "When can we continue with the transaction? Will it be while I'm still here?"

"Give me three weeks to make some moves."

"Done." I extend a hand for him to shake. "I'll be heading out, mate...I'm hungry and need to make another pit stop before heading home." *Is that what she is? My home?*

"Of course, but before you go..." Javier lowers the hood from the two men and stands back while Malcolm pulls out his gun, firing two shots. One in the neck and the other in the chest. The men fall to the ground and no one moves; all eyes are on him. "They weren't very vigilant during their shifts and let people make illegal deals on my property. For that they paid the ultimate price."

"What's fair is fair." I'm not going to argue that point when I'd do the same. Turing to leave, I take two steps when he speaks again.

"There's a simple request that I want witnesses for."

"Of course, brother." I turn back to fully face him and watch as he sets his eyes on the younger man, walks over, and the picks up two photos from the ground. His eyes roam the picture and soften for a split second before hardening all over again. They're cold and threatening as he crouches down to meet the other man's stare. "If you ever lay a finger on her again..." He grabs his hand, the one with what looks to be a dislocated knuckle, and holds it against the cold concrete. Then, without an ounce of care, he slams the butt of the gun down on the bone. Four solid blows and there's a crack; the man doesn't so much as whimper, but the tears in his eyes give away to his pain. "Touch her— fuck with her—and I will dispose of you a small cut at a time. Filet your flesh and then feed it to your dear old father while you watch. It'll be a slow death. Agonizing. One that I will take immense joy in, Foster."

"I love my sister," he chokes out as Malcolm slams the gun down once more.

"As of today, she's mine. I'll be taking her, moving her in with me as part of my payment." I'm surprised by his reaction, but at the same time can't judge. *Seems the arse has met his match, too.*

After a few quick orders to his men and a final warning, we leave, both heading out while cries and whimpers follow in the distance. We don't talk, but I can't help but fuck with him before getting into my car. "You been holding out on me, mate?"

"No more than you have."

"What's that supposed to mean?"

"Means I'll share when you do."

HALF AN HOUR later I'm at her door after dismissing her guard for the night. I want him gone—to go help the others store the cocaine at a warehouse I own here, while the electronics need to be shipped to a seller in South America. They have just a few hours to get it done because everyone except for Jeffrey and Alexander are heading back to England at first light while I enjoy my Gem for a few days.

While I gorge myself on her decadence. While I remind her of just how good we are together.

My breathing is heavy and cock hard as I knock. Almost pounding my fist as the desperation to see her becomes near maddening. It's been too long.

This tiny woman has me going insane, feigning for a taste.

"Christ, woman, open the bloody door," I hiss under my breath, listening for any sign of life from the other side of the door. No more than thirty seconds later I sense her near, that inviting pull ever-present and throbbing the closer to me she gets.

I hear the padding of her feet.

I can just make out the low gasp that escapes her, an almost undetectable little sound that makes my cock throb as she sees my hungry expression through her peephole.

I see the exact moment she begins to turn the doorknob and then yanks it open in her haste to reach me.

Then, we are face to face.

Breathing the same air.

Mirroring the same need.

I have no idea who attacked first or how we ended up an upright mass of tangled limbs, but all is right in my world the second those sweet lips meet my own.

Chapter 18
AURORA

"HOW?" IS ALL I manage to get out between kisses, the slanting of his mouth over mine as he robs me of coherency and the front door slams shut. I'm surrounded by him and yet it's not enough. I don't think anything ever will be.

"Later. Talk later," he hisses as my nails rake down his chest, leaving deep welts behind while I follow the trail down to the waist-band of his jeans. His abs clench the lower I go, muscles contracting as I pop open the button and begin to lower the zipper. My fingers push it down slowly, taunting him, and a rumble builds inside his chest—the vibration running through me a second before I'm turned around by a hand on my hip. The other fists my hair and tugs it back. "Room."

"I want you." I'm breathless and giggling and enjoying the tight hold he has me in. I want to stay as I am, in his arms and being manipulated.

There's something so sexy about it, the way he can pick me up with ease or bend me to his liking. How palpable his hunger is.

It's physical and literal. Can't be denied.

"Room, Gem." His lips trail down my temple and cheek, not pausing until reaching my neck where he embeds his teeth. It stings but feels like heaven. The pleasurable pain flows through my skin and brings every nerve ending to life.

I'm hypersensitive. Throbbing with need.

I shouldn't want him as I do.

I shouldn't give in as easily as I do.

My problem is that every question that starts and ends with him has one answer: I do.

I'm screwed. Utterly screwed.

"Down the hall, first door on the left," I manage to say on a whimper, pointing in the general direction as I throw my head back and close my eyes. Loving the feel of his teeth raking down my skin, how his fingers dig into my hips and hold my ass tightly against his hard length.

Casper nods, the movement subtle as he kisses the spot he's abused. "I've missed you, love. So fucking much and it makes no sense. It's driving me insane."

I'm not sure if those words are meant for me, they are spoken so low, but they warm me from the inside out. Causes my heart's cadence to speed up, a rapid *thump thump thump* that seems to pump only for him.

I've never experienced this type of connection before. This kind of yearning.

I'm afraid and excited and probably stupid for allowing it to continue, but it can't be stopped. This combustion is meant to happen for better or worse.

"I've missed you too." No sooner have the words passed my lips that I find his hold on my hair tightening, forcing my back to arch in a manner that puts his mouth over mine. Devouring. Showing me with his dominion how much of me he already owns.

"Say it again. Tell me." It leaves him on a growl a second before one of his hands leaves my hips and travels to the barely there tank top I'm wearing. Casper fists the material between his fingers and tugs once, forcing the cotton to dig into my skin as the sound of it protesting seems loud within the room. Another pull and it stretches, a tear forming at the thin strap, ripping the elastic material from the seam and exposing half my right breast. "Say it, baby girl. Tell me what you need. What you missed."

"You." And it's the most honest answer I can give him. All these weeks I've been going through the motions, trying to fight my attraction to him or the rabbit hole it could possibly lead to. Deny how much his morning texts mean to me, though sometimes far between, they make me smile. "I just needed you."

"Fuck, I can't go so long without seeing you. Feeling you against me." Another sharp pull and the other shoulder strap breaks, leaving me exposed to the cool air and him. My nipples tighten into stiff peaks and my thighs clench as I wait. Anticipate his next touch. He doesn't make me wait long, though, cupping a breast in each hand as he forces me to take two steps forward. And then another, all the while his lips are at my ear. "Lead me to your room, Gem."

"Please," I whimper, arching my chest into his hands. "Can't wait that long to feel you." Then, to further prove my point, I do what I've been fantasizing about in the darkness of my room late at night.

I walk away from him and step fully into my living room, not stopping until I'm beside the loveseat. His footsteps follow mine; their heaviness causes goose bumps to break out all over my skin. For my thighs to dampen as the soft lace panties I'm wearing become soaked.

There's no need for words. This is a moment to just feel.

To take. To satiate this building fire we have burning within.

Bending over the couch's armrest, I expose my desire to him. "This is what I need."

"Could you be any more bloody perfect." It's a statement that he follows up by dropping to his knees behind me. By pressing his lips to the curve of my ass, the area where cheek and thigh meet, and then skimming across to the other. Casper does this a few times before nipping the skin below the lace as he pulls the material aside with his teeth.

The cool air meets my labia and I shiver. The wetness coating my lips is visible to his hungry eyes.

"Casper, I...*oh God*!" His mouth is against my clit and a harsh shiver rocks through my body. Just the mere act brings me to the precipice of an orgasm. I'm shaking for him, panting for more, but all I get is a low *shhhh* to behave. "Please. *Please.*"

He doesn't hurry, though. Instead, he explores me. Tastes me.

Those lips part and then his tongue flicks at my engorged bundle of nerves. Each swipe, the hungry way he moans into my tender flesh, causes my knees to shake. For my hips to undulate against his perfect mouth as his tongue slips lower until he reaches my entrance.

My entire body clenches as he dips the tip inside and holds still. "More."

I don't receive a verbal response. Instead, there's the sound of his belt coming undone and then the lowering of a zipper. Goose bumps arise on my flesh and I try to push back, to take more, but he pulls back with a tsking sound.

It's a reprimand I meet with defiance as I slip a hand between myself and the armrest, but that doesn't work out; if anything it ignites a ferocious anger in him. His hand meets my cheek, three times in quick succession that steals the air from my lungs.

It stings, but immediately spreads warmth through the area as I choke on a moan.

He spanks me again. Then again. Alternating between the right and left, different areas before giving one last swipe with the flat of his tongue from my clit to rosebud and then he stands.

His pants lower to the ground behind me, trapped by his shoes. His shirt is tossed somewhere, and a second later something made of glass crashes to the ground.

And I don't care. Don't lift my head to look, because nothing matters more to me than the bulbous tip of his cock running through my wetness, coating his flesh before stopping at my entrance.

"Say it again."

"I need you."

One of his hands gathers my hair at the back, fisting the tresses as he turns my head, putting his lips right at the corner of my mouth. "I need you too." Then he slams in, one swift move that causes my toes to curl and eyes to close.

This feeling is what I've been missing. Needing desperately.

Pulling out slowly, he lets me enjoy every solid inch of his cock before sliding to another entrance, one I've never given to anyone. At first, my puckered hole clenches as the fat head and metal slide over, but soon I find myself pushing back beneath his hold. Find myself finishing what I tried to do earlier, and I slip my hand between the couch and my pussy, shaking in his hold as my fingers make contact with my swollen and sensitive flesh.

"Bad girl." It's a growl, a menacing declaration a second before he places his other hand on my hip and pins me against my fingers. Pressing. Giving me just enough friction to keep me on edge. His hips jut forward a little then, the head of his cock pushing against the tight hole, when he pulls back. "That's mine and I'll be coming back for that soon, but for now…"

"Oh, God!" I'm a whimpering, sensitive mess when he enters my core again, and I clench my walls to keep him right where he is. Not that he pauses or lets me. Now he's relentless. Fucking me like I've needed to be all these weeks.

Fast and hard. Almost punishing.

Only he can invoke this painful pleasure; I choke on a scream as

I tremble and my wetness wets us both. It's quick and nothing I was prepared for.

"That's it, love," he grunts above me, lips at the back of my neck. They part and his breath is a caress on my skin a second or two before his teeth lock down. The bite hurts in the most blissful way, taking me higher as he pistons in and out. "You feel...*motherfuck*, you're my ambrosia. My heaven and hell."

But it's those words that put me over the edge. That destroy me.

Between his cock, my fingers against my clit, and how honest he is in his need for me...I'm done.

I'm his. Completely his.

My wetness coats us both, soaking the fabric of my loveseat, but nothing registers more than the pure groan of pleasure from his lips after another pump of his hips. I'm limp beneath him, taking everything he gives, but as I feel that first rope of his come release inside of me, I come alive. My back arches and walls hold him tight as another orgasm rocks me from head to toe.

It's explosive and I'm gasping for breath.

I can't register anything around me but the blissful wake of this release.

"Casper." It leaves me on a reverent moan so low I doubt he even hears me. My eyes are drooping, and sounds are becoming muffled. I'm weightless and falling.

And yet I still hear his whispered words a second before all goes black.

"I'll never let her go."

Chapter 19
AURORA

"**Y**OU LOOK MIGHTY at home in my kitchen, Mr. Jameson."

"I look mighty everywhere, love," he replies, not missing a beat or turning around; instead, he continues to put food on a plate. My eyes shift to the counter beside him and they widen, taking in the crazy number of Chinese cartons on my counter. It smells amazing and my stomach growls. "Grab something for us to drink, and back to the living room you go."

"Aren't you bossy, too."

That earns me a wink from over his shoulder. "Always, so behave."

My thighs clench. "And if I don't?"

The items in his hands are put on the counter and he turns, leaning back against the granite. "Would you like another time-out, Gem? Want me to put you to bed?"

"Please."

"Tease."

"You're the one looking delicious in my home."

"You're the one looking at me with hungry eyes, sweetheart. That's an unfair tactic."

"All's fair."

"Dangerous," he mutters under his breath, but I hear and giggle. "That's it. You brought this upon yourself." I blink twice and he's striding my way, reaching me before I can run, and picks me up. Automatically my legs wrap around his waist, exposing my naked core. The shirt I found of his on my side table—where the picture frame now lying in pieces on the floor once was—is doing a horrible job of covering my body. "Just a bad little girl."

"Is that a deal breaker for you?"

"More like seals the deal." Then his lips are on mine and a hand is exploring lower, over my ass cheek and between my thighs where he encounters my desire for him. Two fingers slide between my slickness, spreading it around before slipping them inside. "But you already know I'm wrapped around your tiny little finger."

"Are you?" I moan as he pumps those digits in and out slowly.

"Irrevocably." But instead of making me come, he pulls those fingers out, dragging them against my walls before circling my entrance twice with the very tips. "And it's because of that pull on me that I'm going to lower you to the ground, pat your arse, and send you to the living room. It's late, and you didn't eat after I attacked you. Let me rectify that."

"Okay." Because what else can I say when he's looking at me

with warmth in his eyes? "What would you like to drink? Beer or a Coke?"

"Lager would be lovely."

Nodding, I walk over to my fridge. "I got you."

"Yes, you do."

"How do you spend four months out of the year in Chicago and have never done the Gangsters and Ghosts tour? This is a staple, dude!" I ask him a few days later after being wrapped up in each other for the last forty-eight hours. The people around us continue to walk diligently behind our tour's host, but we pause with two very different expressions on our faces. I'm almost appalled by this and it shows. "Seriously, I just can't with you right now."

"Gem, think about it." He's chuckling, shoulders shaking as the guide stops at another location on his map of The Loop, this ones near the Asher Building. From where we stand, I can hear him talking about a specific incident that made the headlines in the late 1920s. "Why would I need information like this? I was born into this life. It's who I am."

"Oh, come on! Everyone needs this in their life." At my exasperation, he puts his arm around my shoulders and pulls me in close, pausing while the others doing this tour gasp at the information being given. They're listening intently to the history of this city's most notorious gangster and how prohibition laws brought forth the reign of these men as the need for certain illicit activities grew to high demand.

It's like any business.

If you tell a consumer no, they want it all the more. Good or bad for you; people want what the government says you can't have.

"Sweetheart, look at me."

"Say please."

He turns to fully face me, the hand on my shoulder dropping to my waist, fingers grabbing onto a belt loop. "I'm going to enjoy putting you over my knee."

"Is that so."

"Yes, you lovely little thing." One tug and I stumble forward, chest to chest, leaving no room between us. His heat sears my skin and my nipples tighten, stiff little peaks that poke through the thin material of my bralette and vintage band T-shirt. "But you'd like that, wouldn't you?"

"Maybe."

"Bad girl." His lips meet mine for a quick, passionate kiss before, in a move I'm not expecting, he turns me around and guides me forward. Our group has continued to walk down the street and is currently in front of what used to be a speakeasy owned by the biggest mobster of that era.

"Oh, this is an interesting story from that time." Grabbing his hand, I yank him with me toward the tour guide, forcing myself to ignore the lust he awakens in me with each simple touch. Ignore how right his hand on my lower back feels. "This one is all about alcohol, prostitution, and guns."

"Aren't they all?"

"Just pay attention, Jameson. He's getting to the good part." My voice is louder than I intend, and an older lady with a fanny pack looks back at me with a stink eye. "Sorry." She nods with pursed lips, wrinkles on point and full of displeasure, while I try to fight back my own amusement. "And you..." I shift my eyes to my date and elbow him in the ribs "...don't provoke me."

"What's the fun in that?"

"Learn now and I'll give you a special kiss later."

"That's all you had to say."

"Thank you."

"Can I get a preview of that kiss now?"

"Listen to the middle-aged guy retelling our past."

"And I'm the bossy one, love?" Casper says, then tilts his head to the side, those green eyes still showing mirth. "By the way, how many times have you done this tour?"

I shrug. "A few."

"Dozen?"

"More like five or eight."

"Five or eight?" he whispers, raising a brow.

"We liked the ghost part a little bit more, and it became a tradition to do it every year around Halloween after I turned sixteen. It was our thing, you know?" I look away from him and focus on the building in front of us. There's so much history in this city that people tend to ignore—forget the ways in which it molded who we are today. It's one of the reasons Mom and I did these crazy tours. In a sick way, it keeps us connected to who we are and where we come from. Especially with who my father is and what he represents. "We did corn mazes, old jails, or an asylum or two if the time permitted, and then at the end of the month, this tour. We knew all the monologues by memory, but it's still fun in a morbid sort of way."

"We?"

"Mom and me."

"Sounds like your mum was a lot of fun." The small chuckle that escapes him is a bit wistful, and I can understand it. Mine's been gone a few years, while his has only been a month; thirty days is nothing in the grand scheme of things. "Mine was a chicken when it came to anything like this. Dad, though, he's got issues."

"A fan?"

"A wee too much. Even my curiosity has limits."

"Folks, I'll give you a few minutes to take pictures and wander the area. Our next stop is in fifteen," the guide says, and the murmurs around us grow. People take off in different directions, yet stay close enough to hear further instructions. Us, though...

We stay right where we are. For the third time today, Casper has wrapped an arm around my shoulders and pulled me in to his side, nestling me against his much taller frame. While cameras go off and questions are asked, we breathe in and out while just being.

It's our second official date and while not the norm and probably silly for him, I love that he let me pick our activity. That he's letting me indulge in something I haven't done since my mother passed away, and while it's not October, it's close enough that I feel festive.

Fall is just around the corner, and this year doesn't seem as heavy as the ones in the past. Or maybe it's because I don't feel alone.

I have him here at the moment and that's all that matters. All I will allow myself to focus on.

"How do you feel about blues music?" I ask after a minute or two, trying to hide my smile when his stomach rumbles.

"It's very relaxing when I'm cleaning my guns. Why?"

"And Creole cuisine?"

"Never had it but I'm liking where this is going."

"Good." Turning to face him, I rise to the tips of my toes and nip his chin. "Let's skip the rest of this and get a late dinner. There's an amazing Blues Club not that far from here that serves the best gumbo I've ever had outside of Louisiana."

"You sure? Cause I'll wait until—"

"Come on. Let's get you fed, big boy." At my words, his eyes darken and that cocky smirk spreads across his lips.

"Can I eat you instead?"

"I'm definitely on the dessert menu."

"I REALLY HATE GOODBYES." I also hate the gut feeling that this separation will be a long one.

"Then don't say it." Casper wraps his arms around me tightly, pulling me against his chest as I wipe away a few stray tears that have escaped. "Because I won't. This is more of an *I'll see you later* kind of thing. Besides, we have a date coming up soon and I'm very much looking forward to this Skype sex you mentioned."

At that I look up and find that cocky little smirk on his face. "You're a pervert."

"When it comes to you..." he shrugs "...no doubt. But you already know this, Gem. I don't hide my hunger from you."

No, he doesn't. If anything, the man is the opposite of what I expected in that department. His need to touch—to feel me close at all times—is adorable in the sexiest way possible.

It matches his ruthlessness. The darker edges of his persona that always loom within my fingertips, but I'm yet to fully grasp. But I've heard it, seen the change in his expression when he speaks to those who work for him. Especially Callum, his cousin, who I've yet to meet but have heard them talk on speakerphone when he thought I was still showering the day of the mobster tour.

"What are your plans, Casper?" I ask instead of pulling him into the bathrooms here and bending over a final time before he leaves. We're at the airport now, waiting on word from his employee that the private jet is ready, and holding on for just a little bit longer after five days of normalcy.

Of bliss. Of minimal outside interference.

I took the time off while he delegated. Being the boss has perks, and Ali was nothing short of ecstatic to help me. More so when she heard his voice in the background the morning, I called in. Then there's Casper, and while I know men like him never travel alone, his guard was always out of sight. He kept his distance and I appreciate it— enjoyed every last second because I don't know when I'll see him again.

Something that just last week I thought to be for the best, but today makes me sad. A bit bitter because I wish things—our lives— were different.

In another place and time we would've met, made eye contact while exchanging numbers and then made plans. Then, that one date would've turned into two and then three—months and years with a proposal thrown in the middle—that leads to the elusive happily ever after that all women dream of since childhood.

He would be my prince and I his princess.

However, reality isn't that easy. Nothing in life really is.

I live here, and he's in England.

I want nothing to do with my familial ties, while he's the head of a British mob family.

I promised to never make my mother's mistake, while he is the physical embodiment of a catastrophe waiting to happen.

Would I ever be able to accept him like this? So much like my father?

"Quit overthinking, love. It'll be hard, but we'll make it work." I look up and he's smiling, looking calm and without a care. Nothing like the killer I know he can be.

"Why are you always so sure?" I ask and inhale deeply, pulling that rich scent of woodsy man in that I'll miss like crazy when he's gone. "This is a disaster—"

He cuts me off with a bone-melting kiss.

Casper fists my hair and pulls my head back, slanting his perfect mouth over mine and parting my lips. His tongue caresses mine and I shiver, greedily slipping my fingers through his hair to pull him closer. To express my urgency.

Something he reciprocates.

An animalistic growl builds in his chest and I tug on the longer strands at the back again, nipping his top lip. "Why do I need you so much?" I ask him, but his answer comes in the form of his hold tightening, keeping me in place.

Its sexy and dominating and I whimper for him like the desperate girl I am.

It's the kind of kiss that robs you of all your senses and stops time. The kind where everyone else in the world disappears and it's just you and him.

No one else. All alone and savoring—drowning in each other's taste.

Casper nibbles on my bottom lip, teasing little nips that bring goose bumps to my skin before he trails across my cheek and lower. There's a low whine that comes from me, my need to have his mouth back on mine, but that's silenced quickly as he sucks on my pulse point.

It stings, but I enjoy his marking. Can't find it in me to deny him this.

"You know why I'm calm?" he asks against my neck, tone gravelly. "Know why I can get on that plane without a single shred of doubt?"

"Please." It leaves me on a whimper as he nuzzles my sensitive skin. I *need* his confirmation. *His* word that we won't be another repeated story.

"I can do this because I trust us." He nips my earlobe, and the quick sting travels straight to my clit. My thighs clench. "I can do this..." Casper swallows hard "...because for the first time in my life, I want a relationship. Look forward to this journey and coming back to you, Gem. And lastly, I can do this because in a not-so-distant future, we will always be together."

At his words I freeze and then pull back. Heart racing. "What does that mean?"

"It means that I need you to trust me. That you'll have faith in me."

"How long will you be gone this time?"

"I'll be back the moment I put a bullet between the eyes of those responsible."

"And I'll wait." His conviction—trust in us—helps me make the decision without a single second of hesitation. If he believes, then I will try my best to push all doubts back. I'll give this an honest try.

"And I will come back. Always." Leaning forward, he presses his lips to my forehead and breathes me in, lingering for a minute before walking away. He only looks back once before going through the small tunnel to the plane, and that one look made my heart thump with excitement.

It says he'll be back.

For me. For us.

Chapter 20

AURORA

THERE'S NOTHING WORSE than being roused from a deep sleep by the blaring of your phone in the middle of the night. Your restful dream is interrupted, and the world comes crashing back in full force, startling you. Your heart races, palms begin to sweat, and you immediately begin to think the worse —fear that someone you love is hurt or...

In my haste to grab the small device, I reach over and knock my lamp over where it crashes to the ground and the glass part breaks. *I need to invest in plastic home furnishings. Since meeting Casper, things break all the time.*

"Shit," I mutter under my breath, fingers tapping all around the nightstand until they skim over the screen, and just as I fully grasp it, it stops ringing. I don't move and wait to see if a voicemail or another call comes through...

Nothing. I'm surrounded by absolute silence once more that brings no comfort.

Sitting up with my cell in hand, I bring it toward my face and unlock the screen, directly searching the incoming call log. The last call came from an unknown number; a 609 area code that I've never heard of before.

Seeing that it's not someone I know gives me immediate peace and I calm down. My breathing begins to normalize, and I relax.

They don't call again, and I put the cell back in its place atop my nightstand without giving it a second thought. It's early and I have to be at the home by eight for an early meeting. That, and I'm due for a Skype date tonight after having to cancel last week.

It's the only way to stay sane while Casper and I are apart. In the three weeks since he left, we've made plans and made the effort to keep them. Kept our promises of always talking and no shut-outs.

For this to work, communication is key.

But how long can this long-distance relationship work? Will he ask me to move or will he come here?

Ignoring those plaguing questions, I settle once more and close my eyes. Go back to that last kiss at the airport and remember how at home I felt with him. How right I know we can be for each other if I just trust him not to hurt me.

It's what helps me drift off and forget about the rude wake-up call.

MY ALARM WAKES me up at exactly 7:05 and I glare at the thing while fighting the urge to fling it across the room. I'm tired, hangry, and not in the mood to so much as move a muscle.

I'm sore, and with that soreness comes a kind of cramping I'm all too familiar with.

Aunt Flo is here, and that hateful bitch just loves to annoy me. She appeared somewhere between the wrong number calling, the sweeping of the broken lamp, and then my need for water about an hour later. I hate her, and she made her presence known with a series of vengeful, ovary-crushing cramps that had me near crawling, but like the righteous woman I am, I kept it in check and threw back some ibuprofen with water.

It's what we are taught to do from the moment this *time of the month* arrives.

Throwing my legs over the edge of the mattress, I stand up and stretch my back. It feels tight but eases with every contortion until something pops and I feel the relief. "Much better."

Today is a very important day and I have to be on my A-game; a back spasm is the last thing I need.

After a few more bends and twists, I grab my phone and make my way into the bathroom. There's a certain playlist that I like to use for days like this, and I open the Spotify app on my phone. Before I do that, though, something else catches my eye.

There are a few text messages from an unknown number. Ten to be exact, and I click on the first.

6:00 a.m.

> You will learn your place, little girl. ~Unknown

What the hell?
6:03 a.m.

> I don't tolerate that kind of behavior. ~Unknown

6:07 a.m.

> You touched what isn't yours. ~Unknown

6:10 a.m.

His blood will be on your hands. ~Unknown

They go on, each one showing mounting frustration at being ignored. They also bring a feeling of dread to the pit of my stomach. These messages aren't a mistake.

They are clearly for me. Evidence that I'm being watched.

An observation turned reality when I read the very last message sent.

6:15 a.m.

A whore just like her mother for a man that's a known killer. ~Unknown

The phone slips through my fingers and crashes to the ground, a large crack forming at the upper right-hand corner. This scares me. Brings a series of complications into my life that I don't know how to handle.

It's clear to me that this message came from someone who knew both my mother and father. Of their relationship and my place in that story. I've always been kept on the sidelines, but people talk. They know who I am, and all my life I've been looked at differently because of who Matteo Cancio is.

Something that up until today I've brushed off and kept going. Not letting him define who I am, but this, *this* is very different. There's an underlying threat here. Moreover, they also know of my relationship with Casper—an association that's in its infant stage.

The question now, though, is who? Who would have the guts to send this?

I need to tell Casper.

My first thought is to call him and ask for help. I'm not naïve, nor will I ignore this.

I know better. I have seen things, even as my mother tried to protect me, that other kids haven't. My father never hid who he is, and on the rare occasions where he picked me up for a visit or a weekend stay, he never stopped being boss.

Business is business and to the Cancios, it comes above everything. If it meant making a decision while at the dining room table while his wife glared at me, so be it. If it meant leaving the room and having the cook keep me occupied in the kitchen while profanities were being hurled, so be it. If a sentence had to be carried out somewhere in the backyard of his private estate—deep into the forest behind the property, then so be it.

I know what being in this life entails and as much as I hate what it represents, the family it took from me, it's part of me. A part of me I try to ignore, but it's still there and has come to the forefront now that I've been seeing where this connection with Casper goes.

My second alarm goes off then and I'm pulled from the racing thoughts going through my head. "Shit!" I yell, realizing that in all this craziness I've forgotten to get dressed. "Christ, I'm going to be late today of all days."

This meeting is too important, has the possibility of a large donation that will help us expand the operation to a possible second state.

I'll tell him tonight. Everything will be fine.

Taking a few deep breaths, I calm myself and then send Aliana a quick text.

> Running late. Explain later. Hold the fort until I arrive. ~Roe

At once, three dots appear on the screen.

> And the meeting? Are you okay? ~Ali

> Not really, but I'll explain after. Just keep him there until I arrive. ~Roe

> I got you. ~Ali

Knowing that's taken care of, I walk straight into the bathroom and toward the shower. The motion sensor has already picked up my movement, so I quickly strip and turn on the faucet, letting the water run almost scalding before getting in.

This is a mission-impossible-like situation and I lather, rinse, and repeat faster than I ever thought humanly possible. Once out, I check my phone on the counter for the time and blow out a big breath of air. I have thirty minutes to get dressed and then drive twenty minutes to the home.

"Clothes. I need clothes." Running out, I make a beeline for my closet and pull out a retro three-quarter-sleeve pencil dress with a belt in charcoal that I match with a pair of black leather strappy botties with a platform heel. It's comfortable and cute and after adding a winged liner, leaving my curls down, and adding a nude lip stain, I take a selfie.

This one is for Casper and goes with a caption: *BIG MEETING. WISH ME LUCK!*

I know he's busy and probably won't see it right away, but I send it anyway. Hoping he responds in the off chance. At least that's what I thought because just as I grab my purse, keys, and a bottle of water, my phone rings with his special tone.

And I'm smiling. A real one.

"Hello."

"Morning." He sips something, I can make out the sound of ice inside of a cup, and then there's a groan. It's low and throaty and will be the death of me. "You look beautiful. Absolutely stunning."

My nerves calm at once, and the earlier scare is pushed to the back of my mind until later tonight. "Thank you." It comes out shy and I feel my face heat up. "It's a huge meeting, and I'm kind of nervous. It's the first step into looking for donations to help with our expansion."

"I'll match whatever they give you today."

"You sound so sure."

"How could anyone say no to you. I know I can't." Someone says his name and I know our time is about to end, but it means everything to me that he stopped his day to call. "Sorry about that. My cousin tends to be on the loud side."

"It's okay. I know you're busy."

"I miss you," Casper says then, taking me by surprise. My lips part, and just as I'm going to tell him that I do too, he continues. "And knock them dead, beautiful. Shine like the precious Gem you are. I'll call you later tonight."

Then he's gone and I'm still smiling like a loon. He has no idea how much those words mean to me. How much more at ease I feel now.

They also serve as a reminder that I need to grab my gun from the safe.

It's always better to be safe than sorry and he'd want me to carry.

"Good morning," I say, walking into my office and placing my purse atop a small table against the wall before turning to face the occupants. Ali is looking at me with nothing but relief on her face while my could-be donor gives me a smile. "I apologize for being so late, Mr. Asher. Something came up that I was not prepared for and—"

"No worries, Miss Conte. Things happen." Grabbing his cup of coffee, he takes a sip and then places it back. "And it's Malcolm. Please call me Malcolm."

Behind him Aliana fans herself and it's hard, but I do manage to keep my eye roll in. Yes, the man is handsome and exudes a powerful aura that can't be denied, but I only have eyes for a certain Brit. He haunts me day in and day out without mercy, and I want to keep it that way.

I extend a hand, which he takes and then shakes it. "Then please call me Aurora."

"Deal." He sits back and regards me quietly, and I take that as my cue to move this meeting along. A man like Malcolm Asher doesn't like to waste time.

"Speaking of…?" I trail off as I take a seat behind my desk, matching his cool demeanor.

"Right to the point, Aurora. I appreciate that." Malcolm nods and pulls out a folded piece of paper that resembles a check from the inside of his suit jacket. He places it atop my desk and then pushes it forward in my direction. "If you need more, please don't hesitate to call me. No questions asked."

"I don't understand." For a split second I look over to where Aliana was a minute ago and find her gone and my office door closed.

"Go on. Open it and ask your questions."

Picking up the paper, I unfold and read. "Why?" It's all I can think to ask as I take in the half a million-dollar check in my hand. "Why are you doing this?"

"Look at me, Aurora." And I do, completely flabbergasted and unsettled; I know my expression mirrors this. "There's a reason I am doing this, and her name is London Foster, although, her rightful last name is Conte."

"Wait, what? Who is London Fos—"

"She's your cousin, Aurora," he says softly, but to me it's as if he's shouting the words right into my ear. "Your uncle Julian had a daughter with his wife, Amelia."

"He had…has a daughter?" And I believe him. I grew up hearing that name from time to time—from my mother and grandmother while alive—and how sad they were because of a choice she made. Christ, my head is spinning, and nothing makes sense, but I also can't deny that hearing this makes me smile. A smile that falls just as quickly and I voice my next thought. "But why would my mother hide this from me?"

"Amelia was in a very abusive relationship, Aurora, and out of concern for her daughter, she made your mother promise to stay away. To not get involved, although she did communicate with her every chance she got. It was your mother who helped her change her will and accounts over to London before she died."

I nod, understanding more than he can ever imagine; I see the damage abuse leaves behind every single day. "Is London safe now?"

"She's with me."

"With you?" *Is he saying that...*

"London is my life." And now it all makes sense. She's his girl-friend, because had he married anyone, the entire state of Chicago would know. This most eligible bachelor has a following.

"Does she know about me? About her family?" I can't stop the tears that spring to my eyes, not when the only family I have left on my mother's side was being abused and I couldn't help. Didn't know she needed me. "When can I meet her?"

"Not yet, but I'm sure she will be in contact soon." Malcolm scratches his jaw and then looks down at the watch on his wrist. "I'm not hiding this from her."

"Thank you." It's the least I can say, but those words carry all of my gratitude.

"All I ask is that you're there for her, Aurora. She's going to need you." His eyes are on mine as he says this and, in that moment, I see the other side of him people whisper about. He loves her and is protective. Won't tolerate bullshit when it comes to her.

And that just earned him my respect.

Chapter 21
CASPER

I STARE AT the picture she sent me an hour ago one last time, ignoring Malcolm's confirmation that my wire has been completed before pocketing my mobile and exiting the car. I know he's going to see her today; her guard was able to slip inside her office undetected while she went to the on-site kitchen for lunch and saw his name in her planner. It's how I learned of a few interesting facts after having Ezra look into this for me.

Learned just how tiny this world is.

My girl has a cousin, and my friend is completely taken by her. And it's that small fact that kept me from forgetting our friendship and making a pit stop in Chicago to put a bullet in his brain. He's like a brother to me, but when it comes to Gem, I'd burn the world to the ground for her.

Two car doors close a few seconds after mine, and my men fall in line on this sunny East Coast day as I walk up a pathway that leads to an Ocean City property. We're in New Jersey, and the owner doesn't know I'm here.

Not one person can pinpoint my location, and it will stay that way as I hunt down Mum's killers.

Not even a friend I have in town who's providing me with the facility I'll be using for today's meeting. He knew I'd need it, but not when, and said it was mine for whenever I decide.

Well, today is that day.

"Sir," Archie, a new guard recommended by Jeffrey, calls my name. He's his childhood best friend and an ex-British soldier in need of work with connections that are valuable, especially with the changes that are coming soon to our business.

I pause, tilting my head but don't look back. "Speak."

"Sir, we have confirmation that our guest hasn't left the house since yesterday around eight. He's alone while the new wife is in the Dominican Republic vacationing with girlfriends."

"I see." There is a few-days-old beard on my face at the moment and I rub my chin. "Is there an ex-wife and kids?"

"They live in an apartment complex in Patterson where her older brother and mum also have apartments. She's also had to take a mini-mum-wage job, working overnights at a gas station to make ends meet since he barely passes her a hundred fifty a week."

"What's his net worth?" Because with its size and location two blocks from the beach, this home is easily worth more than seven hundred and fifty thousand.

"Bank statement shows a balance of three hundred thousand, but if we add cars and homes, probably a low million."

I turn my head to look back at Archie. "Transfer every last bloody cent to the children's mother."

"It shall be done," he vows and pulls out his mobile, shooting a quick message to Jeffrey, who is awaiting orders with my hacker in London. It pings a few seconds later and he shows me the screen, confirming my thoughts.

> Ezra is already on it. We were awaiting
> confirmation to proceed. ~Jeffrey

Pocketing the device, he takes his place slightly behind Callum who's been silent. There's something bugging him—he's been off since the last time we were in Chicago—and we haven't had time to talk.

But I see it in the deep pull of his eyebrows and tense posture.

Meeting his eyes, I raise a brow, silently asking if he's good. If he's focused.

His reply comes in the form of a nod and tap to his chest with a closed fist.

Nothing else is said as I turn my head and continue up the path with my gun in hand. It's a sweltering day and I'm glad I dressed down for this occasion. No suit or tie or cuff links—instead, I brought with me a pair of denim trousers and a pullover, both in black. Easier to hide any stains that might come about before we leave.

There are two steps onto a small porch that lead to his door and I don't pause to knock. Raising my foot, I land a solid kick to the wooden structure and send it flying backwards and into the home. It rings loud throughout the silent room, and then we have a commotion upstairs.

Two screams. Two male voices call out to each other at the same time from opposite ends of the second floor and then rush toward the center stairway with weapons drawn.

Two bullets from my gun and the one I'm not here for falls to the ground with a neck and chest wound. He'll bleed out while I deal with this arsehole.

"Who the fuck!" the other yells, switching between panic and worry for the man slowly dying beside his feet. "Luis, get up. I need you to get up, pana."

The man coughs, the spittle red and running down the side of his cheek and onto the floor. This action repeats itself as breathing becomes difficult and his throat cannot perform the simple function of swallowing.

He's choking. Gagging on his life's essence.

And then he stops and the man I came here looking for screams, an agonized sound that brings a smile to my face. It gets the blood pumping harshly through my system. Excites me.

If there are two things in this life that can get me hard, it's the thought of my Gem's pussy and the blood that drips from an enemy's veins.

Seeing their life slip away.

"You have two minutes to come down those stairs." At the sound of my voice, his head snaps up and so does the shit-for-an-excuse gun in his hand. "I'd be very careful with that, mate."

"Hijo de puta, I'm going to...*fuck*!" The gun is no longer in his hand but on the floor, courtesy of Callum who lets out a low chuckle.

"Oi, my apologies, bro. My finger slipped."

My eyes shift to his amused face. "I'm going to start calling you butterfingers."

"I'm not that bad." Callum shrugs and I roll my eyes, looking back at the man bleeding from a hole in his hand.

"You only have a few seconds left, Felix."

"Who are you?" he screams, but I see his intent, taking a few steps back. The cunt wants to run. "What do you want?"

"Your head on my mantle." And just as I predicted, he takes off toward the rooms upstairs, slamming a door closed behind him as the three of us shoot out in different directions.

Archie goes toward the back and out the door.

Callum to the front with his weapon drawn.

And I take my time walking up the stairs. Slowly. Without a single ounce of haste.

At the top of the landing, I turn to the left and turn the handle. It's not locked, and I don't waste my time. The next room is the same, but the third one is the key to finding the slimy fuck.

One kick and it flies open, the cheap wood splintering and flying throughout the room as my eyes land on his huddled form in a corner. He has another gun in his shaky and uninjured hand, pointing at me with the fear of God in his eyes.

"I'll shoot."

"Go ahead," I say and take another few steps in his direction. "It's you or me at this point."

"What do you want?"

"And there's the billion-pound question: *what do I want?*" Scratching my jaw with the barrel of my gun, I continue my walk. Coming closer. Cornering him. "Money, I have. Power is mine. However, there is one thing..."

"I don't know you...you...you break into my home and shoot my brother-in-law. Threaten me." That trembling hand brings the gun up a little higher and he aims it at my head. "Do you have any idea who I am? What I can do to you?"

There's a small wooden chair in the corner of the room and I grabbed it without fear, flipping it around to straddle the seat. Then, I eye him. Just stare from my place near the end of the bed, and as the seconds tick by, his nervousness becomes more pronounced.

"Ask me who I am." Not a question. I'm challenging his bullshit notion of being an alpha in a game where he barely knows how to wipe his arse. "Ask me my *fucking* name, Felix De La Vega."

"Who are—" He's cut off by my bullet to his kneecap. "Motherfuck!"

"Does the name Casper Jameson ring any bells, Felix?"

Felix's face is ashen and his eyes are wide; the anger from before is still there, but now the predominant emotion is fear. "No. No. No."

"Si. Si. Si, motherfucker," I mimic his pathetic tone. "And would you like to tell me why or how you remember my name?"

"I-I took on a—"

"A job that is going to cost you your life, Vega." Standing from my seat, I kick it out of my way as I make my way over and crouch down in front of him. His finger twitches as I do, and his gun goes off, shooting me in the arm. It's a clean entry and exit; I don't flinch. Instead, I bring my face closer to his with my shitty grin firmly in place. "You're the man Nico Savino came to when looking for a trusted contract killer. True or false."

"True," he whimpers out as I dig the barrel of my gun into the wound on his leg.

"And you gave him Mauricio's information?"

"Yes."

"And you know both men well?"

"I do...*please* stop."

"Okay." I pull back and he lets out a breath of relief. "For now."

"For now? What are you—"

"We're going on a little trip, you and I."

Chapter 22
AURORA

"**I**'M GLAD YOU came, Roe," my father says as I step into the all-black Denali SUV outside of the Boston airport. He's sitting in the back as always while two of his men are up front, and I breathe a sigh of relief to see Dominic isn't one of them. "It's good to see you."

"Good to see you too." Pulling my phone out of my small purse, I check once more to see if I have any missed calls or messages. There isn't, and it makes me sad that I've come to expect it. It's been two months since our last call; a Skype date where he was distracted and after five minutes of stilted conversation, was called back to work. Then, there's the last few messages; sporadic at best. They've been short and basic.

I couldn't even come to him with my concern over the anonymous text I received. You can't talk to someone who just isn't there, and I'm thanking my lucky stars that nothing came of it because there's no one to turn to. All I have is my gun and an accurate aim to depend on.

Heck, I don't even trust the man sitting beside me all that much —if anything, his visit is a test to see if we can ever have a normal relationship of any sort.

But Casper and I; we're missing the element of heat that makes me feel alive.

His mind just isn't with me. He's obsessed with vengeance.

Doing something that even though I hate the separation it's created; I understand. Truly do.

Losing his mother the way he did, violently and cruelly, would do that to a person. Casper is out to find those responsible, and all I can do is be supportive and wait. Understand. Because if the shoe was on the other foot, I would expect the same as I hunt down the animal responsible.

I am my father's daughter, and forgiveness is a concept I struggle with. More so if you hurt someone I love.

The traffic at this early hour is heavy and the drivers in a hurry, cutting each other off while others curse and make hand gestures in a lewd fashion. Goes to show you that no matter where you are in the world, rush-hour traffic sucks and brings the worst out in people. "Where are we off to first?"

"You just got here, kid. No rush."

"Really?" Because this man is not known for being laid back.

"Yeah." He chuckles, making a show of silencing his cell phone. "How about we get some breakfast and then go to Salem. You haven't been in ages and the weather's nice out."

"Only if we can go to The Friendly Toast for breakfast."

"Done."

"Thank you." I smile at him, really excited about going to the place Ali talked about after her visit last Halloween. "It comes highly recommended and it's waffles. What's not to love?"

Dad looks at me then, his expression softer than I ever remember seeing. "Believe it or not, your happiness means everything to me, Aurora. And while I've been shit at showing you this in the past, I plan to remedy that."

I don't reply to his statement and he sits back, following my lead. Maybe we can talk more another day, but for now I just want to relax a bit, eat, and spend some time with him where I'm not hurtling reproaches and he's not demanding that I do as he pleases.

For once, I just want to be his daughter and he my father with no anger on either side.

Where are you? ~Casper

IT'S the message I found once dressed this morning after going to bed with a throbbing headache. A headache that's ever-present and won't be getting any better until I put an end to the hot mess I currently find myself in. Because this is exactly what I thought it to be.

True to his word, Matteo kept all talk of business nonexistent for the first forty-eight hours. It was nice. Felt almost normal as we hung out and did things that I never thought we'd do together. Even his security detail made sure to keep a distance—to not disturb—as we reconnected, and I grew at ease with the idea of spending time here. With staying at his home instead of the hotel I'd booked prior to my arrival.

Also, doing something as simple as visiting the Salem Witch Museum and then walking the downtown area afterwards made me realize that a part of me wants him in my life. I'm not fully sure to what capacity and if I can ever depend on him, but I want him there.

The third day was completely different, though. The man I've been expecting made a very memorable appearance...

"You want me to what?" I seethe, gripping onto the chair's armrest and digging my fingernails into the leather. It's the only thing keeping me in place. It's preventing me from hurtling things across the conference room and at his salt-peppered head. "No."

"Just calm down, Roe. It's not that big of a deal and—"

"Christ, something is very wrong with you. How could you even begin to think I'd consider this idiocy? That I want any part in your scheme!"

"You have more of a choice than I ever did, Aurora. More than my father did...please...just consider what I am putting on the table."

"So, let me get this right..." A sardonic laugh escapes as I begin to tap my fingernails on the large wooden table, a long one where he's smart enough to sit on the opposite end with his PowerPoint presentation that must've taken him all night to prepare. *"Either I step up and take over as boss, or find a husband who will? Did I sum that up correctly?"*

"You make it sound—"

"Archaic?" I finish for him, eyes narrowed. *"Because what you're proposing is the same bull crap that took you from us. A marriage of convenience to some random man I've never so much as met before."*

"Dominic isn't a stranger. You've met him in London and he's a great man. A dependable asset who knows the ins and outs of my company and day-to-day activities. He'd be a great husband if you choose to go this route, and who knows, maybe someday you might even fall in love. All is possible if you give it a chance." Matteo's sales pitch is completely in the tank after this.

Had he not said that name. Offered him to me like some prized stallion.

I'm done.

"No," I say and stand up, gathering my purse from beside me.

"*The answer will always be a no. I'm not you, and I'll never play this game.*"

"*Do you have a problem with him? Is there something I'm not aware of?*"

"*How well do you know him?*" I counter, raising my brow.

"*He's been with me for years. Came highly recommended by a family friend of Samantha's.*"

"*I don't like him.*" Plain and simple.

"*What did he do?*" Matteo asks, his tone now serious. Worried.

"*He's pushy and rude and quite honestly, I have no interest in the man. That, and there's something about him that doesn't quite sit well with me. Like his anger when I—*"

"*Okay. I get it,*" he interrupts, rubbing a hand down his face in frustration without letting me finish. "*We can shelve the Dominic subject for the moment, but don't ignore the other half of my proposition, Roe. I also said you could take over on your own and find a husband to stand beside you within the time frame of a year. Find him on your own while I expand the Conte House to an international level.*"

"*Your help isn't needed.*"

"*It was your mother's dream to do so.*"

A low blow and I bristle, gripping onto the wooden edge so hard my knuckles turn white. "*Her dream was to love and grow old with you,* Dad." My barb is just as sharp and it cuts him deep, the immediate flinch as if I've slapped him the perfect tell. "*Something of which you will never know…to be with someone who holds your heart, and I will not follow in your footsteps. I've met someone—*"

"*Who?*"

"*That's none of your concern.*"

"*You're my daughter and I have the right to ask. To make sure he's good enough.*"

"*For me or your precious family affairs?*"

"*You always come first,*" he hisses, slamming a hand down on the folder in front of him. "*You've always come first.*"

"*Bullshit.*" *I don't believe that. He's never proven so.*

"*Just answer me this much?*" *His tone softer now, but I can still detect his own anger beneath the surface.* "*Are you happy with him? Does he treat you right?*"

"*My world is bright when I'm with him.*" *And that's all I will give him. Because the king of* give *and inch and he'll take a mile would make things difficult if he knew who I'm seeing. To be honest, I'm surprised Casper hasn't brought it up after pulling the file on me. Maybe he just doesn't care. But my father is different in that sense and will think it somehow leads back to him. That he'll use me to get to him.* "*This is also where I'm warning you not to interfere if you want me in your life. This is where I draw the line.*"

Instead of the reaction I'm expecting, of demands, Dad just smiles and nods. "*Okay.*"

"*Okay?*" *I raise a brow, not buying it.*

"*I'll drop it for now. Maybe we both need to rethink our approach.*"

"*The answer will still be no tomorrow.*" *Declaring that my third option, I walk over to him and kiss his cheek in a show of mild affection and then walk out without looking back. Knowing that it's best if I book my ticket back home for the following night.*

The phone in my hand goes off, and it's my second alarm. It's fifteen minutes past eleven and I need to get a move on. I promised to meet him at his central office in the heart of downtown Boston, a large building near the center that is recognizable by all that see it.

Because not all Cancio businesses are illicit.

Because his money is not all dirty.

My father has two great passions in his life: power and real estate. He dominates both.

The man is also known for being a real estate mogul with properties, high-rise towers all across the US and a few abroad. It's one of the reasons why nothing has ever really been pinned on him. He's too good. Too smart. He knows too many people in high places who are always willing to help him.

"Just message him back," I mutter under my breath as I pull Casper's text back to the screen, reading it for the tenth time since finding it. It came in sometime during the early morning hours and along with it, there was one missed call a few minutes prior. Nothing else. No voicemail to let me know if something is wrong. If he is okay. *Where are you?* "He would know if he called."

But that's what we've come down to since the last time we were together; a here and there that I hate. I feel disconnected from him, and enough is enough. Considering the time difference between London and Boston, my fingers fly across the screen to reply, but I'm stopped from hitting send by a knock on the door of my room.

Thinking it's the estate manager with some sort of message from my father— a cancellation—I rush to open the door and it's a mistake. The kind that makes your skin crawl and breathing speed up slightly. "How can I help you, Dominic?"

"May I come in?" he asks instead of answering, trying to step around me, but I block his path and keep him on the other side of the threshold. I don't want him inside my room. I don't want him near me.

"No." There's something about this man that rubs me wrong. A gut feeling that makes me cautious. "Whatever you need to discuss can be said downstairs, and I'll meet you in the living room in ten minutes."

A flash of annoyance crosses his face, but it disappears just as quickly and is replaced by a slick smile. "Do I make you uncomfortable, Aurora?"

"Not at all."

"I think I do."

"Good for you." If he thinks I'll back down, he's got another thing coming. "Now, wait for me downstairs and we'll speak then."

"Maybe I don't want to leave. Maybe I want to be closer." Dominic takes a step forward and I do the same, not giving him the opportunity he seeks. At once, the harsh scent of his cologne infiltrates my nostrils, making me want to sneeze. He smells nothing like

Casper. Nothing like the woodsy scent mixed with his natural essence that makes my knees weak. "Maybe I'd like to take you to dinner tonight and get to know you better."

Even upset with him, I miss the jerk. Can't deny it.

"I've already explained that I'm seeing—"

"Casper Jameson isn't good enough for you, Aurora."

Everything within me freezes, and my hands ball into tight fists beside me. I'm angry and uncomfortable and worried. It reminds me of those messages I received. Of their emphasis on my relationship with Casper.

Messages I've pushed to the far back of my mind as the sender hasn't made another move. Messages I'm yet to tell the man I'm supposed to be with about since he's never around. Not here for me like I knew deep down would happen.

"How the..." I'm seething, almost shaking in my indignation "...why the hell are you concerning yourself with my personal business? Who asked you to?"

"It's a personal choice."

"Is it, now? Or are you doing my father's bidding like a good little boy?" I challenge, arching a brow while crossing my arms over my chest. A move he follows with his eyes, licking his bottom lip, and I clear my throat. "Eyes up here, jerk, and answer my question. Did my father put you up to this?"

"No, but I doubt he'd approve of that asshole fucking his little girl."

"Leave."

"There's no need for this hostility, Aurora." Dominic's eyes are still on my chest, and when I clear my throat in annoyance, he just shrugs as if to explain that he can't help himself. "We got off on the wrong foot, but I want to change that. Just give me a chance to—"

"No." I have no interest in him. Not going to beat around the bush. "And I suggest you back off. That man who you claim isn't good enough is a jealous bastard and doesn't take kindly to others sniffing where they don't belong."

"Really?" He laughs, and the sound sends a shiver down my spine. "Is this the same man who's been ignoring you? Who's left you all alone and defenseless?"

"Get out or—"

"I will if you agree to one date."

"You will because just like my father..." I lean in close and make a show of batting my lashes in a dramatic fashion, grabbing the door handle while his attention is on my face "...I have an amazing shot and I carry. Don't test my patience, Dominic."

With that, I slam it in his face and engage the lock.

From this side, I can just make out his low curses and then the sound of him walking away. And it's when I'm sure that he's gone that I breathe out a sigh of relief. For a second my shoulders drop and tension evaporates, but then on my next inhale it all comes rushing back in a chaotic tsunami of emotions. My mind swirls with questions. My body shakes as the hidden fear of the last few minutes makes its appearance.

However, one thing stands out above the rest:

Why does Dominic know about Casper and his absence?

Then, there's a scarier thought: *Why does he care?*

Chapter 23
AURORA

"**H**OW WONDERFUL IT IS that you're still here, Aurora." The last person I thought I'd see says as my foot hits the bottom step. Our eyes meet and at once I'm taken back to all those years of attitude—mistreatments and not-so-subtle jabs at my mother and me. Matteo's ex-wife stands at the entrance to a smaller sitting area to the right of the door, waiting, her look calculating in that fake fondness she's forcing as an expression. "It's been too long since you've come to visit us."

I don't miss her emphasis on the word *us*.

"My apologies, Samantha…I've just been so busy with work."

Matching her bullshit act of decorum, I walk up and give her a kiss on the cheek and pull back. "How have you been? Are you here looking for Dad?"

"No. I came to see you."

"Me? Why?"

"Can't a stepmother—"

"How about we get a little more comfortable?" Walking past her, I step into the small living space and take a seat on one of the over-sized chairs, motioning for her to sit across from me. She follows a few seconds later, taking a pretentiously demure seat with a smile on her face. "Would you like something to drink?"

"No. I'm good."

"Okay then." Crossing my legs, I let my true emotions come through my expression. No more sugar coating or playing pretend. "What do you want, Samantha? You never cared then, and you don't now, so let's stop the games, shall we?"

"You were always so rude."

"And you've always been a horrible actress." Narrowing my eyes, I stare her down. "Again, what do you want?"

"Fine." The smile drops from her face and the sourness I've been accustomed to takes its rightful place. "Did he name you his heir?"

And there it is. Just like I asked him all those months ago in a hotel lobby back in London.

Asked him if she knew. What did the mother to his non-bastard child think?

Because deep down I know she cares. Wants it for Lucas.

"Where is my brother, by the way? I would've liked to see him this trip."

"Answer the question."

"Ask your ex-husband. I owe you no explanation on my life."

"Listen, I'm doing this for your own good." Samantha sits forward then, pulling out a manila envelope from her oversized purse. With her eyes on mine, she pulls out a set of pictures and places each one face up atop the small coffee table between us. "I might not be the warmest or most caring person in the world, but I'm not the asshole you think I am. Your father is under investigation for the murder of a senator that was found dead over five years ago near the harbor. They are looking into everything he owns and are itching to pin this on him one way or another, Aurora. Don't get yourself caught up in something that will destroy you and your mother's legacy. Leave while you can and don't look back."

I don't say anything, and she walks out of the room just the same. My eyes are on the photos staring back at me of a dead body, a man in his mid-forties who looks to be entering decomposition. Then, while holding in my urge to gag, I look at the next three and they are all candid photographs of Lucas and her while out doing random things. They are being watched, and it reminds me of the messages I received.

Is this what that was about? Am I under investigation because of my familial ties?

But why mix Casper into this?

The thoughts plaguing me from all sides are making my temples throb, and I can't help but look back at my brother's face. He's just a kid—innocent and without any stress on his shoulders. It's how every kid should be at his age.

Two things become very clear to me then:

I know what my decision will be, and I can't stay here.

I SEE him before he sees me.

It also doesn't surprise me to find him here, my eyes finding his body facing my living room window as he stares out calmly, without hiding. But then again, the man's impossible to miss. Unafraid to impose his presence.

He's over six feet of solid muscle and tattoos and an aura that draws you in. A charisma that's held me captive since we met months ago.

Christ. It's been months since that night. Since I gave in, knowing the consequences. And it's that same attraction that makes me come a little closer while making little to no noise.

He's deep in thought and ignorant to my eyes. Casper Jameson stands with his back to me and wearing what looks to be a plain white shirt. It's tight to his back, every hard muscle beneath pronounced. Something that makes my mouth water and thighs clench, but I ignore it. That burn. That need.

My eyes shift to his arm and I follow the curve of a tattoo that looks new, but it's a symbol I recognize.

His newest addition is an Ouroboros and I do admire the uniqueness, the way the entire body of a large snake wraps itself around his entire arm and then disappears near the front of his hand. It's bold and done in black and white from my viewpoint, but I'm curious about the head and it's placement. I want to know how the finished interpretations looks; a snake eating its tail.

Death and rebirth in a never-ending cycle.

The early evening sunlight is diminishing as the sun sets, but for now it's hitting just right. Makes the intricate design pop against his lightly tanned skin. Skin, that shows his time out in the sun recently.

It enhances his appeal. The corded muscle rippling down his arm as he clenches both hands.

Casper takes in a deep breath while tilting his head to the side. His dirty blond hair is longer than the last time we were together, and it sweeps across his temple. He doesn't speak, waiting, but I'm in no rush.

I need my wits about me and to ask the right questions, and for it to be a successful talk, I should have a clear head. Too much has happened, and I need to process. To not demand and listen to what he has to say.

He's here for a reason, and I want to know why.

Hope that he's honest with me.

"Go ahead and yell, Gem. I deserve it." His voice is low, so low I almost miss it.

"I'm not going to scream." Leaving my carry-on by the coat closet, I turn and close my front door. Then, after a deep breath in and out, I take a few steps closer. Just a few. I stop in front of my couch while leaving him on the other side of the room with plenty of furniture between us. "To be honest, I'm so exhausted and drained that I'm not sure I'm ready to talk. Just tell me how you got in?"

"Paid a locksmith I know a hefty amount to do me a favor."

A sardonic chuckle leaves me. "At least you're honest."

Casper turns around then, his bright green eyes boring into mine. "I've never lied to you. Things have been hectic, and a promise made has interfered with my plans for us, but I am working on it, Aurora. You're always on my mind."

"I wouldn't know."

"And that's my fault. I'm so sorry, love."

Nodding, I play with the soft blanket strewn across a few decorative pillows. "What happened, Casper?"

"Can we discuss this after? I need you."

I need you.

I need you.

I need you.

Three little words, but they rub me wrong. Anger me.

"Where the hell were you when I received..." I trail off, regretting my emotional mistake. More so when his brows furrow and lips thin. When he takes a step in my direction.

"What do you mean by that, Gem? Explain." His tone is hard, and his steps are loud within the confines of my home. The shift in him is instantaneous, an angry undercurrent that sings through my every limb as I back away and begin to move toward the back of my couch. It's a barrier. A way to put distance and think clearly. "Answer me."

My eyes narrow. "Don't use that tone with me, Jameson. I don't work for you."

"No. Clearly you don't."

"What's that supposed to mean?" I hiss between clenched teeth, hands gripping the back of the sofa. "Is that some kind of a sexist joke? Like women aren't meant to lead or hang with the big boys?"

"Not at all. My mum had a better shot than my dad." And I'm so lost in my moment of indignation that I lose focus as he stops on the other side of the couch. His knee dips into the cushion, the leather groaning under his weight as he positions himself facing me and kneeling. Closer. Almost touching. "That just meant you're not afraid of me." He's quick, and before I move back, Casper's fisting my shirt in his hand and pulling me down, so our faces are but a hair's breadth away. I also don't miss the way he grits his teeth at the move.

"Are you hurt?" I ask, already lifting a trembling hand to check him. My heart can't take anything happening to him no matter how much he's pissing me off today. "And don't think about lying either."

"Clean shot through my arm. It missed the bone and no fragments were left inside."

"Am I supposed to be okay with this?"

"Not at all, but I need you to trust my word. I'm okay, sweetheart." At my *are you kidding me right now* look, he shakes his head. "I'll show you my medical report if it'll help ease your mind."

Nodding, I let out a heavy sigh. Knowing this comes with the territory. It's always a possibility. "I want a copy of it."

"Done. Now, about my earlier clarifications..."

"Yes."

"All I was stating is that people know their place when it comes to me. They're not defiant."

"Should I know mine?" I lick my bottom lip and he follows the movement, his hunger undisguised. "Should I just be a good girl and behave? Is that what you want?"

"No. Never." He leans forward, lips skimming over mine. "I like you wild and sassy and never want you to hold back." Another kiss, softly, before his teeth scrape down to my chin where he bites down. "Now, it's your turn to explain what you meant."

"You'll need to let me go so I can do that." I huff, swallowing back a moan while avoiding his intense gaze. Instead, I trail my eyes down his arm for an up-close view of the snake's head of his tattoo. It's large and encompasses his hand, wrist, and forearm—the body wrapping around his flesh and then meeting on his hand as the mouth bites down on the tail. Like the rest of the piece, the color scheme doesn't change, except for the eyes. Those hypnotizing small orbs stare back at me with the same shade of hazel as mine.

Is this saying I'm his rebirth?

"Why?" There's a minuscule tinge of amusement in his tone which indicates I didn't do as good a job hiding my natural response to his everything. To the ink on his skin that symbolizes a change in him. Possibly us. "I like you just like this."

"And I need my phone." Releasing his hold, he fixes my shirt before using his pointer finger to push me back a bit. He doesn't say anything, and I take that as my opening. My cell is inside my purse, and I walk over to the closet where I left my belongings and pull it out. Turning back to face him, I run into his chest, not having heard him move. I'm distracted. Mind overworking and exhausted. "Sorry."

Casper holds his hand out with a small smile. "Your mobile, Gem." I unlock the screen and hand it over, watching how his facial expression goes from one extreme to the next. From sexy grin to absolute fury. "You should've called me the fucking moment these came in. What were you thinking? What if something—"

"Get out."

"I'm not going anywhere."

"Yes, you are." Snatching my phone from his hand, I take the remaining steps to the door and yank it open. "Now isn't the time for a fight. I'm tired and exhausted, regretting my trip to Boston, and before either of us says something unforgivable, we should walk away."

"Aurora, we need to—"

"I'm not *asking* you, Casper. I need space...time to reevaluate a few things."

"What's that supposed to mean," he asks, tone less acerbic. Casper also doesn't back down, stepping right into my personal space, pressing his body against mine. "And I'm not angry at you. Am I disappointed you didn't come to me? Yes, but I'm more concerned by those messages than anything else."

"And you think I wasn't? I needed you."

"Then why not tell—"

"How do you communicate with someone who isn't there?" Whatever anger he holds evaporates. Metaphorically, it breaks into a thousand tiny shards at my feet. "I didn't take those texts lightly or as a joke...the people who sent them know my family and me. They seem to not want me with you."

"You know who sent them?"

I nod. "I was made aware of an investigation—"

"Into who?"

"My father."

"On what charges."

"Murder."

"I see." That's all he says, and it rubs me wrong, as if he's privy to something I'm not. It's also another reminder of how little he shares back.

"What does 'I see' mean?"

"Your father will be fine, Gem." This confirms that he knows—has known of my familial ties all along. It also shows just how thorough his investigation into me was. "Don't worry. I won't let anyone hurt you."

My smile in response is small and sad. "Can you save me from you?" *From the heartbreak you'll bring?* Casper opens his mouth to reply, but I silence him by standing on the tip of my toes and pressing my lips to his. It's soft and everything I need and hate. It's also over quickly as I pull back before he can wrap me in his arms and deepen the kiss. "I'm going to need some space."

"Gem, I—"

"Please." He doesn't like it but nods. "I'll call you when I'm ready to talk."

"I'll be in Chicago for a few days." That's all he says before proving to me once again why walking away is an impossibility. Grabbing the waistband of my yoga pants, he gives it a hard tug and I'm back in his hold—being held possessively as his mouth slants over mine. Passion ignites and burns me. His mouth devours mine in an almost brutal way and I welcome the sting, the torture as he takes and I give in, until I can't breathe. Until he takes mercy on me and pulls back. "I'll be waiting."

"I promise to call you soon."

"And I promise to always listen. I won't make this mistake twice."

Chapter 24
AURORA

I KNOW WHO she is the moment she steps a foot inside of my office at the Conte House three days later. *Christ,* there's no denying our family's genes. London Foster has my complexion, hair color, and even the slightly fuller lips that everyone this side of the family has.

And we're the last two alive to pass it on to another generation.

It's a sobering and sad fact, but I can't deny how much seeing her means to me. How much I look forward to getting to know her.

"Hi," she says, voice shy and smiling, extending a hand for me to shake while the woman with her takes a stand outside the door. From the looks of her, I think she's my cousin's security. "It's nice to finally meet you."

"Nice to meet you, too," I reply and take the offered hand, pulling her in so I can give her a hug. Furthermore, the moment we do, it brings tears to my eyes and I hear her sniffle, and instead of pulling back, we hold on tighter. Just a little longer, while a piece of my heart gets mended. "You have no idea how much it means to me that you came by today. I've been dying to meet you since Malcolm—"

"Came and spilled the beans?" London finishes for me, laughing at the truth in that. She pulls back from me but keeps my hands in hers, giving them each a squeeze. There's happiness in her face and an honest look of appreciation for this opportunity that has to mirror my own.

We are just two women who lost all we had, our mothers, and were navigating through life missing a link—a bond to the past that will help cement the future. But now we can have that. We'll have each other to keep the Conte legacy alive.

"More like he welcomed *me* to the family."

"He didn't!"

"Totally did in his own sort of gruff-ish way before leaving this office."

"Dear God." Her giggle is loud and boisterous, and she lets go of my hands to wipe at the few stray tears that have fallen. "I'm sorry." Another bubble of laugher. "He's just something else and very determined to lay the world down at my feet. I hope he didn't upset you or was rude while vetting you."

I shake my head, my own smile widening. "So, what you're saying is he's one of the good ones?"

"Absolutely…wait…is it Aurora, or can I nickname you? Because you look like a Roe-Roe to me."

"Go for it. Roe-Roe works for me, but then I get to call you Lo-Lo," I chuckle, her bubbliness reminding me so much of my mother when excited. "I was only ever called Aurora as a child when in trouble, and that was often. I'm too curious for my own good at times, or so I've been told."

"Tell me more. I want to know all about the family I never knew."

"That might take years."

"Good thing I have all the time in the world." London gets a pensive look and then walks out the door to her guard. She says something to her quietly and then comes back in after the woman gives her a nod. "Are you hungry?"

"YOU'RE KIDDING! That's how you two met?" I ask London after almost spitting out my Long Island; we're sitting inside of a sports bar not that far from my apartment and catching up, giving each other little tidbits of information that describe our personas. That show just how similar we are. "You were a private dancer...with a pole and everything? Not judging, by the way..." I tack on, not wanting her to get the wrong impression "...because I've been thinking about taking one of those classes as a surprise for someone."

"Malcolm was my first and last customer."

"Ever?"

"Ever." Her eyes shift around the room once and then come back to mine. I recognize the move, too. She's taking in our surroundings and making sure no one's listening or getting too close, something that the woman with her wouldn't allow anyways. That one looks like she'll snap your neck if you breathe wrong around my cousin. *I like her already.* "That man literally kicked down every door to keep me for himself. To protect me."

"And you're happy, Lo-Lo? Does he take care of you?"

"I'm his equal, Roe-Roe, and we take care of each other. He's never made me feel anything but cherished. Loved." Pausing, she lifts her pop to her lips and takes a few deep sips. "For the first time in my life, I go to bed every night knowing I'm safe. That no one can force me to do anything, and what I give him in return, willingly and because I love him with everything I am, is my heart. That's all he's ever asked for even though he's risked his life to save mine."

"Wow."

"Yes." She waves her manicured fingers in a *hurry up* motion. "Now, your turn."

"Um, what? I don't have anything like—"

"The guy you want to learn to dance for...is he your boyfriend?" she asks, smirking at me. Enjoying my impersonation of a tomato. "This has to be good if you're blushing this hard."

I shake my head, averting my eyes. "We shall put him under the *it's complicated* section for now."

"Why are you looking away?"

"No reason." Another mistake on my behalf as I look over and begin to fidget in my seat. "Quit looking at me like that. He and I are not serious." *But I want to be. Need him to want it.*

London tilts her head to the side, appraising me. "But can you see yourself with him? Like long term?"

"Yes." No doubt. No hesitation. "But who knows what the future will bring, though. Life changes in the blink of an eye and right now, whatever we are is up in the air."

It's the truth. Nothing in life is guaranteed and a relationship like ours is doomed from the very beginning. All the cards are stacked against us.

We live on separate continents.

I hate the business, and it's a huge part of who he is.

He's always disappearing without a trace for weeks as he searches for the man who pulled the trigger.

I'm afraid to fall and crash.

"Why?" She gives me an apologetic look, picking up on my change in mood. "If you don't mind me asking, of course."

"Not at all." Smiling to show her that it's really okay, I sit back and pop a fry in my mouth, chewing slowly to give me a few extra minutes to word this right and control my tells.

"You're killing me here."

"So impatient," I mock grumble, a bit chastising in genuine fun, just like my mother did to me as a kid. I have no chill. Almost zero when I'm curious about something and so far, the only person that keeps me waiting is Casper. He's become my exception to the rules on every subject it seems. "But..."

"Woman, I will throw a piece of bacon at your head."

"You wouldn't dare."

"Yes, I would." Her light blue eyes turn to slits, daring me to keep making her wait as she tears a tiny piece of bacon from her club sandwich. "Five, four, three—"

"You little shit! Okay. Okay." I'm laughing at the absurdity of this. Just how at ease I am with her and how much it's helping my self-inflicted loneliness after I sent Casper away. "I give."

"Spill."

"You and my best friend Aliana are going to get along beautifully."

"Great, and two."

"I met him in London and had a one-night stand," I spit out *a la Band-Aid* effect.

"Oh my!" She sits forward and places both elbows on the table, cradling her face and looking at me as if I'm an interesting soap opera. "Please continue."

"Dork."

"Takes one to know one, and keep going. Because he had to have left quite the impression for you to get all red and—"

"I did not."

"You did."

"Do you want the story or not?"

"Proceed."

"You're so kind." Discreetly, she flips me off and I can't help but crack up. It's insane to me how effortlessly this has all been. How fast we've clicked.

It's easy and comfortable, as if we've known each other our entire lives.

"Yup, and it was totally cliché too. Just like the movies." Closing my eyes for a minute, I'm transported back to that day. Moreover, my lips begin to paint her a picture of that night. The pub, the pulsing music blaring through its speakers, the intense green eyes watching me across the room. The connection and draw, the moment he stepped in behind me, and then the moment his lips skimmed my earlobe as he spoke against my skin.

My skin breaks out in goose bumps. My heart races.

And through it all, I get hit with a pang of longing because I'm the one stepping back.

I need to call him. I miss him.

When I'm done, I open my eyes and meet London's wide ones. She's smiling. "Not serious my ass, chick. That was hot and sexy and intense and I'm running out of words to describe a smidgen of what you just told me. Don't be blind or stubborn. Don't deny what is clear to see…that man is under your skin."

"And who's under yours, Twirl?" a male voice says from behind her, and our heads snap back simultaneously toward the intruder. When we realize just who it is, we have two very different reactions. Lo-Lo is elated, while I'm embarrassed.

How much did he hear?

"You," is her automatic response before slipping from the booth and throwing her arms around the no-nonsense CEO's neck, something that with his demeanor I'd think he'd be against, but it's the opposite. The extreme opposite.

Malcolm Asher is all smiles for his girl and doesn't give a damn who sees it. The look in his eyes is that of a man in love. The sweet kiss he gives her is drowning in adoration.

It pours from them. The love.

And seeing it with my own eyes gives me hope. Literal hope that maybe someday this can be Casper and me.

"I NEED TO CALL HIM," I whisper to myself as the elevator door opens on my floor. It's been a long day, but amazing, and with it came enlightenment:

If we really want to, we can make this work. I had the perfect example of it in my face all evening, and everyone knows who Malcolm Asher is. What he does. What they have never been able to prove, but people talk.

And others, like my father, have done business with the man and his father before him.

"Gem," Casper says out of nowhere and I scream, a gut-curdling yell that makes him step back with both hands up. "What's wrong with you?"

"Why would...are you...you scared ten years off my life!" I'm in his face, moving in closer and fighting to ignore just how good he smells. How good he looks in a leather jacket, simple white shirt, and old jeans. My pointer finger digs into his pec as I jab him, angry that he both scared and made me wet at once. *Handsome bastard.*

"Love, I said your name three times. Is something wrong?" There's genuine concern in his tone, and my annoyance simmers into a near nothing throb. "Did you get another one of those messages?"

"No. Nothing like that."

"Then?" he asks, taking advantage of our nearness to slip an arm around my waist to pull me against his chest. And I don't fight his hold, if anything, I let him. Enjoy it. His touch.

"I met someone today that I didn't know existed."

"Met someone?"

"A cousin. I have a cousin here in Chicago and had no idea all these years."

"I'm so happy for you, Gem. Family is the most important thing in the world." Ducking his head a bit, he kisses my temple and then across to my forehead. "I like knowing you have someone to turn to here."

"Thank you." I nuzzle his chest and give him a small kiss of my own there. "Now, what are you doing here? I thought you'd wait for my call."

"Something happened—"

"You need to leave again?" Disappointment hits and he sees it. I've gone from happy to my shoulders dropping.

"They found my mum's killer in Cuba." As much as I hate it, I understand. Agree, even. Casper won't move on until he finishes what he started months ago after her death.

"Go. I'll still be here when you get back."

"You promise we can talk then? There are some things I need to explain. Plans to discuss."

"More reason for me to wait. Go," I whisper shakily, emotions rising to the surface. "Just come back to me in one piece, and no more bullet holes. If you do, I'll add the next one myself."

"Is that your way of saying you care?"

Rising up onto the tips of my toes, I peck his lips twice before speaking against them. "That's my way of saying I want to be with you."

Chapter 25
CASPER

EARLY YESTERDAY MORNING...

MY MOBILE RINGS atop my nightstand and I reach over, almost knocking my bottle of water to the ground before bringing the device to my face. It's a number I don't recognize but the area code is a similar one: 305, and that means Miami.

And there's only one bloody bastard that I know in the area personally.

Thiago Rivera is one of my biggest and most loyal business

associates/clients. He's a man of his word and an unapologetic cunt to everyone but those closest to him, and also a damn good friend. Furthermore, in this business I only trust two men: Malcolm and him.

I pick up on the next ring. "About time you called, you arse. How's life treating you on the outside?"

"It's getting there." His voice is a bit rough, as if he's been out all night drinking, and he clears his throat. "Adjusting."

"That's good to hear. Are you free, or…?"

"Probation for two years." Through his side of the line there are some loud voices—they're yelling something in Spanish, and I sit up on the bed. I have a feeling this isn't a social call. There's too much commotion. Too much cursing.

"Everything okay, mate?"

"Is the pigeon in its cage?" he asks, and it's his way of asking if the line is safe to speak on.

"Ezra keeps it clean and maintained."

"Good." The sound of ice clinking inside of a glass follows as he moves to another room, the yelling around him ceasing as the door slams shut. "You in the States?"

"In Chicago. Why?" Without conscious thought, I grab my pajama bottoms and put them on before heading out into the main living area of my penthouse. I'm alone, but Callum isn't far with Archie. They're at the unit across from mine, more than likely sleeping after being up until three a.m. going over intel one of my men gathered on the Cancio organizations—trying to find a connection to the Savino siblings.

And we learned three very fascinating things:

That name doesn't exist in New Jersey. Not a single fucking Savino family.

Matteo wants to retire and wants his heir, *my Gem*, to take over.

I have a bullet with the name of his second-in-command on it.

He wants Aurora, and I'll have his head mounted on my wall

before he lays a single finger on her. Fuck that, I'll never allow him the chance to even attempt to get close.

Dominic Bruno is a dead man walking.

"…because you're needed in Cuba tonight, my friend."

"Tonight?" I ask, walking into the other penthouse, and Callum looks up at me mid-bite. He places his bowl of cereal down—the man has an obsession with Lucky Charms—and stands, awaiting orders. "What's going on? Why is your little brother in Cuba?"

"Because Ivan has your mother's killer in a holding cell in Havana."

I miss you. ~Gem

Wish you were here, but I understand. Do what you must and come back to me safe. ~Gem

HER MESSAGES COME in as I step off the small chartered aircraft we switched to after touching down in Miami the following night. It's just a little over nine in Havana when we land, and it's hot. The temperature is in the high 80s while Miami's wasn't any better. We were in the beautifully sweltering city for less than thirty minutes before leaving, and then inside of Cuban airspace a little over an hour later.

With each step down from the small plane, I feel my state of mind change. I'm wound tight and full of restless energy. Angry and needing to unleash my wrath.

To begin paying them back for what they've done.

A life for a life multiplied by my ire.

Thank you, love, for always understanding and being amazing. I'll be seeing you soon. ~Casper

Then I pocket the device, putting it on silent so as to not be interrupted, at least for the next few hours as I go and make new friends.

At the end of the small private airstrip that belongs to the Riveras is an older gentleman holding a sign with my last name on it. Behind him there's a classic car, an open door, and the man I owe a very large favor to.

"It's been a very long time, Ivan," I say, extending my hand out once I reach him. "How have you been?"

"Can't complain." He smiles, and it's just like looking at a younger version of Thiago. "Happy to have him home...Mom's ecstatic and planning a wedding."

"He's getting married? But I thought—"

"Luna is giving him hell, but it'll happen." Callum stops to shake his hand and then slips inside the car, followed by Archie. Both are silent for distinct reasons. One is trying to clear his head, while the other is working with Ezra via text to wipe our information from all flight logs. As far as Interpol and the US government knows, I'm still in London. We all are.

And I want it to stay that way.

My comings and goings aren't something I want to be public knowledge or publicized anywhere. Anonymity is key in my business, and I adopted that teaching into my daily living.

The less people know, the more successful you'll be. The less you're likely to run into hypocrisy disguised as friendship.

The less bullshit tries to infiltrate your life with false pretenses.

Trust very few people and those you keep close. Because bad intentions and envy run rampant in today's society, and when the going gets tough, very few stick around.

"My money is on her drawing blood first."

"More than likely." Ivan shifts his eyes to the driver, who's already put our carry-ons into the trunk of a mint 1950s Chevy Bel Air and nods, signaling for him to get back inside and wait. "But this clusterfuck is a long time coming. He brought this mess upon himself."

"Agreed, but we both know he'll wear her scratches with a smile on his face and a drink in his hand."

Ivan throws his head back and laughs at that. "Very true."

"So, about this little visitor you have…"

He sobers at once, features turning hard. "Some motherfuckers have a big mouth and love to run it, Jameson."

"Drunk?"

"Off his ass." Stepping aside from the door, he comes and puts his hand on my shoulder, squeezing it, while his dark brown eyes meet mine. "You have our deepest condolences, Casper. What they did is unforgivable, and whatever you need to avenge her is yours."

"Thank you, my friend."

"Ready to go?"

"Please lead the way."

THEIR HOME HERE IS LARGE: a colonial monstrosity with a twenty-four-hour staff, transportation, and full-sized jail at the far end of the compound. There is one way in and one way out, with a crematory inside the same building.

No neighbors. No questions. No one knows they are here.

The government here is too cocky to realize what's happening beneath their noses. How people are slowly rising up to take back what has always been theirs. They were just too afraid to strike back without help. However, it's coming. That day that all Cubans dream of is on the horizon, with help from the Riveras and two more families silently working in the background.

They will have freedom.

We will have an open port to negotiate from.

However, this visit is for a very different purpose and as we exit the car right in front of a building's door, I walk calmly to the trunk and pop it open before their driver can assist.

I won't need much for this visit.

One gun and my two knives.

"Mate, were you able to get what I asked for?" I hear Callum ask Ivan as they come to the back as well. "How much?"

"Yes, and not a thing."

"Owe you one. Just ask." They stop beside me and Ivan pulls a package from deep inside the trunk—a box—and hands it to my cousin. I don't ask about the contents. I'm sure it'll come in handy, but for now, I take my time preparing.

My vest comes off and the all-black suspenders fall down to my thighs. Next, I remove my mobile and wallet—handing them over to Archie—and then pull out the chain inside the front pocket of my trousers. It's a special medallion my mum had blessed by the pope on a visit to England after I was born. On the round, quarter-sized piece is the symbol of Ares, the God of War: an ancient helmet from gladiator times and two swords in the form of an X behind it in white gold.

It's intricate and bold, and I very much doubt the highest-ranking member of the Catholic church noticed it when giving the blessing.

A pulsing energy fills my body and all around me the noises begin to dull. I put the piece around my neck—securing it before moving my neck from side to side. It cracks, my back loosens a bit, and I close my eyes for a minute.

That's when I hear it. This minuscule sound that I pick up while the other two continue to talk and Archie stands to the side with the two guards standing outside the door. He knows his role here—to keep watch and help them clean up after, nothing more.

This will be a family-only event.

I take a step toward the entrance and the sound becomes a tiny bit clearer. Low, but more coherent.

It's screaming. Male. Afraid.

"Ivan, I'm going to need a desk chair than can spin, please."

"I'll have someone bring one down."

"Thank you."

"Whatever you need." Ivan walks past me and his guards open

the doors wide, letting us see into the long corridor up ahead. Everything is dark. In need of repairs, but then again, if you're brought to a place like this, it's for a reason. You're here to receive sentencing, not have a drink.

At the end of this hall there's a large metal door and the further inside we walk, the more his words become pronounced. Clear.

Where the fuck am I?

Let me go, cabron!

I'm going to kill you.

He's a defiant little arse, and I'm going to enjoy every minute of his end.

There is a total of twenty steps before we meet the entrance and I open the door.

At once, the scent hits my nostrils; it's putrid and stomach turning, but more than that, the scene that greets my eyes when the lights are switched on is beautiful in all its gory glory.

Mauricio is standing in the middle of the room surrounded by cells with open doors, and inside of each is an animal. Large hogs; angry and feral swine that the minute we walk in become quiet. They're deathly still and silent as we make our way toward the almost naked man with his arms bound high above his head.

Mauricio fucking Hernandez is dirty, angry, and a lot older than I thought he'd be.

"Evening," I say. His eyes snap in my direction, and he hisses as once again the brightness from the lights angled toward his face, hurt his eyes.

"Who are you?" he asks, squinting hard. "Why am I here?"

"Why is he here?" I parrot, looking back at my cousin and Ivan. "The poor man is asking why he's here? Why this is happening to him?"

"Poor lad." Callum comes to stand beside me with the package Ivan gave him in hand. "This is a horrible predicament to find yourself in."

"It is."

Ivan steps into the light, places the chair in front of Mauricio, and steps back, but not before the cocksucker gets a good look at his face.

"You," he grunts out, fighting against his bonds to reach Ivan. "You were at the bar—"

"Yes. I was." The door to this room slams shut and a lock is engaged. "And it was an interesting night, indeed. Many stories shared over a bottle of Havana Club. Do you remember that?" Ivan pulls out a remote from his pocket and hits the button at the center, dimming the lights a bit. Enough that he can now see me and pales. "Remember the story you shared of your recent time in London?"

Chapter 26
CASPER

"I DON'T REMEMBER."

My eyes narrow, but I keep my tone of voice calm. "I'm going to give you a minute to go through your memories, Mr. Mauricio Hernandez. Use your time wisely."

"You have the wrong man," he says instead. Too quickly. Stupidly. Sweat begins to build at his temples and then the shivers begin to run down his body. With each tick of the clock, his fear is becoming all the more palpable. It's pulsing throughout the room. "I'm innocent."

"I haven't accused you of anything yet, mate." Turning my face, I look at Ivan. "Have you?"

"Not at all."

"And you?"

My cousin beside him snorts and shakes his head in the negative. "I haven't said a word."

Looking back at the guilty fuck, I shrug. "See? No accusations. However, I do believe you have a story to tell."

"I'm not him."

"Him who?"

From the corner of my eye, I see Callum and Ivan step away from us and head toward the very last cell. Once inside there's some racket, the sound of metal items being pushed around and then the wheels of a creaky old cart coming toward us. The thing is old and definitely belongs in here with the trash, but the laptop atop it is new and so is the camera hookup beside it.

It clicks then what he meant outside, and I'm glad he thought that far ahead to prepare. My father will very much appreciate it.

But first...

I take the remaining steps between us and with a quick flick of my wrist deliver the first of many cuts to come with my karambit, two identical slices behind the ankles that sever his tendons. Even if he could, the man can no longer lift his foot off the ground and walk.

"Motherfucker!" he screams out, and the agony in that high pitch does two very important things:

It makes me smile.

Makes the large hogs in the room grow loud and rowdy.

Another click of his remote and the cells close, leaving two of these beasts on the loose and roaming the room. They're running, squealing—coming closer to him but not attacking yet. They will, though. It's only a matter of time before the hunger overtakes all thinking.

An important fact about pigs; they can be cannibals. A small horde can clean a body down to the bones without any problem. For this very reason, I asked my friend to not feed his lot today after finding out that on his compound, they had livestock for different purposes.

A hungry animal is dangerous.

A hungry and agitated animal is a killer.

"I'm going to ask you one last time, Hernandez. Tell me the story you shared with my friend here? Last chance."

"He's lying!" The more he fights his bonds, the tighter they become, and I can see the tip of his fingers turning a darker purple. Take in the way the ropes are cutting deeper into the wound I created. *Ouch.* "I was just at that bar celebrating my wedding anniversary."

"Really?" Ivan looks at him from behind the laptop's screen, in his hand an HDMI cord. "Because there was no one with you but the prostitute you bought for the night. And don't worry, I left her every single cent you had in your wallet and back at the cheap hotel you were hiding in. Those two hundred thousand in cash will be used by her family and friends to survive and have a better life."

"You piece of shit...I will kill you!"

"That's a mighty big threat from an innocent man."

"Do you know who I am? I will...*fuck*!" Another cut. This time, though, to his leg, and it runs the length going from knee to upper thigh where his boxer briefs end. I went deeper this time. I made sure to take my time and enjoy the way his flesh gives way underneath my sharp blade.

The only way to describe is it is like slicing through butter, smooth and precise.

Blood rushes to the top of the wound and rolls down his leg, pooling on the floor beneath his feet. The puddle grows quickly, calling the attention of the animals. One almost gets close enough to bite, but Ivan slaps his behind hard enough that he rushes away on a squeal.

"Feel like telling me that story now? Come one, Mauricio. Let's reminisce."

"Maybe he just needs a little help getting there. Something to remember?" Callum walks over with the calmness of a saint and opens a bottle of the same rum he got piss drunk with. "Right, friend?"

"Don't. Please don't." Mauricio's head is shaking hard from side to side, his eyes on the bottle in my cousin's hand. "I'll talk."

"So you do remember?" Callum lets a small amount fall from the bottle's opening onto his leg but avoiding the cut altogether.

"Don't do this."

"Do what?" Another small stream. This time, a few drops fall into the open wound and his body bows into itself. Crying out, he blubbers something that we can't quite make out. "Repeat that?"

"I'll tell you what you want to know, just let me walk out of here alive. Promise not to kill me."

"But first, let's start with a slide show. A beautiful message from a friend?" Callum asks and I nod, loving the idea.

What do you think, Hernandez?" Ivan takes that as a cue to turn the laptop on. He does so, and then pushes the creaking cart closer until its literally touching his skin, the rust from the metal smearing across his abdomen and thighs.

And because I'm an arsehole with no remorse, I slice across his stomach—a shallow cut—from side to side right over his dirty flesh.

At his curse of pain, I smile, but I sober just as quick. He killed my mum. This bloody cunt took from me the most important woman in my life until just recently, a move she would've approved whole-heartedly if it meant her son is happy. That she would've gotten those grandkids she dreamed of and never once stopped giving me shit over.

"Where are they?" I ask Callum who looks back at the computer, pointing at the app next to the Skype button. Pressing it, I remove myself from them and let the entire album play out. I let him see just how depraved and sick I can be. I let him watch picture by picture as his good-for-nothing friend, the rubbish that got him my mother's job, is sentenced.

Felix Vega was useful until he wasn't and for his role in her death, he received a penance that no man, misogynist or not, can handle. For the couple of days that Gem made me wait for her, I tortured him. A burn at a time. A strike at a time. A loss of an appendage at a time.

Alexander is Aurora's bodyguard for a reason, and it's his brutality that has kept him under my employ. Without an ounce of concern or care, I watched the man from a comfortable seat as he cut an inch off his dick at a time. One every hour and the wanker only made it to number five before there was nothing left.

Then, he removed his balls. One at a time too.

From the very beginning to the end where Felix takes the offered gun with a shaky hand and pulls the trigger is all documented. Saved for him to enjoy, and on the second go-around, his watery eyes meet mine.

"I'm sorry," Mauricio says as I hold a hand up for Callum and point toward the laptop. He set this up so my father wouldn't miss this moment from his home in London. Everything happened too quickly for him to meet us, but this is the next best thing, and after a few clicks of the mouse, he's on the screen.

I look over and he nods in greeting but we exchange no words. None are needed at this moment.

It's a time for actions, and they speak louder than any words ever will.

Flipping my attention back to the prisoner, I raise a brow. "So, you do know who I am?"

"Yes. I studied your picture and file for two weeks before the hit took place."

"Who sent you?" He doesn't answer right away, and Callum does me the favor of pushing the bottle's opening into the wound and tipping the alcohol over. Mauricio's screams of agony rile up the hogs again; this time they begin to bang against the metal bars keeping them back, while the ones that are loose come sniffing, licking the floor, snorting, pushing forward until they are just below his bloodied feet. Just when they prepare to bite, Ivan pushes them back with a metal pole he procured while we watched the photo film. "This will only work for so long, Hernandez. Tell me their real names and not the bullshit Felix gave me."

"No one knows their real names and I didn't care enough to ask." It's an honest answer, I'll give him that, but not what I want. So to edge him along, I give him an almost identical slice across his other leg to match the first.

"Tell me what you know. All of it."

"Nico and Antonella are the children of Giada Savino. These three hate Matteo Cancio for something that happened between their father and the Boston mob boss a very long time ago. They never told me what, but from what Felix said it all started a year after Aurora, Cancio's daughter, was born."

"Matteo wasn't in charge then."

"The father. Matteo Cancio Sr. was."

"Okay." Placing my knife onto the cart, I extend a hand out to Callum for the bottle. He hands it over, and I bring it to Mauricio's lips. "Drink. It'll help."

"Just kill me."

"I will, but I need something first..."

Opening his mouth, he lets me pour a generous amount and swallows. "You want to talk about your mother?"

"She wasn't your intended target." Not a question, and he nods. "Then why shoot an innocent woman."

"They doubled the offer." He shrugs and lifts his head toward the bottle in my hand, and I pour another shot in his mouth. After swallowing, he releases a hiss as some of the spirits spilled onto his leg. "Those are a bitch...hurt like hell."

"That's the point." I hand the rum back to Callum. "Now, about the money?"

"I was supposed to receive the other half a mil next week to an account I have in Guatemala City. The national bank doesn't ask questions and after slipping the manager a couple of bucks, he speeds the process up personally."

"What day next week?"

"Wednesday."

"Thank you for your cooperation." With that, I pull out my gun and shoot him four times in the upper torso. That's the signal. The beginning of his end as Callum cuts him down, letting the almost dead weight drop to the ground without a care.

His groan is loud and pulls the attention of the two pigs on the floor. They come closer and we pull back toward the exit, and once there, Ivan presses the button on his remote that opens the cells for the other hogs to come out.

Within a minute, the screams inside the room are deafening. Would make a weaker man sick to his stomach.

Not me.

It's almost poetic, really. A disgusting cunt ending his life as nothing more than pig food.

After a minute, I step outside while the other two stay on the other side of the door talking, catching up, and I'll do that tonight, but first...

I find Archie right where we left him, standing to the left of Ivan's men and watching the door. Once I step through, he wordlessly hands me my belongings and then retakes his position. The other two give me a nod, but also remain quiet as they know to wait for all three of us to walk out before they remove what's left and dispose of all evidence.

Swiping a finger across the screen of my phone, I scroll through my contacts and find the phone number I need and type out a message.

It's time we sit down and talk ~Casper.

Within seconds there are three little dots on the screen letting me know my message was received. It starts and stops a few times, but I'm pleased with their response and agree.

Name the time and date. ~Cancio

Chapter 27
CASPER

"I'M VERY SORRY to hear about what happened to your mother, Casper. That's unacceptable and if you need anything, let me know." Matteo extends his hand out for me to shake as we meet in the lobby of his downtown office a week after I came back from Cuba. I've spoken to his daughter three times since then, explained what happened, but I never told her I'd be coming here.

Not yet. Not until I've handled a few loose ends.

The first is making her father understand my intentions. What I think of his plans for Gem.

Hopefully, my beauty understands why I do what I do. For her. For the us we will be.

The entire top floor of this building houses Matteo's office and that of another man I'll be visiting before walking out today because I'm here for two reasons:

To lay my cards down on the table. To warn him of what's to come.

Both reasons begin and end at the exact same spot:

Don't touch what's mine.

Looking at Gem's father, I take in the similarities between him and his daughter. Like now, as I take the offered hand and give it a firm shake, his brows give a small furrow as he tries to read me. Then, there's the tightening of his jaw when I give nothing away.

Two small expressions that match ones I've seen on Gem's face whenever her piqued curiosity isn't fed. On her it's cute, on him it's amusing, but I rein it in.

"Thank you. The offer is much appreciated since we have a mutual interest to take care of."

"We do?"

"Yes."

Matteo nods and then points over to the sitting area near his floor-to-ceiling windows. "Right to the point, I can appreciate that."

He has no idea just how direct it's about to get.

We take seats across from each other; he's watching me, and I'm dissecting what I know about the man and his relationships thus far. "Who are the Savinos?"

"Savinos?" His expression is confused because that not where he thought I'd begin. If he isn't aware of my relationship with Gem, then he thinks this is about business. "I don't know anyone with that name." *My information was correct. They don't exist.*

"They seem to know you, though."

At my response, he shakes his head. "Never heard of the name. Are they from Boston?"

"From my understanding, they're from New Jersey but want a

permanent seat of power here. They know you, your family, your business dealings, and want it all."

"What the fuck are you talking about? Who are these people?" His face has gone from lost to red in anger, jaw ticking. "How do you know this, and no one under my employ has—"

"I'm involved for two very specific reasons, Cancio. Both of which involve the women in my life." Sitting forward, I let my hands fall between my parted thighs. "They stole a gun shipment from me around the time you were in London a few months back."

"I had nothing to do with that."

"Something I already know, but at the time, blamed you." My phone pings with a message, and the special tone is his daughter's. For the moment I ignore it. I'll call her when I leave. "It became pretty clear soon after that you had no direct involvement and were in town for personal reasons."

"Direct involvement? I had no knowledge of anything happening."

"It involves you because of those fucking cunts. This is the second time they've tried to mix me in their mess...do their dirty work and have failed. They want you dead, want your territory, and then the male of the trio desires your daughter for himself. That last one will only happen over my dead body."

"How do you know my daughter?" As he says this, his eyes narrow. "Wait. Why are you really here? What does my Aurora have to do with this?"

"Why do you *think* I'm here?" Does he not look into her life at all? Does the bloody arsehole not care?

"Business. Maybe an expansion of operations."

"Are *you* looking to expand. Is the UK attractive to you?" I counter, instead. My expression is one of annoyance.

"Always has."

"Nice to know, but I'm not here for that...this time."

"Then why?"

"Because Aurora is mine." My tone leaves no room for argument. End of.

"Shouldn't you be asking me—"

"For shit." My voice is even, but the threat hangs in the air. I'm not a child and I ask permission from no one but Gem. Hers is the only one I need. "What happens between us is just that...between us. My relationship is with Aurora, and I will never ask nor apologize for being with her."

"And if I forbid this?" He's toying with me now—testing—and doing a shit job at it; the smile he's fighting back isn't helping his case. To him, this would play out perfectly in his desire for her to take over, and I could be the man to guide and stand with her.

Problem with this is he just doesn't realize how much of a wall I can be.

"Your approval isn't needed or wanted."

Matteo doesn't like my reply and his eyes narrow. "You have balls, Casper. This isn't England."

"I do, and I'm not afraid. Trust me when I tell you my connections run deeper than yours."

"Is that a threat?" he spits out through clenching teeth; hands are on the armrests and placed strategically to launch himself forward if need be.

"That's a fact." I shrug and then sit back to show I'm not at all intimidated. "Now, to get back on track. Nico, Antonella, and Giada Savino set things in motion to make it look like you were involved and responsible for the stolen shipment...hoping I would link you to my mum's death and retaliate. But like all rubbish, the stink comes to the top and people talk. It's how I found out about these three, the others involved, and disposed of a few."

"We're not done talking about my daughter."

"My intentions are clear, and I'm not going anywhere."

"We'll deal with that later." Matteo rubs a hand down his face, spitting out a few curses in Italian under his breath. Once he regains his composure, he looks at me again and this time all amusement is gone. The man looking at me now is the one people fear in Boston. "How do I find these assholes?"

"*We* find," I correct, and he nods, accepting my position in this. "Do those names ring a bell? Any of the three?"

"No. Not at all," he says, standing from his seat and walking over to the windows where he just looks out. He doesn't say anything. He doesn't move a muscle. Just stares until there's a knock at the door. It's timid and stops after three taps. "Come in."

The door opens and his secretary's head pops in, a woman in her early forties that looks afraid of her own shadow. "I'm so sorry for interrupting, sir. Mrs. Cancio is on line one and demands you take the call."

He doesn't turn around to address her. "No worries, Lisa. Pass her through."

"Thank you, sir."

Once the door closes, he releases a rough exhale. "Will you protect my daughter before your own life?"

"Yes."

"Will she be taken care of and respected?"

"Yes."

"Do you love her?"

"I'm not going to answer that." Matteo turns around at my reply, but before the man can utter a single syllable, I shake my head. "When I say the words, they will be to her. Not you. Not anyone. Just her."

"I can respect that."

"Good." Standing from my seat, I fix my cuff links. "Answer your call, and we'll finish this conversation at a later time. For now, you have my mobile's number and can reach me if needed. Watch your back, Matteo, and keep this information to yourself. You don't know if they have help on the inside."

"Even Dominic? I trust him and as my second—"

"Especially not him. There's something about the wanker that doesn't sit well with me, and if he ever so much as breathes wrong in her direction again, he's a dead man. A message I will be delivering personally once I leave this office."

"I can't allow that."

"Yes, you will." I crack my neck to alleviate a bit of the tension there. "For this meeting I gave you the courtesy of no guns and none of my men entered this floor. As a matter of fact, I left them downstairs waiting for me with strict instructions on how to proceed if things became *unpleasant* between us. Now, it's your turn to play nice. Where is he?"

"Just to have words."

"I'm going to kindly explain a few things."

He lets out a sigh but relents. Not that he has much of a choice. "Opposite end of the floor, only door on that wall."

"Thank you, and don't forget that your ex-wife's call is on line one."

———

TO DOMINIC'S SHITTY LUCK, he's not in his office when I seek him out, but I do find him a little later entering the building as I exit.

His eyes are down and oblivious to my persona as he tries to slip into my slot in the large revolving door. He's a bloody fucking idiot and it's time he learns a bit of respect.

"The fuck?" he yells the second my shoulder slams into him, sending him back onto the concrete outside the Cancio building. His phone, the one he was so lost in, goes flying toward the street and I see Callum walk toward it while a few of Cancio's guards take their positions.

No guns are drawn. Not while we're out in public like this.

Archie stands to my right with Jeffrey and a minute later Callum does as well.

I don't touch the idiot, but I do stand above him. "Get up."

There's a flash of fear in his eyes, but he hides it behind a sneer. "Touch me again, Jameson, and it'll be the last thing that you do."

Those are the wrong words to tell a man like me, something he learns a second later when I place my foot on his neck. Not to choke, but to prove a point. He's still a nobody. Will never be on the same level as me. "You have five seconds to remove it and leave. Matteo will see this as an act of—"

"Matteo gave me his blessing to deliver a message personally." At this, his features harden and the hand trying to push my foot off clenches. So I do him the favor, removing it only so I can yank him up by the hand and help the tosser stand to his full height. Dominic tries to distance himself, but I don't let go, and the next time he tries to forcefully do so, I take my karambit out and flip it open while stepping into his personal space so to everyone passing by, it looks like I'm giving him a friendly hug. With my lips at his ear, I bring the blade to his neck—enjoying how hard he swallows when he feels the sharp steel—and let out a chuckle. "If you come near Aurora again, I will find out and I will kill you. Make no mistake, Dominic, she is mine and this is the only warning I will give you as the second-in-command for the Cancio family. Don't force my hand. Back down and learn your place."

Then, I step back as if nothing has happened. I even pat him on the back and wish them all a nice afternoon.

I'm done in Boston, and I have a girl to go see.

Why are you in Boston? ~Aurora

Why didn't you tell me you were back? ~Aurora

You know what, never mind. I don't like to chase people. ~Aurora

THOSE THREE MESSAGES came in two hours apart and I made the mistake of not calling her back like I promised I always would. I bodged up. Not going to deny it, but I wasn't in a good place and never want her to see me like that.

Maybe it was everything that's happened over the last few days catching up to me, or my talk with her father, or even the four pints I had with dinner, but I let myself mourn my mum. I said goodbye in my own way and privately without anyone there to witness my grief.

Her killer has paid his price for taking her life, and I said my goodbyes.

Now, though, as I dial her number forty-eight hours later and find a recording telling me that *the number you've dialed has been disconnected*, I realize my mistake. Taking the time to myself isn't the problem. Not at all. All I had to do is tell her to give me a moment and that I would get back to her.

Aurora is tired of waiting for me.

Aurora misses me.

My Gem needs me the same way I crave her constantly.

"You're in a shit mood tonight, mate. What gives?" Callum asks from beside me in a pub back in Chicago, but I pay him no mind. I'm preoccupied. Taken in by the memory of her smile when I promised outside her apartment door to always come back. I remember the sweetness of her lips as she pressed them briefly to mine and then told me to go.

That she would wait for me.

"He looks like a man who's in the doghouse." Malcolm brings the gin and tonic in front of him to his lips and takes a sip. "Want to share with the class? I'm an expert on relationships nowadays."

"Back off, Asher."

"I'm not the enemy, Casper." Malcolm regards me with a cool look, at ease. "But something is up, and it isn't business related. Fuck that—since when do you spend so much time in Chicago?"

"My apologies," I say, but I neither confirm nor deny his suspicions. "Just have a lot going on in my head."

"Want to talk about it?"

"Not really." Callum clears his throat, ready to add his two cents, but at my glare closes his mouth. I'm sure he'll bring it up again. That he'll tell me I'm being an idiot, but now isn't the right fucking time to meddle. Cousin or not, I'm not in the mood for anyone's bullshit.

"Fair enough." Malcolm then pulls out an envelope from his suit jacket and pushes it across the table. It's an invitation of some sort and I raise a brow at him. "London and I would like to invite the Jamesons to our wedding. It's taking place in a couple of months here and I'd like for you to be a part of the wedding party. It'll give you a chance to get to know London and meet her cousin Aurora. She'll be the maid of honor—"

I don't let him finish. "Count me in."

"That easy?"

"You're someone I consider family. End of." *Perfect opportunity to fix this.* "Do you know who I'll be walking down the aisle with?"

Callum coughs, and Malcolm glances back over at him with a questioning look. "You okay?"

"Yeah…" my cousin bangs a hand on his chest at bit "…beer went down the wrong pipe."

"Oi. Be careful."

"Thanks." He gives me a shitty grin. "Must be some bullshit in the air that caused it."

"You're the only tosser choking on nothing. All you, bro."

Malcolm clears his throat; the man doesn't quite know what to think. "Any request?"

"Her cousin." No hesitation from me, and if he notices, Asher doesn't call me out on it. Something I'm grateful for. "It'll give me a chance to get to know her as well." *To win her back.*

Chapter 28
AURORA

"THAT WAS A BIT extra of you, Roe-Roe."

"I agree with her, chick. A bit much," Aliana adds after London, looking at me like I'm insane for having changed my number. And maybe it is a bit much, but what's done is done and so be it. "Especially since you swear, he means nothing and isn't worth mentioning."

"She has a point." London picks up a piece of apple with Brie, pops it into her mouth, chews, and then gives me the stink eye. "Why can't you at the very least give us his name?"

We're at the house she shares with Malcolm and in the middle of some serious wedding planning. There are samples everywhere: flowers, fabric swatches, and a few place settings to choose from that the planner dropped off for us to go through. The menu is pretty much set, and I'm just adding notes for the caterer on different RSVPs with allergies while Aliana serves us drinks. Bottle number three, a light Pinot has been the group's favorite so far.

"Because it's not important."

"Says the woman still harping on it."

"That's mean, Lo-Lo."

"Calls it like I sees it." She shrugs, waving her hand in the air. "Prove me wrong. Tell us."

I shake my head. "Not happening."

"You suck." Then she's distracted by a pretty napkin and the ring that goes with it. It's in a soft champagne color with a gold trim. "I like this one. What do you think?"

"Beautiful and delicate. I'm digging it." This all feels like it's happening overnight; we met, I blinked, and they disappeared for a few days, coming back engaged. And I can't deny that a small piece of me is jealous. That I want this for myself. She's so happy, vibrating, and this newly found confidence looks good on her.

My beautiful cousin is free, and it's because those two pieces of shit are dead. *May they rot in hell where they belong.* Her past isn't pretty, but my girl has risen above the bull crap and is building a good life with Malcolm. He's good to her. Looks at her the way Casper would look at me whenever our eyes met. Like I was his everything.

Maybe I am overreacting. Maybe I should just let him explain why he went to see my father.

"You look like you want to spill," Ali whispers beside me and I jump, wanting to punch her while she refills my glass. Her giggles are not helping her one bit.

"Nope," I hiss.

"Yes," they say in unison.

"Not happening."

"Why not?" my best friend whines, and I can't stop the epic eye roll that follows. These two are relentless. "Why can't you admit you like him and tell us who he is? Do we know him?"

"Because she's being selfish." Mariah, Malcolm's cousin, walks into the Asher kitchen then with two more bottles of wine in hand and a delivery boy behind her that looks ready to pee his pants. It's priceless, what I come to expect when we convene and gossip. It's nice. Fun. We go together in a way that's seamless.

"Withholding information from friends is a punishable offense, Aurora. I'm both hurt and disappointed," Ali says, a fake innocent expression on her face.

"Really? Who sent you a text last week that turned you tomato red?"

The other two turn their heads and narrow their eyes.

"It was a wrong number."

"Those make you blush and smile?" I question, hoping it takes the attention off me.

"Whoever it was had sent someone a dirty joke. Sue me..." Ali shrugs, trying to be nonchalant but I'm not buying it "...and I didn't know that finding something amusing was such an issue. Unlike you, I haven't been on a date in a long time. Too freaking long."

"You guys suck as friends," I say, schooling my facial features for half a second, because then like a domino effect, we all crack up. One by one laughter rings up and it's in the middle of it that someone clears their throat.

The delivery boy is still there and standing awkwardly by the counter near the fridge. "Can I leave?"

Christ. We begin all over again. I've never laughed so hard in my life.

Tears. Hiccups. The whole nine.

And right now, when I want to give in and call him—see him— it's needed. It hurts like hell, this separation, but we can't go on like this. I'm here and he's there. And while I know that it won't fix our situation, our relationship can go one of two ways at this point…

Together, or not at all. The ball is in his court, and I hope he seeks me out.

That he makes the right move.

London is the first to calm down, and her eyes gets this evil twinkle in them. "You know, Malcolm has a good friend flying in for the wedding that I could set you up with. He's handsome, in his thirties, and Asher approved."

"No."

"Why not?" This time it's Aliana.

"Prove us wrong." Mariah is looking at me with a raised brow. Knowing that if I fight it, it's because of the mystery man they're dying to know about.

I'm a cheater if I do and damned if I don't. *Fake it for now and call it off before the date.*

"Fine. I'll go on one date if he agrees." The hoots and hollers that follow make me forget we're grown women and not a bunch of prepubescent tweens at a boy band concert. "What's his name, by the way? The friend?"

"Not telling," London says with a giggle, high-fiving the other two. "It'll be a surprise."

Crap.

IT's around midnight when I finally make it back home, and just like the last few days, there's a long-stemmed white rose on my door. A first, because the others have been on the windshield of my car or my office door at The Conte House.

It's taped, and with a folded note attached that I grab, opening it right there before entering my apartment.

I'm going to give you the world, Aurora.
Just hear me out.
Let me in.

The girly girl deep within makes an appearance and I squeak. Squeal. I make all kinds of embarrassing noises that I'm incredibly thankful no one sees, this display of weakness.

This little act of affection means more to me than any ostentatious gift would. It soothes me. Makes me think that maybe, just maybe, I'm wrong and he's not the jerk I've made him out to be in my head.

That maybe there's a reason for how he handled things. For why he went to see my father, a father who's gone silent since that visit. Not a single peep in days, and had it not been for Samantha letting me know to stay clear—in a text—because a mob boss from England was visiting, I wouldn't have known.

It's just too much of a coincidence, and his lack of denial is all the confirmation I need.

Or maybe I'm looking too deep into this and I just need to let it play out.

My mind likes that conclusion while my heart thunders in my chest. There's no denying that I miss Casper. That I want him here, but I'm going to need something more profound than a flower and note.

What I need is to know how he feels about me. To know that he cares.

That maybe someday soon he will love me like I already love him.

A sobering truth that sends me rushing inside and to bed. It's better to not think about things I can't fix; this is on him.

Casper needs to show me before we can move forward.

THERE'S a hard knock on my door the next morning, startling me awake. It's constant, loud, and I find myself stumbling down the hall toward the front door without a second thought.

My hope is that it's Casper, but as I look through the peephole, I realize it's a woman. She's dressed in black and looking straight ahead, letting me take in her face without her knowledge.

Light complexion, jet-black hair, and high cheek bones. Her lips are also in a bright shade of red.

I've never seen her before, and I open the door. "May I help you?"

"Aurora Conte?" she asks, and the second I nod, the woman brings her badge into view. She's BPD and at once I'm fully alert. "I'm detective Corrine Santos and I have a few questions for you. Do you have a few minutes?"

"Sure." I step to the side, giving her room to enter. "Come inside."

"Thank you." Officer Santos crosses the threshold, then waits, following me into the living room a minute after and takes a seat on the oversized chair. I take the loveseat. "I hope I'm not interrupting anything, and I appreciate you taking the time to speak with me."

"No problem." Grabbing the afghan from the back of the couch, I lay it over my lap. "I'm sorry, but why are you here again?"

"I have some questions regarding your relationship with a Matteo Cancio."

"You mean my father." My conversation with Samantha comes to the forefront of my mind. Once again, she wasn't lying.

"Yes, your father." Pulling a small recorder from her blazer, she gives me a smile. "Do I have your permission to record this conversation?"

"Yes."

"And you understand that anything you say can be used as evidence in a criminal investigation."

"Yes."

"Great. Let's begin." She crosses her legs and sits a bit forward, keeping her eyes on mine. "Once more, how do you know Matteo Cancio?"

"He's my father."

"But do you know him personally? This is a yes or no question, Miss Conte."

"He's my father."

Her eyes narrow a bit and lips thin. "What was he like as a father."

"Absent."

"And his relationship with your mother?"

"Is none of your business."

"Miss Conte, for this to work I need you to answer—"

"Why are you really here?" For a split second there's a bit of worry, a hint of fear, but she schools her expression quickly. This is all beginning to smell fishy. "What are you looking for?"

"I'm sorry..." she gives me what she thinks is a sincere smile "...but that information is pertaining to a criminal investigation and I can't divulge."

"Then I see no reason for you to be in my home, and this is where I ask you to leave."

"You need to answer my questions."

"No. I don't." At my response, she clenches the hand in her lap; her entire posture stiffens. "Leave."

"I can charge you with—"

"Nothing, Officer Santos. I have broken no laws, and at the moment, I feel as though you're harassing me. Leave my home and stay away, or I will place a formal complaint with your department regarding this visit and your treatment."

"Are you threatening me?"

"That's a promise." Standing from my chair, I calmly walk over to the front door and pull it wide open. She follows a minute later, an angry expression on her face. "Have a good day."

Officer Santos walks by me and out the door but pauses a few steps from me. She doesn't turn around. "Be very careful with the company you keep, Aurora. You're walking a fine line between loyalty and stupidity. Don't get caught on the wrong side of this war."

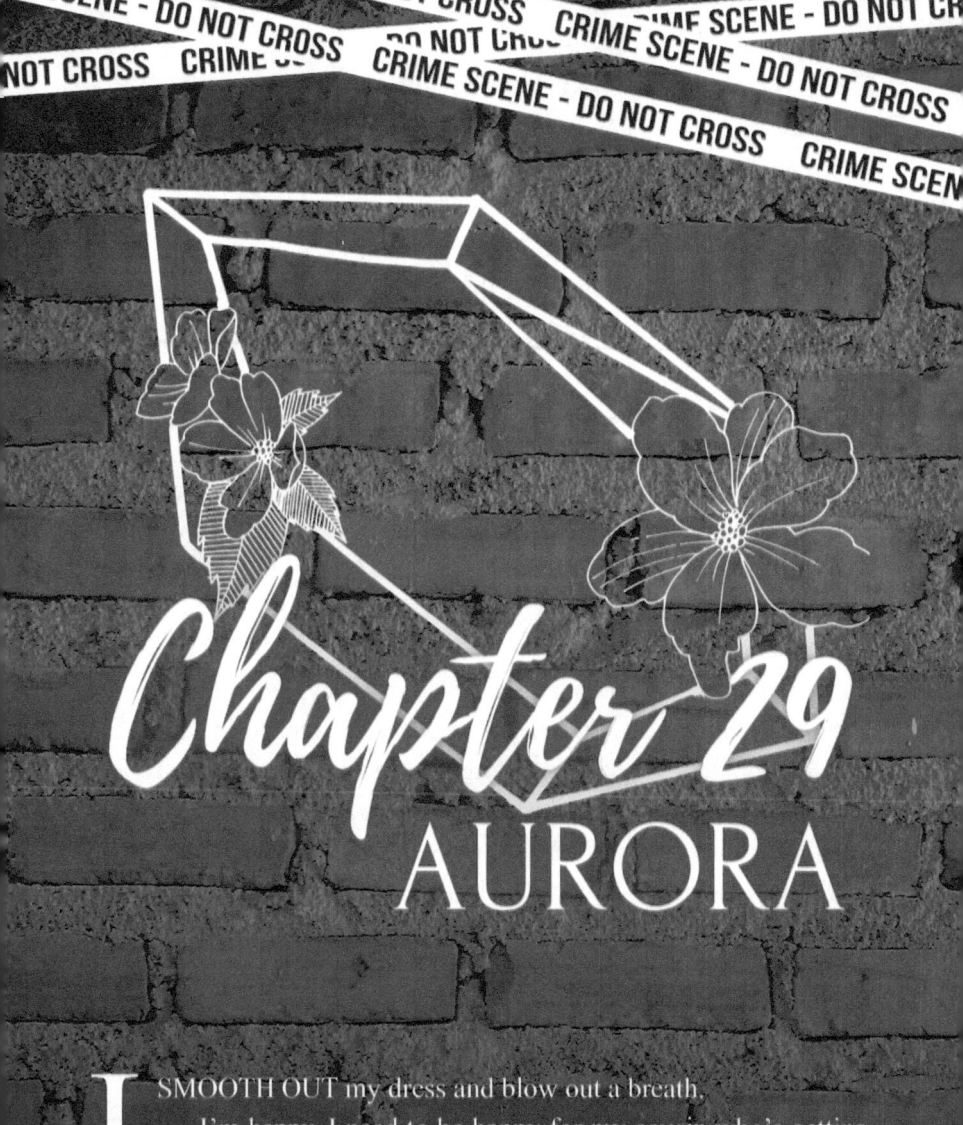

Chapter 29
AURORA

I SMOOTH OUT my dress and blow out a breath.

I'm happy. I need to be happy for my cousin who's getting married in a few short hours, and although my heart hurts and I'm inexplicably jealous, I'll put on a brave face and smile for the cameras. I'll say the right things and be giddy, but I can't help but think back on what I never truly got to enjoy.

It's been months since Casper looked at me the same way, since I've seen him.

Sure, the jerk has left me roses and notes, but that's it. Nothing more. No more visits or calls letting me know he's never too far

Why does he decide to listen to me now and give me the space I asked for?

"Roe-Roe!" London squeals as she wraps her arms around me. The hold is tight and near suffocating, but it does the job of erasing the sudden pang in my chest the thought of him brings. All the darkness is washed away by the happiness London soon-to-be Asher exudes.

"Hey there!" I am blown away by the smile on her face and I find myself matching hers. It's contagious. So honest.

"You ready to meet your date?" London asks with a waggle of her eyebrows, but then she's looking past me, and a hint of blush appears on her cheeks. My money is on Mr. Asher being close by.

I roll my eyes, suddenly regretting that I agreed to this. "Yeah. Fine. Where is he?"

"Right here," a low rumble of a voice says with that British accent that makes my knees go weak and I turn, losing the very breath in my lungs at the sight of him. In a suit. Hair perfectly styled. With that hellish five o'clock shadow that I miss between my thighs.

Christ, woman. Get a hold of yourself.

In the distance, someone calls for London and I hear her say something to me, but I can't make out the words. I'm trapped, lost in the man in front of me. In the sudden burst of desire that ignites at his mere presence. That won't let me go.

Of course Casper and Malcolm would know each other. Two peas in a criminal pod.

"What are you doing here?" I ask, my brow furrowed, inconspicuously trying to take a step back and create space between his body and mine.

He glances over toward Malcolm and London before reaching out and taking my hand. "Come," he says, pulling me away from the rest of the bridal party. Casper doesn't stop until we reach an empty corridor, away from prying eyes and ears.

Once there, I pull my arm from him and cross them over my chest. "What do you want?"

"We need to talk, Gem."

"Why now, Casper? Where have you been?"

"I've been trying to give you space," he says, and it holds a hint of bitterness. As if he hated doing so. "To not overwhelm you, but I miss you, Gem. I'm sorry if you're angry with me—"

"You know where I live."

"Yes, but I've been unable to come. I'm wrapping things up."

"Then call." It's simple. He has ways to do so.

A flash of annoyance crosses his features. "You changed your number."

"I know you could have gotten my new number if you tried."

"If you wanted me to have it, you would have contacted me."

"That didn't stop you last time."

A chuckle leaves him. "No, I suppose you're right." He steps forward then and rests his hands on my hips, fingers digging in. The fire from his touch seeps through my skin and into my muscles, and even though I shouldn't, I relax into him, my hands finding purchase against his chest.

"I was away for too long, but I swear it's for the last time."

"Months," I seethe, even as I draw closer to him. I ignore how he says it's the last time, because I don't want to believe what I know will be nothing more than another broken promise.

"Roe-Roe, where are you?" London calls out and I force myself to step away, my eyes never leaving Casper's.

We return to the group and go through the motions, my heart skipping when I wrap my arm around his and we walk down the aisle together. Each step the need for him grows. Each moment near him weakens my resolve to stay away.

To not let him in.

When the schedule for the next day is gone over and we disperse, the group all in a chatter as we depart to dinner, I fall silently behind with Casper right next to me. When they turn right, I go left, and still, he follows. And when I stop to demand he quit playing with me, Casper spins me around and I fall into his chest. A low growl rumbles beneath my hands, but I barely get a squeak out before his lips crash to mine. Hands grip, digging in, pulling me closer as he kisses deeper. Breath leaves me and I fight to control the kiss, which only makes him fight harder.

"You're mine, Gem. Will always be mine."

"YOU LOOK BEAUTIFUL, cousin. The bracelet from Grandma Isadora looks perfect," I say from behind her, watching with amusement as she adjusts the crown Malcolm demanded she wear again. He was adamant on this; no veil or anything that would cover her face because in his words: *his queen never hides*. But then again, London loves his obsession with her. How much he wants her and shows it without a single ounce of shame.

The place or time doesn't matter.

"Thank you so much for coming, and for this." Lo-Lo lifts her wrist and inspects the delicate tennis bracelet with diamonds and sapphires throughout. It's her something borrowed and blue. "Having a piece of the family to wear today means more than you'll ever know." She turns to face me then and does to me what I find myself doing all the time. It's crazy and wonderful how much we look alike. To take in the familial resemblances after spending so much time alone without knowing the other existed. "It means a lot that you could make it. That you wanted to do this."

"I'm going to flick you if you thank me again, chica. Stop it." My eyes are watery, and my bottom lip trembles a bit.

"Ass," London mutters in the same emotional tone, but before we ruin our makeup, I smack her arm.

"Dork."

"You bruise me, and you'll deal with Malcolm."

In the last few months since we connected, if she says something like this, I laugh and hit her again.

Our relationship is very sibling like.

Like what I've missed out on my whole life.

Which brings forth questions that have been plaguing me for a few days now.

How long have they known each other?

How well does London know him?

Is that why they want to hook me up with him?

"What gives? What's with the look?"

"How well do you know his groomsmen?" I ask, keeping my expression as neutral as possible.

"Which one?"

"British and a complete lying asshole." *Christ*, I suck at this. How could I just blurt that out? *Get a hold of yourself. She'll put two and two together.*

"Casper?" she asks, thrown off by my yo-yoing change in demeanor. From almost weepy to hormonal in the blink of an eye. *I need help.* "Did he do something to you?"

"Other than exist?" And because I'm certifiable, I nod with an added huff for good measure. *Is this what an out-of-body experience feels like?* My curiosity is going to get me in trouble if I don't shut up. "We don't click."

Lies. All lies.

The way he grabbed and kissed me—full of passion and need—after the rehearsal dinner in an empty corridor re-confirmed this.

I can't escape him. I want him.

"Why? Do I need to involve—"

"No. It's me."

"Do you like—"

"I'm coming in," Malcolm calls out through the door a second before barging in, and I thank Jesus above for this interruption. The groom has the most amazing timing, and as he takes her in, I know I'm going to be asked to leave, something I'm internally doing the Nae Nae over. *Thank you and amen.* "Aurora, we need a moment before the ceremony. Please find Casper and let him know I'll be down soon."

I'm already fluffing my hair before the last word passes through his lips. "Of course. Just behave, kiddos. Leave the fun stuff for after..." I trail off, heading straight for the door because while I adore them both, I'm not trying to see what comes next.

"Oh, God!"

London moans before the door is fully closed and yup. Just say no.

NERVOUS BUTTERFLIES OVERTAKE me as I lift a hand to knock on the door of the men's dressing room. I know he's there. I can feel him near.

Sense that overwhelming electrical current that flows through my limbs each time we're near. It's palpable. Heart thumping.

My thighs clench, and I place my knuckles on the wooden door to hold myself up. I don't knock, not yet, but as if sensing me too, Casper swings the door open.

And then, I'm tumbling right into his arms. Feeling whole again.

"Get in here." His voice is gritty. Holds a tinge of near demonic desperation that makes me whimper, and I move closer to his body. Chest to chest. His hard cock against my mound.

I can't help myself. I can't stop this.

At that moment, I thank the inventor of the high heel for making me the few inches taller I need to enjoy this. To feel him throb, pulsing against me where I'm longing to have him again.

"Please." That one word from my lips and his pupils dilate, lids becoming heavy as he sees just how much I missed him, too. How my own hunger matches his.

Then my feet are off the ground and my dress rides up, bunching around my hips as he lifts me with one arm beneath my butt. This puts him right there, my wetness to his tuxedo-covered cock, and my legs go around his waist to hold him tight.

So I can gyrate softly.

So I can quell some of this mounting heat burning me from the inside.

Casper lets out a curse and pivots us both, my back slamming against the door. "I've missed you," he whispers low, but to me, it's as if the man shouted it from the rooftops. Our faces come closer and those lips I've missed so much hover over mine. They sweep gently across once and then pull back, tempting with his denial, until I can't take it anymore and I'm the one that caves.

I submit. I can't fight this anymore.

Embedding my fingers in his hair, I yank his mouth to mine and let go. I just let go.

He has me. Always will.

Thank God this room inside the church is empty because we can't control ourselves. The bubble of lust we're trapped within squeezes tighter, so tight that as his hands wander lower, I begin to shake. As he fists the back of my lace thong and pulls, ripping the fabric in pieces, I moan. That the moment two of his fingers swipe over my wetness, I come for him.

It's automatic and wild and I can't breathe.

I can't focus on anything but his harsh breathing against my neck as I throw my head back with eyes closed. Savoring. Letting the relief wash over me while I whisper his name like a sacred mantra.

"Fuck, Gem. Give me more, baby," he rasps, nipping my collarbones while a hand takes hold of my hip, anchoring me to the wooden surface. "I want to walk down that aisle with your scent all over me. Marking me."

"Oh God." Another harsh shiver and I'm panting. I can't think as the world around us fades and the pleasure overtakes my senses. That is until he's right there.

His flesh on mine.

His cock against my entrance.

Just there. Not moving.

When he pulled himself out, I have no clue, but bless him for being coherent when I'm not. In that moment, I'm useless. His to enjoy. His to take.

And I want it that way. Crave it more than I thought could be possible.

Casper slips the head inside and it's like breathing again after being deprived of sustenance for an extended period of time. Another inch and I cry out, fingertips tugging on fistfuls of hair as my body arches, fighting his tight hold on my hips.

"Tell me you want me. That you need *me*," he demands and pulls out. My eyes narrow and my lips part, the expletives sitting on the tip of my tongue, but they die down when he pushes forward, sliding the bulbous tip through my folds and over my clit. "Say the words and I'll fuck you...break you...then when you let go, I'll put those beautiful pieces back together again."

To anyone else those words would be demanding and forceful, but the look in his eyes tells a different story. This man is barely holding on to his sanity. Showing me his weakness; my hold on him.

"From the very beginning, it's always been you. I just want you."

"Christ, I need you. We can't be apart for so long again...I don't function that way." I want to tell him that I feel the same, that I agree, but before I can, he slams in to the hilt in one smooth stroke. His hips are punishing, bouncing me on his cock at a rapid pace, and I can't do anything but hold on and let him.

My hands fall from his hair and my head bangs against the door, the sound loud. "So good. Always so good."

"Shhhh." He nips my chin and the action brings his chest against mine. This changes the angle of his thrust and I clench down hard, moaning out my approval. "Quiet, Gem. Or do you want everyone outside this room to hear how much you love my cock? How much of a filthy little girl you are." He doesn't realize how I love his dirty mouth. How wet hearing him talk makes me. "*Fuck*, baby. You like that, don't you. Like the thought of being caught."

"No," I whimper out, fighting against his hold. Wanting to move but can't.

He places his hand over my neck, gently squeezing. "Explain."

"I don't care what anyone outside this room thinks, Casper. Truly don't give a fuck." His thrusts are languid, savoring, waiting for my explanation—it's worse than when he lets go. Because right now, as he pulls all the way out and pushes in slowly, I can feel every ridge and the metal of his piercing against my walls. "You make me delirious with need. You make me wet. Your dirty words are what throw me over the edge every single time. Just you."

"You're it for me too." His hold on my neck and hip tighten, and my body responds with another rush of wetness, coating him. The groan he releases is a delicious torment before he picks up speed, angling my hips while keeping my shoulders on the door by his hold on my neck.

On the next pump of his hips, I see little white dots dance across my line of sight. He finds that spot, the one that he's claimed as his, and presses against it with each inward stroke. Hard. Precise. Each thrust holds an edge of pleasurable pain that pushes me headfirst into another orgasm.

This one is stronger than the last, and a few tears run down my cheeks. "I can't...*oh God*," I whimper into his ear as he envelops me in his arms, pulling me against his chest as he lets go with a hissed *fuck* next to my cheek.

We don't move for a few minutes. To be honest, I don't think either of us has any strength left in our bodies, but Casper still manages to not trip and sits with me astride his lap on the leather chair across the room.

Across from a mirror. Where I can see the mess we are.

And as he releases a chuckle, it hits me all at once just what we did and where.

I'm going to hell for this.

This is so wrong.

"Quit overthinking things, Gem. Relax."

My eyes shift back to his warm green eyes and I forget my

reproachful words. Instead, I go shy and feel the heat sweep across my cheeks. "Hi."

"Hello, love."

"I was sent here with a message from the groom."

"Which is?"

"He'll be back down after he sexes up my cousin." No sooner has the last word passed through my lips than the sexy Brit beneath me is laughing. Hard and long. Unrestrained. Moreover, a minute later I follow.

We are ridiculous and I love him all the more for it. I can't help myself.

Somewhere along the line without thinking, I gave him my heart and the jerk, unknowingly, won't give it back. *Now I just need to tell him this.*

IT's our turn to walk down, and my hand in his trembles. The entire church is looking at us, and I can't help but fear that they know. That even after fixing what he got messy, they are judging.

Hell, I'm judging myself for just how easy I am when it comes to the man.

What is wrong with me? Why do I let him?

"Relax, Gem. I got you." His voice is soft and at once soothes my fragile nerves. He helps me breathe easier as we make it to the front where he drops me off with a kiss to the cheek that makes my face bloom.

Aliana is looking at me, but I ignore her. Instead, I focus on the maid of honor and her man walking up to the front. Mariah and Javier are adorable in that *I will cut you* kind of way. They reach the front and after Javi lets her hand go, she hugs her cousin and pulls back, wiping under her eyes.

They share a look—a silent conversation—before Mariah takes her place next to us, and then the music changes.

Every person in the church stands as London comes into view. She's beautiful. Absolutely breathtaking, and while Malcolm takes her hand in his at the end of the aisle and the priest begins his sermon, my eyes turn to Casper.

He's looking at me with a dirty little smile that makes my own lips quirk up. It's like we're having a private conversation, saying what we can't with words.

I'm sorry.

I need you.

I can't be without you.

The world around us continues, but we're lost in each other's eyes, listening as the vows are shared. The promises our loved ones make hit home for me, and as they say I do, I can't stop myself from mouthing *I love you.*

But what surprises me the most, what takes my breath away and centers me all in one breath, is his *I love you* back.

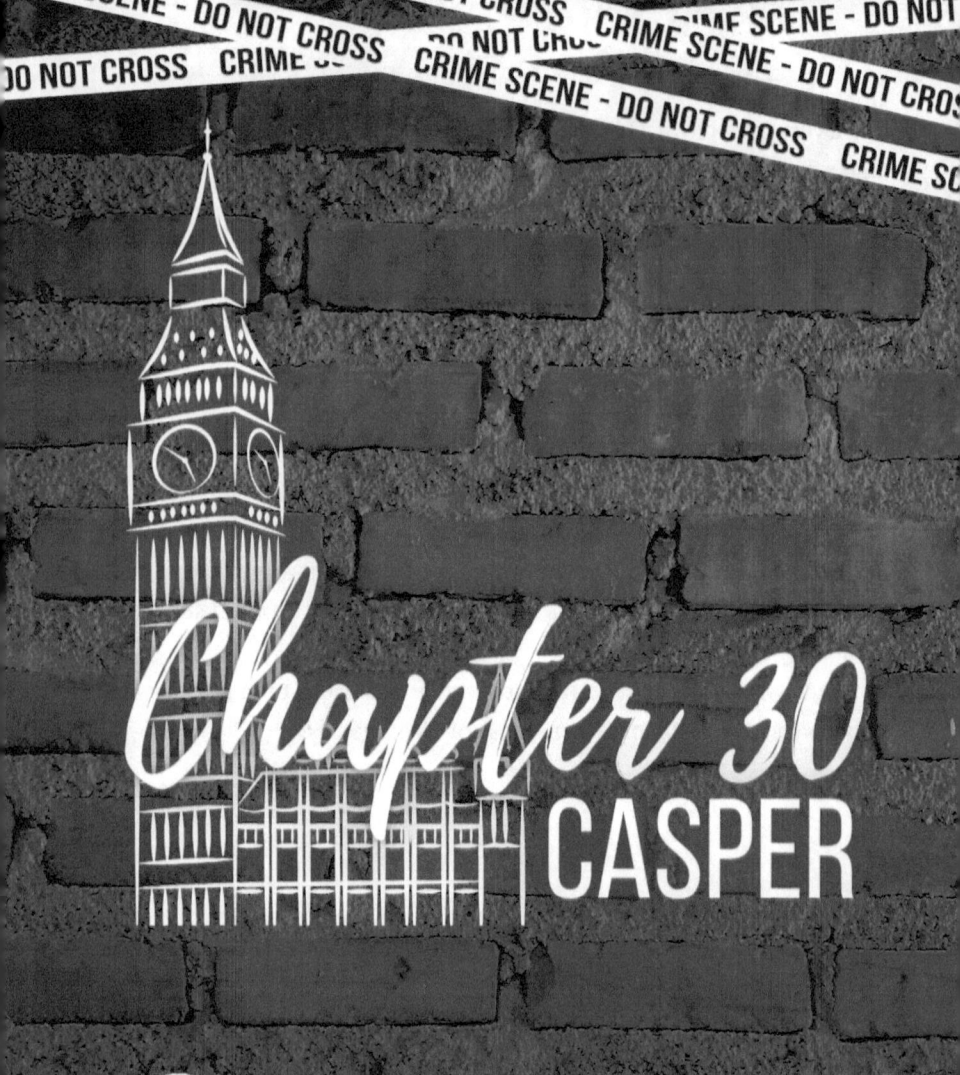

Chapter 30
CASPER

"**C**OME WITH ME," I whisper into her ear, watching as the two lovebirds leave. Everyone's following them out; some wish them well while others keep to the time-honored tradition of throwing rice at the newlyweds.

We're neither of the two. Instead, we pull back and out of sight, slipping away from the group and back inside the hotel. Let them party—we have more important things to discuss.

Like the three little words we said during their wedding.

Gem places her hand in mine and gives my fingers a squeeze, not saying a word as I lead her through the open lobby where anyone could see us and right into the elevator that leads to the penthouse.

Once inside, she stands beside me and watches the numbers go up as we ascend. Little does my girl know what awaits her once inside. What I've had planned since Malcolm told me the reception would be held for the guests inside the Peninsula's largest ballroom.

They wouldn't stay to enjoy it, and as much as I care for the two, I want my girl. Alone. Unfiltered. Open to my plans.

The elevator dings, announcing our arrival, and I let her exit first, guiding her with a hand low on her back toward the room's door. This is the largest suite the hotel offers and has the most privacy. Especially for what I have planned.

I give her the keycard. "Open the door, love."

"Okay." It's shaky and low and *fuck*, she smells amazing. Like cherry blossoms and sex; a little bit of her and me combined to create the most decadent scent. The card goes in and the light blinks green, a lock is disengaged, and when I push it open for her, she gasps, seeing my surprise for her from the very entrance and leading toward the outside terrace. "Casper? What did you...how? When did you have time to do all this?"

There are rose petals along the floor, a sweet blush red that reminds me of her cheeks when I embarrass her with something inappropriate. Something that we both know she loves. Then, there's the soft glow from the lit candles placed strategically along the room to show us the way.

"I've known you were in the wedding party for a while, Gem." Giving her hand a gentle pull, I bring her to my chest. Loving how she wraps her arms around my neck loosely, because even though those sexy heels help her in the height department, she's still so much shorter than me. She always the perfect little doll to my much harsher planes. Soft to my hard. My other half. "For much longer than you think, and I began to plan that very night. I need you to know...show you...that I want this. That I want you."

"I know you do. That part was never in doubt." Her eyes are bright and her smile so fucking sweet. "I'm just selfish and want you here all the time. That's on me. I need to—"

I silence her with a kiss. Taste her the way I wanted to earlier but couldn't because of her makeup. Now, there's no photographer or people to please. No friends or interruptions and I embed my fingers in her hair, tipping her head back to my liking.

And I devour her. Kiss her with every bit of the hunger I live with day in and day out for her.

Always her. Always burning.

"I want to be with you, Aurora. Always." Turning with her lips still on mine, I guide us slowly outside, one foot at a time and between her pleas for more and my wandering hands. I touch her everywhere I can and before she reaches the open balcony doors, I lower the zipper at the back of her dress, letting the silky black fabric fall to the floor at her feet.

It pools there, and just like at the church, I place my hand beneath her arse and lift her up. One cheek in my hand, I squeeze the flesh and step over the threshold where the cool night air meets her overheated skin.

It's the perfect time of year here. Not too hot. Not too cold.

And yet, my girl shivers in my hold. Goose bumps arise on her skin and it's a motherfucking heady notion to know it's solely because of me.

"Is this going to become a regular occurrence? I can walk, you know." She's a cheeky little thing and it also earns her a quick smack to the arse, one that I soothe with the tip of my fingertips. Caressing. Massaging the sting away.

"And if it is?" With her in my hold, I take us straight toward the private jacuzzi in the far corner of the terrace and the table beside it. There, I have an assortment of fruit, cheeses, melted chocolate, and a chilled bottle of champagne, a delicious spread that I'm going to enjoy either feeding her or licking from her skin. "Do you have a problem with that?"

Placing her on her feet, I peck those bee-stung lips and then turn, picking up the bottle and pouring us each a glass. I'm also trying to calm myself, to not attack like I want to. Because dear God, this woman is a sinful delight wrapped in a pretty little bow just for me.

When did she have time to change her lingerie?

The color of her underwear—the indecent scrap of satin covering her pussy and tits—almost matches her skin tone. A light tan shade with a hint of rose. It's soft and molds over her curves, showing me every little secret she hides, like the wet spot over her mound. The proof of her desire for me.

"You like?" she asks, but I don't need to turn around to know what she's talking about.

"How did you—"

"A truth or a lie?"

"Always the truth," I grind out, bringing a hand to my cock and squeezing.

"I carried an extra set in my small clutch just in case. I knew you'd be there today and…"

Fuck, this girl. "So, you came prepared."

"Yes." Aurora's tone is a bit breathy, holds a sultry edge that brings a shiver down my spine. "And to answer your earlier question…No. No, I don't."

"Good answer." I turn then, because I just can't hold back, and groan at the sight that greets me. That barely there silk is no longer on her skin. It's on the floor, tossed without care, while the moonlight illuminates her soft skin. Aurora looks ethereal. Like a goddess.

Like my favorite kind of sin.

"You're wearing entirely too many clothes, Casper. Aren't you hot, baby?" she asks coyly, batting her lashes while twirling a long curl around her finger. The few pins that held one side back so that it all cascaded over the opposite shoulder are gone, and the loose strands now flow around her bare shoulders with the soft breeze.

"Can I have that?" Aurora asks coyly, batting her lashes.

"I'll give you anything you want." I hand over the flute, watching in silence as she brings it to her lips and takes a sip. She moans at the taste, and my cock throbs, pushing against the confines of my trousers. "I meant the words, Aurora…I do love you."

"I love you, too." She takes another sip and hands it back to me. "Hold that for me."

"Okay." And then Gem does the sexiest motherfucking thing in the world; she begins to undress me. I'd long taken off my jacket and bowtie—left them with Callum who was busy talking to Aliana downstairs—so she untucks my shirt and begins with the very last button.

One by one, and at a torturous pace. Slowly. Her nimble fingers undo each one and then push the material off my shoulders, exposing my torso to her lips. Lips that begin to kiss every inch of exposed skin.

She licks and nips. Traces the contour of my six-pack and then lower to the waist of my trousers. There, she dips her tongue beneath the edge, encountering the head of my throbbing cock.

Another lick and she hums in the back of her throat. "No underwear?"

"Don't like them." My voice is gruff, rough as I try to keep still and see where my naughty nymph is taking this. "Never have."

"Sexy." She whimpers a second before dropping to her knees. Naked, beautiful, and trusting. Nimble fingers undo the button and then lower the zipper, giving the bulbous tip another lick before pushing the material down to the floor. "Even your cock is perfect."

"The only perfection here is you, Gem. My perfection."

"I love you." Then her breath is on the head of my cock, fingers surrounding my girth in a tight grip. She pumps me once, twice, and on the third swipes her tongue over the slit at the top. "And you're delicious."

I grip her chin and force her eyes to mine. "Open, baby. Take me in your mouth."

"No." Shaking her head, she removes my fingers from her face and then comes back to my cock. Her lips are against my skin, breath kissing the tip. "I'm going to enjoy you at my pace." Gem runs her tongue over the head, swirling before going lower where she lays a tiny kiss over my piercing. "Slowly."

"Be nice, baby girl," I warn, body coiling tight as my need to take control begins to claw at me. "Just remember that I'll return the favor tenfold. I'll make you cry with desperation."

"When I'm done, do your worst," is all she says a second before taking me in her mouth, sucking me in deep and then pulling back slowly. She does this three times, hollowing her cheeks each time and then adding pressure with her tongue on the underside.

All the while her gorgeous hazel eyes are on mine, watching my reaction each time she takes me a little deeper, opens a little wider—how good she looks with her lips all shiny from my pre-come.

This woman is my demise and rebirth. My everything.

She feels so good, and yet I need more. To dominate her.

"Son of a bitch," I grunt, bringing a hand to the back of her head and pumping in and out a few times. Her fingernails are digging into my arse while a hum reverberates through my shaft. "Open wider, Gem. Let me fuck that pretty little mouth."

"*Oh God.*" It's a moan and it causes a lick of heat to rush down my spine and settle on my heavy balls. "I want to taste you."

Wrapping a fistful of hair in my hand I pull, forcing her to arch prettily for me. Her breasts are perky and nipples hard. Her inner thighs shine with her wetness.

Her lips are open and as I slide to the back of her throat, I moan. *Motherfuck.*

Warm. Wet. Fuck.

Gem whimpers around my length, the sound traveling through every nerve ending while she relaxes her throat and I slide in a little deeper. Slowly. She lets me fuck her mouth with measured strokes until her lips kiss the base and my eyes roll back.

"So close," I hiss, throwing my head back when she cups my balls. Squeezing them. "Where do you want my come, beautiful? Your tongue or tits?"

She doesn't hesitate to answer when I pull back, leaving just the tip over her lips. Lips she licks while those heavy-lidded eyes watch me. "Come in my mouth."

"Good girl. Now open wide and show me your tongue." Doing as I say, she waits with a hungry expression. Showing me that she wants this. Me.

I slide back inside and this time I'm not gentle. I use her, pumping my hips as my hand on her head pushes her forward, meeting my thrust. Her mouth is warm and her tongue eager, swirling around my length as she pulls me in deeper.

Then those lips close around my girth and her cheeks hollow.

Her teeth scrape over the piercing with the right amount of pressure to cause my eyes to roll back.

But nothing...not a motherfucking thing compares to the lust in her eyes and the word *come* slipping from her lips.

One word. Four letters.

And I give in to her command.

"Swallow," I manage to grit out, hand tightening in her hair as the first rope of come coats her tongue. The second and third do the same, but on the fourth, I pull out and dribble down her chin and onto her chest. "*Christ*, Gem. Hot little mouth."

Aurora pulls back, a sassy smile on her lips as she licks them. "Yummy."

My knees are weak and body thrumming with the aftershocks of pleasure, but I still manage to scoop her up off that floor and bring her to my chest. "You're amazing."

After what we've shared, you'd think she wouldn't get shy, but Aurora does, and her cheeks pink up. "I've been wanting to do that for some time."

"Have you, now?" I chuckle, lips at her temple. "Because I will volunteer my cock every day for the rest of my life."

"Perv."

"Absolutely." Taking us to the jacuzzi, I sit her on the edge, remove the rest of my clothes, and then get in. The water is hot, and the night air is a tiny bit cool—feels amazing—but it becomes pure perfection when I pull her to sit between my thighs. "Now, how about we talk for a bit. I have something I want to run by you."

"Good or bad news?"

"It's the best decision I've ever made."

Chapter 31
AURORA

"YOU WOULD DO that for me?" I ask from my seat across from him in the jacuzzi a few hours later. Because a blow job led to his face between my thighs and then my body being bent over the large tub's ledge. We can't be trusted. Can't help but attack. It's the only way we can talk and be close without going at it like sex-starved animals. "Just like that? You want to step down as the head of the Jameson family, buy a house here or in Boston, and help me run my father's organization?"

"There's more to it than that, love, but in a nutshell, yeah. Pretty accurate summary."

"Why?"

"Why?" Casper smiles at me and shrugs. "Why not."

"You need to give me more than that, Jameson. Why would you do this for—"

"Because I love you. Because I want to build a life with you. Because running a criminal organization is not your dream, not where your heart lies, but it is what I know. We could do it together —grow it together—have it all, and you'd still be able to do what you love. It's a lot of work, a huge learning curve for you, and I'll help. Money isn't an issue nor is where we live. All that matters is that I come home to you and you greet me with a kiss."

"I like that," I say, but then scrunch up my nose. "I'm also scared of agreeing. He wants to hand it over in a year...I don't have a clue what I'll need to do or how I go about handing it over to you."

"I said together. We have time to figure it out."

"Thank you."

Because what he just laid out is everything I want and more than I can hope for. Especially after making up my mind regarding my father's proposal.

I'll step in with the condition he leaves Lucas alone. He's a child and I want him to enjoy that the way I never did. To just be happy and for Matteo to be there when he needs him.

To show up at baseball games and practice because from my understanding, the kid is very good.

To show up for school functions.

To show up just because he wants to see his kid and decides to kidnap him for the afternoon to go and goof off.

I want that for my brother. I honest to God do, and with Casper offering me the world at my feet, I can do this. I'll have him to lean on. To take over because that would be the best scenario for me.

"I know what I am offering, Gem. I also know that more than anything, you need me here."

"But what about your family?" I'm grasping at straws because what sounds too good to be true usually is. "Your responsibilities?"

How the hell can he just pack up and go when my father married out of duty. The man always acts as if he had a gun to his head when he agreed to that sham of a marriage. "Don't they need you to—"

Casper crosses the tub, silencing me with a finger over my lips. "Breathe, sweet girl. Breathe."

"I'm fine. It's just that I don't understand how you can make a change so grand when my own father abandoned us over duty."

"That's a simple answer." He leans toward me, kneeling by my feet and with his face inches from mine. If I shift just the slightest bit forward, our lips will touch once more. "Focus, Aurora. I'll fuck you after if you behave."

My eyes narrow. "I can always head inside and take care of myself."

"But you won't. You want me to touch you...make you come." He accentuates his point while running his strong hands up my thighs, kneading the pliant flesh until he has my hips once more in his hands. Then, I'm straddling him in the water, my core over his throbbing cock.

"You're cheating." I pout.

"And I need you to pay attention to what I'm going to say." The seriousness in his tone grounds me and I stop, no more teasing or messing around. Instead, I scoot back an inch and closer to his knee, creating some distance.

"Go on."

"Thank you." Casper takes one of my hands in his and brings it to his chest, right over his heart where it pumps fast beneath my palm. "A man in love can do some crazy and stupid things. Sometimes it's a combination of both. Your father does care, Aurora, but circumstances put him in a position where he didn't have a choice. I'm telling you this because when the time comes, I need you to listen to what he has to say. Really listen and try not to judge too harshly when there was more than one player involved."

"What do you know that I don't?"

"That it's time for you two to talk without anger or guilt. For him to tell you the truth."

"You're scaring me."

"There's no need to be scared. I swear that it'll bring you peace and help you heal...and while I want to tell you, that's a conversation best had between the two of you. Trust me."

"I do." My heart knows that this man won't let me down or put me in a position to be hurt. That I *can* trust him if nothing else. "Should I just pop up for a visit or call first?"

"How about we call his secretary after we talk to someone else."

"Who?"

"It's time you meet your new family, Gem."

He had it all set up.

Sneaky, sneaky man.

After getting out of the tub, I rushed inside and straight for the shower without contemplating one very important factor...

I have no clothes here.

Nothing but the dress I wore for the wedding and that's the last thing I wanted to wear when meeting the important people in his life. Which is how he found me forty minutes later inside the bathroom near panic and trying to get ahold of Aliana to come and drop something off.

Problem is, she isn't answering her phone. Two rings and it goes straight to voicemail with that generic recording that most of the population uses for their inbox.

"Pick up, chica. For the love of all things holy...pick up," I hiss into my cell, cursing my luck for getting stuck like this without a backup. Being that the wedding was local, and I was taking an Uber home with Ali, we left our Athleta wear in the dressing room at the church. The priest's secretary told us to do as much and to just come pick it up the following day. Today. "Dammit. Where are you?"

"Everything okay?"

"Jesus!" I grab my chest, holding the towel covering me tightly. "You scared me."

"And you look like you're having a heart attack. What's going on?"

"I don't have anything to wear."

"That's all?"

"What do you mean *that's all*? I'm not meeting your family in the nude."

"Fuck and no. No one sees you but me."

"Possessive much?"

"And?" The man has no shame, even shrugs at me as if to say *so what*. "But to help you with the first part, I already had something brought up. Just come and grab it when you're ready. My cousin already called and should be here in twenty minutes or so."

"You know what? I'm not even going to question a thing." I drop my towel, turn him around, and push the man out the door. "Just lead the way and I'll get dressed."

"You're naked and that's not fair."

"Neither is my freak-out." Reaching down, I pinch his butt hard.

He yelps and swats my hand away. "That hurt."

"Don't be a baby."

"I'm going to fuck that sassiness right out—"

There's a knock at the door followed by a very loud *Oi* that blocks him from any form of retaliation. Serves him right, and I pinch him one last time after grabbing the bag on the bed and running back to the safety of the bathroom.

———

WE'RE SITTING in the penthouse overlooking the Chicago skyline and silence hangs in the air. Casper just told them his plans. His desire to move to the States and help me run the soon to be renamed Cancio empire. It's the one thing I will go to war over.

What's fair is fair, and it won't just be my father anymore. It'll be a mixture of the two; the Jameson name will be just as attached and none more important than the other.

We will be one.

He didn't make some long-winded speech or gave them multiple reasons why either.

Not at all. Casper is a straight-to-the-point, take-him-or-leave-him kind of man, and I appreciate that if no one else does.

Callum is across from us, his face impassive and eyes on me. "And how do you feel about this, Miss Conte? How do you feel about my cousin coming to live in the States? Why won't *you* move to England?"

"Watch it, Callum. Don't get ballsy on me—you more than anyone should know I won't hesitate to shoot."

"Let her answer."

"She doesn't need to."

"I'm right fucking here," I hiss out, standing from my seat beside Casper and moving to the center of the room. "Callum, watch the condescending tone. All right?" Then I shift my eyes to the man I love. "Casper, I'm not a child nor do I need to be spoken for...let me say my piece."

Both men sit back and look at me while I turn my attention to Jameson Sr. He's an older version of his son with a sweet face, but I see the pain that lingers in his eyes. The sadness.

"I'm going to take this moment to extend my condolences to you, Mr. Jameson. What happened to your wife is horrible, and I'm truly sad that I will never get the chance to meet Casper's mother and tell her that I love her son." From his side of the video screen, he swallows hard and nods. The first hint of a smile appears on his lips since the video call began. "Now, as for Callum's question, which was rude by the way, my answer is simple...I cannot leave the Conte House. That place is all I have left of my own mother—her legacy—and I will continue it. As for Casper moving here? When he told me, I was shocked, happy, confused, and so on. I still don't fully understand how he could leave your family to come and help me take over the reins here, but I appreciate it more than you could ever understand. I also hope that this will be the start of a strong alliance between the two families and we can work as one to grow as an empire. Because make no mistake, I might not want to be involved in the day to day, but I will have a seat at the table. I will be made aware of important decisions and my vote will count...will be higher than anyone's outside of Casper. Is that clear enough, or do I need to say a little more?"

"No. That's enough." Callum stands from his seat and walks over to me, extending his hand. "Please accept my apologies if I offended you. I love that bloke and just want him happy."

"Accepted and forgotten."

"Well, I guess there's only one thing left to say after that." His father gives me a nod full of respect and then claps his hand once. All the men stand at that and look at me. All wearing the same shit-eating grin on their faces. "Welcome to the family, Aurora."

Chapter 32
CASPER

I T'S LATE IN THE evening when the arsehole leaves and I'm alone with my Gem once more. Callum has plans he's not divulging and to be honest, I'm not worrying over it. When he's ready, he'll come find me.

Until then, I'm going to enjoy the next few days with Aurora before leaving for London. Because while Callum accepted the position to take over, I still have a few things to deal with, the main being our contracts and having a meeting with certain suppliers.

This merging of families will work for all involved and could be very profitable. Matteo has a lot of businesses, legal ones like the real estate firm where his head office is located.

The man is good with the housing market, but more importantly moves a lot of money each month through it: bonuses, client gifts, and the cocaine he peddles through those same avenues.

I've done my research, and the arse is smart.

While he does buy, flip, and sell a lot or properties—he also has a high turn-around for failed negotiations. While to most that would be a red flag to never work with him, it's the opposite, really; those checks that go through his bank account with large sums and fall through are how he moves his product.

Those home showings are nothing more than a pickup and delivery.

And the businessman in me likes that. A lot.

Easy and once learned could be implemented across the globe through different partnerships, Miami and Vegas being the main two that come to mind outside of the Boston/London union. One is a large-quantity buyer and the other transports across state lines and into Mexico for me.

And while her father isn't retiring this very moment, it's never too soon to start putting your ducks in a row when it comes to a change in power like that. There are things Gem needs to learn. That she can only understand from a hands-on approach.

"You're thinking awfully loud in there," Aurora says, giggling as she taps the top of my head with her small fist. "Are you having second thoughts?"

"No. Not at all." Turning my head, I meet her eyes beside me on the bed. She's fresh out of the shower and as naked as I am, scent sweet and feeling like the softest silk beneath my hand. I can't stop myself from reaching out and caressing her arm and lower to her hip where her hand lies. "Just planning. Figuring out in my head how to make this merger happen quickly and without incident, because there's always some wanker that has a problem with change."

"You think we'll have some resistance?"

"Possibly, but I'll be bringing half of my men back here with me. Including the one that works for you."

Her brows do that adorable pucker in the middle that makes her look grumpy. "What are you talking about? I don't have anyone—"

"I put a bodyguard on you the very day you tried to sneak out of my house after the night we met." Gem looks at me like she's not understanding, and I lean over to kiss her cheek. "Sweetheart, just because I haven't been around doesn't mean I left you alone. You've always had someone there ready to intervene if necessary and he quite likes you, so it works out."

"He likes me. You've been watching out for me?"

I nod, happy that she's not screaming at me. "His name is Alexander, and he's the older gentleman that drove you to the hotel where you later met with your father."

"So then you know about Dominic and the weird detective who came to my—"

"I do. Does that bother you?" Turning onto my side, I bring her thigh over my hip and pull her close. Her naked flesh is against mine, though this time it's in a comforting gesture. This is something she needs to know and accept, more so as she steps into her new role. Aurora might not want to be the head of the soon-to-be-renamed Cancio family, but her role will bring just as much attention.

People who've always wondered about her affiliations with the mob will now have concrete proof and will come forward, looking for a handout. It might be money or a connection for something they want...but the rubbish always comes to the surface when it can bring them a gain.

"It should, but it doesn't," she says, her nails tracing the pattern of my chest tattoo. "And I was going to tell you about them. Especially Dominic's behavior. The guy is an asshole, but I'm not afraid of him. He's just another pompous jerk."

"He's a dead man walking."

"You could just fire him?"

"Or I could shoot him."

"We'll revisit him later." Her pointed look only makes my cock twitch and she notices, rolling her eyes. "What about the woman?"

"My hacker tapped into the BPD mainframe and pulled her file. She *is* a detective and has two years of experience under her belt. However, her quest for fame is your father's case."

"Samantha told me about it, but I didn't want to believe her."

"Samantha?"

"His ex-wife. She came to see me while I was in Boston." Gem is pensive and I don't interrupt her. Anything she remembers could help us get to the bottom of this bloody mess sooner. "It just doesn't make any sense to me that out of everyone, I'm the one she tries to interview. What about Samantha or Lucas? Associates and that one senile brother he has that is around from time to time?"

"Uncle? Matteo has a brother?"

"Half-brother, and the guy is weird. Has been put on a seventy-two-hour hold more than once."

"This didn't show up in the police file Ezra has been working on for days. None of those people you just named do." Tapping her thigh, I wait until she moves and I grab my phone, sending a quick email to Ezra with the new information. Something isn't right. More so when the only name that repeatedly shows up is hers.

That, and we are missing the identity of their informant. I have a feeling this is an inside job.

―――――

"WHAT DO you mean it was seized?" I hiss into the phone, pacing the length of the penthouse terrace. I'm furious. Wanting to break something, but Gem is inside sleeping, and I don't want her to worry. "When did this happen?"

"A few hours ago." Thiago's voice is gruff, thick with sleep. It's barely seven in the morning there and he's been at the Port of Miami since six thirty. "Don't worry. We got the motherfucker responsible and he's being taken to his room as we speak."

Running an agitated hand down my face, I close my eyes for a moment and think. Analyze the situation.

Transporting through state lines isn't my usual mode of delivery, unless it's a pickup from Mexico to the US and I have a courier for that, but this is different. The product is already sold, and Thiago's buyer is waiting.

This client has already paid him half of its street value and needs it for a week-long party he's throwing in the Bahamas. CEOs of Fortune 500 companies imbibe more than your average citizen and harder. They want to get high, have sex, then repeat the cycle all over again and for extended periods of time.

Hell, look at the little blue pill industry. Who buys that?

Old men with money and in copious quantities so they can fuck their newest wife like the pool boy can.

"I'll be there soon," I say after a minute, feeling her near but I don't turn around. Not until I get hold of my anger. "Please send a car to take me straight there."

"Not a problem, Jameson." The sirens of a cop car become louder on his end, and then it shuts off. "How's it looking, Officer Alejos?"

"It's hot, Thiago. You shouldn't be anywhere near here, especially if you just got out."

"And I'll stay out. Luna will kill me if I go back."

"She talking to you yet?"

"Since when have you known your niece to be anything but hardheaded." The man laughs at Thiago's statement, but quiets just as fast when his radio goes off. There are a few codes that come through, a woman letting him know there's a robbery in progress and units are needed.

"I'm out, Rivera, but I'll let you know. The initial report should be ready by tonight and it'll show what they know. You'll have the upper hand, but the window is small. Act fast." The siren blares a few seconds later and then quiets as he drives away.

"You heard him?" he asks as my girl wraps her arms around my midsection. "We need to move fast while they'll be preoccupied. Question is; how are we replacing? How long will it take?"

"Buy me a few days." My fingers entwine with hers, holding them tight against my midsection. "There's enough in Chicago thanks to a gift from Asher and it's here in a warehouse. I'll have it driven down."

"Perfect. Shoot me a message with your flight info."

"Will do." I hang up and turn around to look down at Aurora. "Did you hear?"

"I did."

"I'm sorry."

"Not your fault." Rising onto the tip of her toes, she bites my chin. "Now, let's go back inside and book your flight so I can take you back to bed before you leave. I'm thinking you owe me that wicked tongue between my thighs as an apology."

"Done," I growl, throwing her over my shoulder and heading back inside. She wants me again and I'll give her my mouth, fingers, and cock.

It's time for my breakfast.

"RISE AND SHINE, ARSEHOLE," I say, kicking the man responsible for all of this. He stirs, grunting a little as he comes to, but I don't have time for slow awareness.

My next blow comes from a closed fist straight to his jaw, causing a piece of tooth to fly out.

We're in the Rivera home in Miami. They own an entire street, no neighbors, and have a small building where they hold detainees for transport to Cuba. It's away from the main house, their adorable mum, and completely soundproof. I'm really loving the space.

It gives me ideas for my future home with Gem.

The punch to the face catches his attention and he comes to, searching for the culprit. Those muddy brown eyes land on me and widen, and as blood rushes down his lip and chin, he looks to his left and finds Thiago. "What's going on?" he asks, fear radiating from his every pore, more so when he takes in Ivan to the right and Callum behind him.

Surrounded on all sides and tied to a kitchen stool, he's bare chested and hunching over a bit, hands and feet bound by rope through the wooden legs.

If he moves wrong, he'll tip over.

If he pisses me off to quickly, I'll slit his throat.

Sitting forward in my chair, I get in his face. "How have you been, Mr. Arroyo?"

"Why am I here?" His eyes keep shifting between myself and the raging lion beside him. Thiago's looking at him through narrowed eyes and a snarling lip—it curls over his teeth at the corner while he chews on a toothpick. "Mr. Rivera, what's going on? I—"

He's cut off by another strike. This time it comes from Ivan and the four-inch blade in his hand. A quick jab and it's embedded deep into his right side, causing him to choke on a scream.

Pulling the blade out, he cleans it on the man's bare skin. "Answer Mr. Jameson when he asks you a direct question."

"Mr. J-Jameson." His voice breaks while his limbs begin to shake. *Good, he knows who I am.* "This is a mistake."

"People who usually say that without any prompting or accusations being presented are usually guilty." My eyes shift to Callum who quickly does as Ivan did, stabbing him in the back area, near the kidneys. "Now, let's try this again, shall we?"

"Yes," he cries out, body wanting to bow in on itself, but the bindings don't let him. Instead, every move he makes creates a shooting pain that races through his limbs. Causes more rivulets of red to stain the floor below.

"Good boy." And I pet his head like I do my dogs back in London. *I need to buy a house in both Chicago and Boston...bring my boys with me.* "How are you today?"

"Scared. In pain."

"Honest. I like that. Don't you, Thiago?" The man just grunts in affirmation, eyes hard on the cunt responsible. "We'll take that as a yes."

"Now, do you know why you're here?"

"No...*fuck*...okay!" Thiago chose his spot with precision, stabbing him in the thigh and with the blade inside to the handle, he twists his wrist, tearing through the muscle in the most painful way. This isn't a straight cut; it's jagged and rough. "Please, I'll tell you what you need to know."

"So speak. Tell me why you snitched to the feds, got our shipment seized, and then cost us a lot of money?" I tick each one with the tip of my karambit, slicing the very tip of my pointer as I do. "Talk."

"It was to get you out of Chicago."

"The fuck did you just say?" I'm hearing myself talk, but it sounds far away. Fury ignites within my veins, my worry for Aurora overtaking all of my senses. "You have ten bloody seconds to explain yourself."

"The Savino family paid me a lot of money to—" I don't need to hear him finish—I've already slit his throat and I'm rushing out of the room. The other three are following close behind as I leave the building with my mobile in hand.

"Call Malcolm and tell him to take her to his house." Callum moves past me, already dialing while Thiago places a hand on my shoulder to stop me. "Not now."

"What's going on? How can we help?"

"They're going after my girl, brother."

"Then we're *all* going to Chicago, Jameson. Nobody touches family."

Chapter 33
AURORA

"SO," I say, drawing out the word as I stare at the rearview mirror and the man reflected there.

"So," he replies.

"Interesting to see you again."

"I saw this coming," Alexander says. He's driving me to work. It was a promise I made to Casper before he left for Miami, and the man can be very persuasive. With his mouth between my thighs, he can get me to agree to just about anything and knows it. "Besides, have you not noticed just how determined he is when wanting something?"

"Touché. But in my defense—" I'm interrupted by the ringing of my cell phone. It's a Boston area code and I pick up. "Hello?"

"Aurora?" It's a woman, and the voice is familiar.

"Yeah. Who's this?"

"Oh! Umm, it's Lisa...your father's secretary."

"Good morning, Lisa." Alexander eyes me from the rear view, brow raised high. I put my hand over the phone's receiver. "My dad's secretary. Not sure what she wants."

He nods, and Lisa on the phone clears her throat a few times. "Miss Conte? Are you there?"

"Sorry. You caught me mid coffee order." It's the first thing that comes to mind and when Alexander snickers, I roll my eyes. "How can I help you?"

"I apologize for the interruption, but your father would like to invite you to lunch today. He's in Chicago, and wants to know if you're free from twelve to two?"

"Why is my father in Chicago?"

"There's some commercial property he's looking into buying near West Hubbard Street and would like to see you."

"Why didn't he call me himself?" Even at his most neglectful, Dad never involved his staff. This is weird. "Better yet, tell him to call me. I'll make the time if he does."

"Please don't get me in trouble." And it's the fear in her voice that makes me pause. The last thing I want to do is take my annoyance out on an innocent bystander.

"Fine. Tell him to meet me for lunch at the Mexican place. He knows which one."

Upon arrival at the Conte House, I dig into my daily tasks. Catching up on email takes up most of my morning, and shortly before noon Alexander taps on my office door, ready to take me to meet my father for lunch.

"Go get yourself some lunch," I tell Alexander, exiting the vehicle in the back parking lot area. I'm but a few feet from the door and my father should already be inside waiting. Not that Matteo bothered to call me. Lisa was the one to confirm the place and time an hour later.

"No," he says without pause.

"I'm safe with my father," I argue.

Alexander's expression is dead serious as he regards me. "No."

"Yes."

"Miss Conte, I have strict orders from Mr. Jameson to not let you out of my sight. Let's not ruin my track record here."

"You weren't there in Boston," I point out, remembering how uncomfortable Dominic made me feel. "Where were you then?"

His gaze holds a hint of something. A secret he feels ready to spill. "The room next to yours is a storage dump-all where your father shoved whatever his ex-wife didn't take. I was in there, gun up and ready to shoot, but you handled yourself impeccably."

My eyes widen as I stare at him. "Wow." Once again, Casper amazes me. I had no idea Alexander had followed me a thousand miles to keep watch. More than that, he managed to get inside without detection in a home that should be a fortress with how serious my father takes his security. He can be a bit paranoid at times.

"He cares. Has from the very start."

My lips pull up into a smile. "I do too, you know."

"And I think you shouldn't." It comes from behind me, and before I can take in Alexander's expression, fear locks me in place. Everything happens around me in slow motion; one minute we're holding a normal conversation, and the next I'm being pushed out of the way as a gun goes off.

My head hits the hard pavement, bouncing twice, and my vision blurs a bit.

"Run!" It's my guard's voice I hear, and it snaps me out of my momentary shock. More bullets fly. Different directions. So much noise. And as I try to reach for my Glock within my purse, I'm being yanked up by the hair, forcibly shoved and made to face Alexander's kneeling form on the ground.

A strike to my cheek snaps my head to the side. A cry leaves me as pain floods in from the impact, radiating through my face.

But that pain helps me focus; it brings my attention to the woman to my right as she unloads another shot into Alexander's body.

He falls back and the gun slips from his hand.

There's no time to react, to attempt to get away—there's just a pinprick to my arm.

The last thing I remember is saying her name.

"Detective Santos?"

I DON'T KNOW where I am.

I don't know what time it is.

I can't see anything but darkness all around me.

Everything is slowly coming back into focus and my body hurts —my head feels as though it's going to explode.

Shifting to draw my hands to my temples, I realize I'm bound and the continuous movement all around me is that of a car. Or van.

I can't see, and the scratch of cloth across my skin tells me it's because of a blindfold covering my eyes. But more worrisome than anything, what has me near tears, is the hand slowly stroking my hair as if I were a pet.

An unknown caress that sends a chill down my spine while I lie as still as I can.

"I do love a woman who plays hard to get. Breaking them is much more rewarding," a male voice says and it's familiar, has a certain lilt to it that makes me cringe, and that's a huge mistake. He notices, letting out a low chuckle before there's another pinprick on my arm. "Sleep, Miss Conte. We'll be playing a special game soon enough."

"He'll find me," is all I manage to say before it all goes black.

I'M ON A BED. It's comfortable and smells clean, but definitely not one I know. That, and I'm not a fan of the harsh citrusy scent inside the room.

The more awareness looms on the edges of my subconscious, the colder I become, and the thin blanket thrown over my body doesn't help much. I don't move, though, lying completely still in order to pick up noises all around me.

It's quiet, but I don't trust it.

I don't trust anything at the moment.

It's fight or flight, and I need to keep my wits about me if I'm going to escape these lunatics. Especially the man.

There's something familiar about him, a natural disgust, that reminds me of Dominic. Even his voice held a similar tone.

"Open your eyes, Aurora." My eyes snap open and my worst nightmare is confirmed. "Hello, beautiful. Ready to get married?"

Chapter 34
CASPER

Message received at 12:00 p.m.

Mr. Jameson, I've spotted Cancio's second-in-command lurking around her apartment building. He didn't see me, but the bloke walked up and down the street twice, phone in his ear, and then left. I'm on my way to the Conte House now, and will be calling Alexander shortly. I'll await your call on how to proceed.

Message received @12:30 p.m.

Sir, I need you to call me. Aurora went to meet with her father for lunch and has gone missing. Alexander has been shot, two to the chest and one to the arm. Police are involved, happened outside a Mexican restaurant, and he's being attended at Northwestern... Casper, we don't know where Aurora is.

Message received @12:40 p.m.

Sir, it's Ezra. I was able to get through the encryption and found some alarming facts. Detective Santos is none other than Antonella Savino. Her alias was given by the department head in BPD, a family member of Matteo's deceased mother-in-law, her last name before marriage was Savino. Giada Savino at that. This is larger than we suspected, more so because she and her brother, Dominic, are the older children of one Samantha Cancio. They were before their marriage occurred and were raised by a family friend—away from Matteo, Aurora, and Lucas. Samantha is also the informant for this case. I'll be emailing you the proof shortly.

T HAT'S WHAT GREETS me as the plane touches down in Chicago. It's been five hours since the son of a bitch in Miami let me know that it was all a setup. Five hours since my world was taken from me, and I want to kill every motherfucker that so much as breathes in my direction.

No one knows where Gem is. They've disappeared.

"We'll find her, Casper." Callum squeezes my shoulder, jumping into an all-black SUV waiting for me. Jeffrey is behind the wheel and he nods in greeting, slowly pulling away from the curb as Thiago and

Ivan jump into another vehicle. I don't know who the driver is, nor do I care, but my guess is my employees knew I'd want my space at the moment.

I'm not thinking rationally. The anger is consuming me.

"Head to his flat," Callum tells Jeffrey and the man nods. My place here is not that far from Aurora's, maybe a ten-minute drive at the most, and I need to head there first. "Do I bring Archie here? I'll call and have him on a plane if you think we need him."

"No. Leave him with Dad just in case." Which reminds me. "Has anyone called her father? Where the fuck is he?"

"No," Jeffrey interjects from the front. "And from my under-standing, the one that called to set up the lunch meeting was the secretary. Alex was semi-conscious when I got to the restaurant, was just being put on a gurney, and he told me this. Dominic and Antonella have her."

"I want their blood on my hands," I ground out.

"Ezra's doing his thing and says he'll have something soon. He's tracking Aurora's phone signal. It's last ping was near the Missouri border."

"They're heading west." It's not a question.

"Seems so."

"Okay. Okay." I need to get home and prepare. "Get her father on the phone for me. He needs to get his arse here, and the secretary has some explaining to do."

THE SPECIAL REPORT bulletin has been running on the bottom of the television screen over and over for the past few hours. It's the same for every major news network.

And that explains where her father has been.

So far, they have no leads or motives, and his secretary is with the police. She was the last to be with him, just ten minutes prior to him leaving the building, and is being interrogated.

My money is on her being involved somehow.

I look at Callum and tilt my head in the direction of the balcony. He follows me, leaving the other two inside, passing me a cigarette before lighting his own.

"Something isn't right with that," Callum says.

"No. It isn't." Pulling the smoke into my lungs, I hold it for a few seconds and exhale. "Have you heard from Ezra? Has Samantha been found?" Because she's also gone missing, while Lucas is staying at his dad's home. The staff there is watching him —keeping him away from the news—until I know what we're facing.

Funny enough, they called me when the first report released, telling me they were under strict instructions to take direction from me—or Aurora. No questions asked. Period.

"Still gone and—" We're interrupted by the Face Time application on my mobile. I hit accept at once. "What do you have for me?"

Ezra comes onto the screen from his home office, hair a mess and bags under his eyes. "Sir, I have visual from an airport in St. Louis where Antonella caught a cheap flight out, and the destination is Vegas. The name it was booked under matches her work I.D. and Casper; she wasn't alone. Samantha, Cancio's ex-wife, boarded the same flight under the name Giada Savino."

"Both heading to Vegas?"

"Yes. It was a direct flight." There's an alert coming from his screen then, a loud blaring sound, and he looks away from me. Placing the phone down, I watch as his fingers fly over his keyboard and then a wicked grin overtakes his features. "Gotcha."

"What's going on, mate? Did you—"

Ezra cuts me off, his eyes scanning the screen in front of him. "He chartered a small aircraft in St. Louis after going their separate ways and has now been in the air for two hours. Destination is also Las Vegas."

Finally. Direction to my Gem. "You're getting a bonus for all these extra hours."

"Not needed. Just kill the bloody bastards...they deserve every last bit of karma coming their way."

THE BRIGHT LIGHTS of the Las Vegas sign welcome us six hours later. After hanging up with Ezra, we got things done quickly. A change of clothes and out the door—my only pit stop was to her flat, where I grabbed something for Gem to change into.

After the day she's had, my girl will need the comfort.

> They're staying at the Venetian. Top floor. ~Ezra

> The credit card on hold for the hotel is Aurora's ~Ezra

Typing out a quick "Thanks" I pocket my phone and walk out with the others. I called in a favor before boarding the plane back in Chicago to my colleague in Vegas.

Julio Villanueva is not a trafficker but a runner, and his MC is my go-between for the States and the largest Cartel south of the border. He knows people. Knows the city like the back of his hand and can get me anything I need for my buyers overseas.

Or, like now, he can find a few unmarked cars and the weapons I need.

"Good to see you, Jameson." He pulls me into a one-arm hug. "Wish it was under better circumstances."

"Me too." Walking to the trunk of the first car, I hold my hand in the air waiting for the keys—he tosses, and I catch them, popping the back using the key fob. The compartment is fully loaded. Inside, I have everything I need and a few extras: guns, bulletproof vests, magazines, cans of gasoline, and even a machete or two. "Thank you, mate. This is perfect."

"Do you know where they have her?"

"Why do people come to Vegas?" I ask instead, slamming the trunks closed. "Why is Sin City so bloody popular to tourists?"

"Gambling—"

"And bullshit wedding chapels with twenty-four-hour service." My mobile pings then with an incoming text from Gem's phone and I pull it out, opening my messages to find my suspicions confirmed.

There, with her back against a car door and with tears in her eyes, is my girl. They put a cheap veil on her and a sash that reads *Bride-to-be* over the clothes she was taken in.

But more important than that, Julio beside me cocks his gun. "I know exactly where they are. It's fifteen minutes from here and behind a dingy strip mall away from the main casino area. It's the part of Vegas most don't see. The fucker who owns it will marry her against her will. Suit up. I'll take you."

Chapter 35
CASPER

THE PLACE IS just as Julio described.

Filthy.

Bad area.

A low-level criminal's playground.

The chapel with its neon sign half working is isolated at the very end of this street and away from the normal traffic route—no walkways or performers working the passing crowds.

The place is perfect for the illicit, but today it will meet its end.

Outside the small building, we park our cars, closing in on the two already in the attached lot. There's a newer-model Mercedes and a Toyota Prius, both tags from Nevada, and Julio makes quick work of slashing the tires with the two men he brought with him.

They'll be staying outside and acting as guards because one way or another, this little family and the shop's owner won't be making it out alive.

Taking my gun from the back of my trousers, I walk up the small concrete pathway that leads toward two steps and the main entrance. The entrance is locked, and I stepped aside so Callum can shoot the lock using his silencer.

I chose not to use one. I want them to hear me.

A quick *pop pop* and he pushes the double doors open with his foot, leaving them open wide. There's no movement from inside, no running or cursing, and we walk quietly through the small lobby and right into the room where an older gentleman sits at the organ playing the traditional wedding march.

Nobody's standing, but there is a woman—familiar in her role as Aurora's stepmother—all but dragging her down the narrow aisle while a group of ten random strangers watch this all unfold.

"Don't do this, Samantha. Let me go!"

"Shut the fuck up, brat. I should've had you disposed of years ago."

No one steps in.

No one moves a muscle to help a crying woman.

And yet, when I raise my gun and shoot the officiant in the neck, all hell breaks loose.

Now, they run. Like bloody cockroaches, they try and scatter but one by one begin to fall as bullets rain down on the sick bunch. Men and women, I no longer care as I aim and shoot.

The man on the organ.

The fucker sitting near the back drinking a beer from a paper bag.

Dominic's sister who comes toward me with her own gun raised, firing off a bullet that grazes my sides as I reciprocate. "You had to make this difficult. You should've chosen me."

The difference between her and I—I didn't miss. I also don't respond to her asinine bullshit.

Antonella Savino falls to the ground with a chest wound, bleeding out fast but still trying to reach for the gun that fell from her hand a few feet away. She's determined if nothing else, dragging herself, and I follow behind her as she grunts in pain. It only takes a minute or two at best for her fingers to grip the handle, and when she does, I shoot the back of her skull, killing her instantly.

Then, there's a sound I've come to enjoy over the years. Truly savor.

A loud screech that rents the air then, an agonized yell, and I meet the eyes of someone who should've known better. Who should've protected my Gem as if she were her own.

Prim and proper looking, her face is pinched tight—pure agony in her expression—before she takes off running in a ridiculous pair of heels.

"Ivan," I yell, and he looks over. "The mom. Through the door on the left."

"Got it." Then he takes off, and as Thiago and Callum make quick work of everyone else—the entire staff on the clock included —I walk toward a scared Gem and a nearly pissing himself Dominic.

No one has touched them. They left him for me.

"Let her go."

"I'll kill her."

"No, you won't." My eyes meet Aurora's hazel ones and I smile. "Close your eyes and walk toward the sound of my voice, sweetheart." The last body falls to the ground and the men with me turn and point at him. "Trust me, baby. Nothing will happen to you."

"He's got a gun to my back," she whimpers, but I also take in how her shoulders pull back a bit. How she's fighting the natural instinct to crumble in fear.

"He'll die before a single bullet dislodges from his gun."

"I'm right here, you piece of shit."

Ignoring his idiotic cry for attention, I wink at Gem. She smiles back at me; it's a tiny one, but there, and it grows just a little bit more when a crying banshee in the form of her stepmother is dragged in a minute later.

"Nico! Baby!"

"Mom!" Dominic yells out, and it's his last mistake because he pulls the gun away from the only person keeping him alive.

The moment he does, Gem ducks and begins to crawl away as every gun goes off, emptying their rounds into his body. From the barrage he flies back against the wall, pulsating against the shattered mirror behind him.

And when the last bullet leaves my gun, hitting his mouth and ripping a part of his face wide open, his lifeless body falls to the ground riddled with holes. His blood is on the ground and splattered across the walls. His bullshit legacy, the one they were forcibly trying to create, will be nothing but a memory because in the very next moment, I have Gem back in my arms.

She's all that matters. My entire world is back where it belongs, and I never want to be apart again.

"From now on..." my lips skim down her temple and cheek "...where you go, I go, and vice versa."

"Deal." Gem pulls back and tilts her head up, locking those watery eyes with mine, and the world fades away. "I knew you were going to come for me."

"Always, Gem. I'll always be but two steps behind you." Then I'm kissing her. Completely losing myself in her taste in the middle of a corrupt wedding chapel littered with dead bodies. I ignore the hysterical stepmother and her pleas while she's being removed. I ignore someone pouring gasoline throughout the room until we need to leave.

And yet, I'll always remember the very moment I fell in love with her all over again.

Once outside, Aurora walks up to each man and gives them a hug, the last being me—she held me tighter. Longer. And when she pulls back, Gem holds out her hand for the box of matches Julio had given me when we exited the building.

"Let me do the honors," she says, and I couldn't be prouder.

In that moment, I know she'll be okay. That she'll stand beside me through anything the world sends our way.

WE LEAVE Vegas without looking back two days after seeing the others off. Thiago and Ivan flew back to Miami that same evening while Callum disappeared last night after dinner.

We don't know where he went or why, but the man had a look of determination that rivaled mine when it comes to Gem.

On the news, the incident was reported as a gang-affiliated crime, a local dispute between the owners of the shady chapel and a meth ring that left a total of fifteen dead. The authorities are asking the community to come forward with any information that can help locate those responsible, but no one will say a word.

Not when they fear becoming the next victim on the five o'clock news. Not when the bodies were burned to a crisp, and the medical examiner is having to pull dental records to identify each one.

"You are thinking hard again, Mr. Jameson?"

"More like missing you, Mrs. Jameson." I hum and look over, catching her wicked grin a second before she unclips her seatbelt, ignoring the sign. Then, she's up and shaking those hips, exaggerating the four steps it takes to make it across the aisle and into my lap where she burrows her face into the crook of my neck. "Are we a little needy after our nap, love?"

"Always want you close."

"I love you, Gem." Bringing her face up to mine with the tips of two fingers, I stare deeply into her hazel eyes. Let her feel the full weight of my words—almost the exact same ones— before saying I do in our private ceremony inside the Bellagio with no one but Callum in attendance.

"Gem, since the moment I saw your beautiful face across the room from me, I've been yours. Completely and irrevocably owned." Callum snickers beside us and I subtly flip him off, making Aurora giggle. *And because I'm a man with zero patience, I bend down quickly and steal a kiss. She gasps and I wink, squeezing her hands once before continuing.* *"You make me want to be a better version of myself each day, and I hope that over the next fifty or more years, I can make you proud to be my wife. I promise to always be faithful, honest, and more than anything else...to be your best friend and partner in crime. I love you, beautiful, and I can't wait to spend the rest of my life waking up to your smile every day that the Lord blesses me with life."*

We got married our way.

Privately, and inside the room we stayed in with an officiant that for a few extra grand made the early morning trip to see us. She wore a simple cotton dress I brought with me in a pale lavender color, and I wore a button-down and a pair of trousers, both in black. Our rings are basic and not the ones I'll have her design with me and the family jeweler, however, if I go by the smile on her face each time she sees the solid band, I'd say these aren't going anywhere.

That I'll just have to find a way to incorporate them into the new set.

"I can't wait to start this next chapter of our lives, Casper. To move on from the bad and build a new world together."

"You rocked my world in a way I wasn't prepared for, Mr. Jameson. You were determined, hardheaded..." I couldn't help but laugh at that *"...and ready to bulldoze your way through all of my preconceived notions of what a man like you* is *and not who you are. And I couldn't love you more for that. For not giving up on me when I was lost and afraid. For not walking away when I made things tough."* Aurora's voice becomes thick then, her emotions rising to the surface as I fight back my own. These words are the greatest gift she could ever have given me. *"You've always had my back, let me lean on you, and now it's my turn to show you that I got you. That I'm where*

you can rest your head at night because I will protect you just as fiercely. I love you, Casper. Love you with every bit of my heart, and I promise to always be faithful, honest, and stand by your side through the good and bad."

And I believe her. Wholeheartedly.

Because my girl is strong. Her heart is pure.

And while the road to forgetting this entire ordeal won't be easy, she showed her determination by turning this negative into a positive. This, as crazy as it may sound, is where our life together begins.

We still have a mess to deal with back home and with her father, but we'll be okay. She'll get through the trauma, will come out stronger, and I will cheer her on every fucking step of the way because that's what love does to you. You live for your other half and become what they need at any given moment.

As long as we have each other, everything else can go and fuck itself.

Epilogue 1

AURORA

FOUR MONTHS LATER...

"DAD, THIS CAN wait. She isn't going anywhere," I say, trying to make the stubborn man back down. There's no reason, no value, in seeing Samantha at all. For me, she could rot away for the rest of her life right where she is.

A location that only Casper knows about and is keeping it that way. He's handling her. He's delivering her punishment for what he considers to be an unforgivable crime: touching me.

"No, Roe. It's time that you learned the truth on a few things.

You need to hear the real story of how this mess began," he grunts from the back seat. He's still in some pain. The pothole we hit isn't helping, and yet he still wants to do this. "I need you to see...to understand why things happened as they did. To realize that I do love you and always have."

His words stop me, and I look toward the man driving us to her location. His words to me out on that private terrace slam into my consciousness and I nod.

A man in love can do some crazy and stupid things. Sometimes it's a combination of both. Your father does care, Aurora, but circumstances put him in a position where he didn't have a choice. I'm telling you this because when the time comes, I need you to listen to what he has to say. Really listen and try not to judge too harshly when there was more than one player involved.

Casper asked me all those months ago to listen. To really listen and try to understand that life isn't always a cup of sugar sprinkled with rainbows, and I get that now. After Vegas, I see the world differently.

It's one thing to know what people do and another to witness it firsthand. To be made a pawn in someone's sick game.

Turning in my seat, I look at my father in the eye. "Okay. If you need to do this, then we will go, but I need you to understand something before we enter this building...I already know you love me. You showed it by discharging yourself out of a Boston hospital against their wishes and flying to see me in Chicago three days after you woke up. You proved it when you grabbed me and hugged me tight, begging for forgiveness for a crime you didn't commit—"

"I am to blame, kid. This mess began a long time ago, and it's because of love for family that I didn't do what I should have." And that right there is his demon. The cross that he shoulders.

"Dad, I don't care—"

"We're here." Casper's voice cuts through our conversation and we both turn to look out of the car's window. The place is not what I thought it would be. Not at all, but I can see the why behind his actions.

Her home is nothing more than a private facility that takes in those that society won't. Those that, for the right price, will lock you away in a padded room with nothing but a mattress in the corner. Most people don't know that this asylum still exists; it's not open to the public, but for criminals, the rules change.

They bend and don't break.

"Nice," my father says, opening his door and stepping out without help. I glare at that, but the man waves me off and walks toward the entrance where a large man dressed in scrubs awaits.

"Name?"

"Giada Savino and the code is 1982," Casper says, stopping behind me.

He types the information into his tablet and then gives us a smile. "Thank you for your patronage, Mr. Jameson. Please enjoy your visit."

"Cheers." Then, he's guiding me forward without a word. Dad follows; he's looking around the place and chuckling to himself now and then. The place is creepy and nothing holds humor, but I can see how having a woman like *her* here is hilarious.

She went from everything to nothing in the blink of an eye.

At the end of the long hall to the right, there's an elevator and we take that to the fourth floor. The door dings, we step outside, and right across from the only way out is her room. And more than that, she's standing there looking at us through the small window.

I wave and her scowl deepens.

Casper takes a step forward, and she rushes away like the dogs of hell are after her.

He's the first to step through, and I take in the empty room with nothing but a mattress on the floor. *How the mighty have fallen.*

"Take a seat." My husband points at a small dinette set near the opposite wall that I didn't take into account, I've been too busy looking in the general direction of where she is. "That was placed here for your use only."

I take the offered seating while my father doesn't. Instead, he walks slowly over to his ex-wife and when in reach, caresses her cheek. "How are you, Samantha? How's this life treating you, princess?"

"Fuck you," she sneers and tries to slap his hand away, but that's a mistake on her part. Before she can take in her next lungful of air, my father has her throat in his hands and is squeezing, slamming her body hard against the wall behind them.

She turns red right away, her panicked eyes looking to me of all people for help.

"You do not look at her," Matteo snarls; his demeanor is one I've never seen before. Never had to experience. "How fucking dare you...after everything I gave up helping you...to save your life and that of my brother."

"Your brother?" I ask myself, not realizing I said it aloud until Dad turns his head toward me.

"I agreed to marry her because of a bounty placed on both you and your mother's head, by her father. See, being the next in line, I was promised to her without my knowledge by our fathers. They wanted to join the families—our underworld dealings with their pharmaceutical company—and take over the global pandemic that was growing at the time for opioids."

"How? But, I... what about Mom!" I'm not making any sense. This information cuts deep—is almost too much at once.

"She knew. I never hid who I was to her and after an attempt was made—"

"They tried to kill her?" I interrupt, angry at the fact that they tried.

"No." His eyes are sad. "They tried to kill you by injection at a routine doctor's appointment. I caught them, and after taking both of you home, I disposed of every employee at that office."

"Then what happened?" Because I need to know. I want to have this hole inside my chest, the one that missed her father growing up, to be sealed. My heart needs to know that he didn't abandon us. Me.

"I went back to the apartment I shared with your mother and found her bags packed. It hurt, but I understood. You were and will always be our greatest achievement, Roe, and above our love, your life came first. We spoke, planned, and made the right moves to keep you safe. If I gave in to their demands, nothing of this world would touch you."

"I'm sorry."

"Don't be. I'm not an angel and this has been my penance."

"But when you took over, why didn't you just come back? Mom would've—"

"When Lucas was born, I made a promise to God and him that I wouldn't fuck that relationship up, Aurora. I couldn't live with another child hating me."

"I don't hate you."

"Thank you." Then, he's turning to look at the woman who is close to turning blue beneath his hand. He eases up but doesn't move. "Now, for the rest of this story—"

"I have a gift," Casper speaks up from the doorway, and I never even saw him move. "This is my early birthday gift to you, Cancio. Enjoy."

No sooner has he said the words that Callum enters, all but dragging a dirty man behind him. A gasp leaves my throat because I know him. I have seen him from time to time over the years, but there's no denying the resemblance between him and my father.

"Ah, Mario." Dad looks at Casper and gives him a smile. The British bastard has officially become his favorite person. "So good to see you."

The edge in his voice causes the man to jerk back, but Callum isn't having that and shoves him forward where he lands on his knees a few feet from his brother. A move that makes whatever her real name is whimper.

Mario's head snaps up and the moment he sees her, rage builds behind his eyes. "Get your hands off her," he sneers, spittle flying from his mouth. "She's mine and you stole her from me! You took everything from me!"

"Did I?" Releasing her, he lets Samantha fall to the ground and turns toward his brother, taking the remaining steps between them. There is no remorse or pause in his actions, but Dad pulls a gun from the waistband of his pants and forces it into his mouth. "Because I didn't want to become the head of this family, but you were irresponsible and had a drug habit that would've created problems. You slept with her and got her pregnant. You refused to step forward and let them force me into that sham. You put me in the position to lose it all so your life could be spared, and yet, I did take care of *your* responsibilities and lost my world." *Is he saying that Dominic and Antonella were my cousins? That* they *had kids together?*

"But you offered me an arranged marriage to—"

"I didn't know, kid." The remorse in his expression guts me. "These two pieces-of-shit faked the children's death shortly after they turned fourteen. And I believed her. Bought the tears and screams of pain." Dad turns his eyes back to his brother. The iciness in them makes everyone in the room pause. "Your idiocy has cost me a lot over the years, but I forgave because that's what families do, but trying to overthrow me while touching the one thing I told you to never come near...you crossed the line, brother."

"Please don't. Don't take him from me, too."

"When I married you, I told you to never betray me. I took care of your kids with *him*," he sneers, "as best I could, given the situation. I maintained them while Lisa raised them. I warned you that I'd given my arm to bend once, that I signed my name on that dotted line so that both of you wouldn't be killed, to stay away from my daughter. You didn't listen, and this is your penance." Without another thought, my father pulls the trigger, ending his own brother's life.

His body falls and I'm immune to it. After what he confessed, I'm an emotional ball of a different kind. I'm angry for what they did to us—to my family—but more than that, I see a man who gave up everything to protect me. So that I could live a normal life.

That's a sacrifice most people will never have to make.

That's the most unselfish act a parent can do.

And all I can do in that moment, as his ex-wife crawls over to my uncle's dead body and Dad steps back, is rush forward and hug him tight. I understand. What he did for us... "I love you, Dad. I'm sorry it took me this long to say it back."

Epilogue 2

CASPER

FOUR YEARS LATER...

"**Y**OU TWO WILL have issues with that one," Malcolm says from beside me. We're outside in London's child-hood home barbecuing, waiting for Callum to arrive with Aliana, and for the girls to come downstairs. He's taking too long and is making the wife a wee bit antsy. Then, we have one heavily pregnant woman covering for the other who thinks she's slick and is taking multiple tests upstairs.

This family is crazy but keeps me entertained. Everyone thinks they can keep secrets, but we all know the other too well. Have too many resources at our disposal.

Aurora gave birth to our precious Penelope Bianca Jameson a little over a year ago and has already been wanting another one. She wants a huge family and I do too. With everything that happened, the heartache and obstacles, getting pregnant wasn't easy. Cost a year of tears and frustration for her, but when that little stick held those two pink lines, everything became worth it.

However, what I still don't get—what's beyond my comprehension—is how Gem thinks I wouldn't know? That I don't pay attention.

When it comes to her, I don't miss a single detail. Especially, one as blatant as chugging a gallon of water this morning without rhyme or reason.

"Why do you say that?" I ask, watching Maximus, his son, come closer to my Penelope and I smile. That little dictator-like arse is going to come in helpful when boys come knocking. Heck, he'll save me the time of shooting them myself.

Like now, Thiago's son waddles toward a sleeping Penelope in his mother's arms and Max pulls him away, all but dragging the child by the vest toward the sandbox we put up for the kids yesterday.

We're here for the next three weeks to unwind for a bit and celebrate my woman's birthday. That, and let things die down in Boston. Business is business and a dead body near the Boston harbor will bring forth questions.

Questions, that will be thrown our way because of who the bodies belonged to. Samantha and Lisa—who'd gone missing after being released from her interrogation—were both found dead and tied together last night. Both spent the last few years together inside the asylum as neighbors, like the good little cousins they were, and died by suffocation the night before being found by a worker there.

Good riddance. None of us care.

Even Matteo has moved on and likes the retired life down in Boca. He's popular among the women there and while Aurora finds that disgusting, she agrees he needs to move on.

To find someone.

"I'm going to set up a bodyguard business for Max and I'll charge you for him."

"Will he know how to use a gun?" Because Romeo has a little backbone on him already, pushing the other away so he can reclaim his spot near my little girl. *Arsehole.* "That might bring in bigger clients with heftier pockets. He'd be golden for the fathers trying to keep their hands clean."

"Maybe when he's eight." Malcolm nods; I can see the wheels already turning in his head. "London will kill me if it's before...she even made me sign an agreement on this."

"You tried teaching him?" The kid's only four and a mini replica of his father down to the attitude and brow-raising. Fuck, even the way he talks reflects the man. "That would be kind of cool."

"It is." Yeah, the lad isn't waiting, and his wife will have his head for it. "Now, back to your weirdness..."

"Speak up, arse. I don't have all day here."

"You remember my inauguration of the Hong Kong building?"

"I do. Why?"

"You said that Chicago would become your permanent home base?"

"That's because I plan to retire here...eventually." I shrug, watching the stubborn bloke trying to rouse my princess from sleep. He's playing with her toes and I want to punch the lad. "My plans have deviated a bit."

"Is this change happening any time soon?" Malcolm laughs now, but wait until London delivers his next child. A girl. "Need help?"

"When Lucas is ready, I'll be making some changes. Might settle the family here first, for a little while at least, and then move." At that, he nods in understanding. Since his mother went away and father decided to live in Florida, the kid's been with us, going to school during the day and being trained at night. Aurora was against it at first, but she sees and accepts his desire to carry on the family legacy.

And I agree. My sights are on a different city.

Much larger. Grander scale.

"Out East or West."

"East first—"

"Malcolm!" we hear the women yell and take off running.

Malcolm enters the kitchen first, coming to a stop in front of an already waiting London. "What's wrong? What happened?"

"It's time," is all she says, and he's picking her up and heading toward the front door; the man barely has enough of a conscious thought to ask that we watch Max for them. The front door slams shut after my confirmation, tires peel out, and through it all, I'm watching a smiling Gem.

"We'll be there soon, love,' I croon into her ear as I turn and place my hand on her flat stomach. "Just a few months."

"You know?"

"That's a silly question, love."

"A boy this time? To have a pair?"

"I'm happy with whatever the Lord blesses us with."

Her head turns in my direction and those hazel eyes are bright. She's smiling at me so beautifully. "I love you, Casper, and I'm so blessed to have met you."

"And I'm thankful to call you mine." Then, my mouth is on hers. Pouring every bit of the love I have for her into that kiss, because I do. I adore this woman.

She's my heart. My soulmate. The mother of my children.

And I'll never let a single day pass without her knowing this.

She'll always be my greatest treasure. My Gem.

The End For Now…

. . .

Turn the page for an Outtake of SIN as a special gift to you!
Elena xoxo

Outtake

LONDON

"**W**HAT THE FUCK?" everyone in the room hears Malcolm whisper-shout from his office. It's not in anger, but more of a weirded-out confusion that makes the nosy folk in this family head in his direction.

Of course, I'm the sacrificial lamb since I'm untouchable, with everyone else following close behind. Roe and Mariah are a few steps behind me, almost tiptoeing, and their men cover the rear.

Pun intended. Literally.

"Who the fuck left this in here?"

And while we're all lost, Javier is chuckling to himself. As if he knows what's happening.

"Babe? Are you okay?" I call out, announcing the brigade because the man hates people barging in. Except me. I get a total pass, and more so since he knocked me up. "What's wrong?"

However, before we can enter, the man himself appears in the doorway in all his devilish glory with a set of keys in his hand, clenching them tightly. "Is there something you'd like to explain, Twirl?"

My brows furrow, head shaking at his tone. "Not that I can think of. Why?"

"Are you missing anything? Maybe misplaced something?"

"My Chapstick, but I highly doubt you'd be upset by that." That's the only thing that comes to mind.

"I'll order five cases tonight."

I cringe. "Did I leave it on your desk?"

"No."

"Laundry?" Because that's happened a time or three, ruining a shirt or pair of pants, and all incidents damaged something of his. Not that he cared. I was more upset than he was.

"No." Malcolm shakes his head, less tense now. If I'm reading him right, he's becoming amused. "Think, baby. Are you missing *anything* personal."

"Did I leave out one of our—"

"No. Not that." This pregnancy has done a number on my memory. If it's lost in this house, ten times out of ten it's mine, but even so, I don't understand Malcolm. *What the hell did I do?*

And then the tears come.

I can't help myself.

I'm five months pregnant with the following uncontrollable symptoms: hungry, horny all day, and hormonal. I cry if the breeze is too hard while munching on my newest obsession: pickle chips.

I'm down to my last bag. Need to have more delivered.

"I'm sorry." It's a hiccup as I look up through watery eyes.

"What the hell is wrong with you," Mariah seethes at her cousin, coming to my defense, which makes me sniffle harder. "How can you pick on a pregnant woman?"

"I didn't—"

"Casper, give me your gun." That's Roe-Roe for you. After discovering her long lost love affair with the shooting range, she wants to shoot everything.

"Cool it or get the fuck out," he hisses, and another round of tears hit.

"But the barbecue!" Cause I'm also hungry.

"Oh for the love of..." my husband trails off, picking me up in his arms and walking me toward his display case inside the office. It's a creepy addition he had custom built a few months back.

The large trophy-like case takes up the entire wall to the left of the entrance and holds nothing but guns; old and new ones, some going as far back as the early 1900s which were given by a client as a gift. Then, right at the center of the case, he put his retired Desert Eagle.

The same one I used to shoot Alton.

Placing me back on my feet, Malcolm wipes the few tears that have fallen and kisses my lips. A quick yet passionate peck that makes me forget my name, and once I'm calmer, he turns me to face the glass structure. *Oh my God!*

"Hmmm," that's all I manage to get out, biting my bottom lip to fight back the laughter building. "That's..."

"So you recognize it?"

"Maybe."

"Maybe?"

"Kinda."

"Twirl?" When I don't answer, he turns me around and tips my chin up with two fingers. His lip is twitching and mine aren't any better. "How did an old and worn copy of *Emma* end up in there?"

"Are you mad? Because my answer depends on that."

"And my answer will depend on who did it."

Widening my eyes, I give him my most innocent expression. "Me?"

"Why are you framing this as a question?"

"Just in case your answer was a trick."

"Christ, baby." Then he's laughing, cracking up in a way I've never seen him do before. The serious businessman I know and love is gone, and this one is almost choking on his amusement. "London, sweetheart...you...I love you."

"I love you, too."

"And you owe me some money, Mrs. Asher." Javier says from behind me and I pout, because he was right. Malcolm isn't mad and is laughing, pulling me close to his chest and kissing my temple between chuckles.

"She owes you shit, and I should shoot you for this. This bullshit has your idiocy written all over it."

"I'm insulted." Javier's mock indignation should earn him a slap to the back of the head. He's a horrible actor.

"Try threatening him when you can breathe, babe."

Malcolm looks down at me, still wearing a grin. "Get the book out of my case, Twirl." Then, because the jerk loves to use my neediness against me, he leans down and places a kiss below my ear. "You'll pay for this tonight, baby. Over my knee and you'll count each one; ten spanks in total." I swallow hard and nod, afraid to speak. "Then, I'm going to fuck your ass slowly, agonizingly, because I want you desperate."

"Please," I whisper under my breath, hoping no one notices, but he does. His hum against my skin is the proof.

"You will beg. You will cry."

"Malcolm," I whine, at this point ready to say goodbye to everyone and take him upstairs. "Don't be mean."

"You will say my name, but more importantly...you will soak our sheets and my cock."

Okay. That's it.

"Everybody out."

"Lo-Lo, you okay?" Aurora asks, but the moment my eyes shift to hers, she gets it. I don't have to say a word because she's dragging Casper out of the room. "We'll be back in two hours. Have fun!"

God, I love her.

"I owe you double, now get lost." Javier nods, giving me a quick high-five before pulling a confused Mariah behind him. She's asking him what's going on as the door locks behind them, demanding to know why they had to leave, but I drown it all out the moment Malcolm takes ahold of my hips and grinds his hardness against my ass.

The world fades and it's just us.

"So beautifully needy." Gathering my hair, he moves it over to the opposite shoulder and nips my exposed neck, each bite a little harder than the last. "My perfect girl."

"Yes," I moan, pushing back against him. "All yours."

"To have and to hold." He walks us back to his desk, stopping once my hands find purchase on the edge.

"Always." I'm panting, skin prickling with excitement.

"In sickness and health." Strong hands wander across my chest, squeezing my tits before pinching each nipple through the thin cotton of my shirt.

"We will never part."

"Never."

"Good girl." His hands wander to the front of my maternity jeans and lowers them carefully over my belly, shimmying them down my hips and lower until they pool at the floor. I'm not wearing any underwear and he hisses out a curse in appreciation. "Now, bend over and count each one, Twirl. Let's not keep our guests waiting."

"But you...*fuck*! One!"

"I decide the when, sweet girl. Not you." His lips are at my ear, releasing a rough exhale over my skin. "This is to punish you for taking bets from an idiot." His hand comes down again, three times in rapid succession and he doesn't wait for my count. I can't. Not when he's squeezing the hot skin with one hand and rubbing my clit with the other. I'm wet and swollen and already close to the edge.

But he does that to me. Drives me insane.

Another two swats and my legs shake.

Another to the opposite cheek and my back arches.

I don't think I'll make it through the next three without coming, I'm right there and those tight circles he's rubbing over my bundle of nerves...

"Oh God!" I scream, every muscle in my body locking down as he spanks my pussy with three fingers. That's all it takes. I'm falling over the edge and crying, lost in the sensation as he gathers me in his arms and walks us around the desk to his chair.

We don't talk.

We don't move.

Malcolm lets me close my eyes and rest, giving me exactly what I've been needing for the past two hours.

An orgasm and then a nap.

And it's as I'm drifting off that I hear him, his deep baritone softly in my ear. *"I'm still taking your ass tonight."*

MY SINFUL VALENTINE

The only thing that can crumble a KING is disappointing his QUEEN. So what do my Beautiful Sinners do on Valentine's Day for their women? They spoil and lick and eat...

Worship: Malcolm and London
Say My Name: Casper and Aurora
One More: Thiago and Luna
You've Been Bad: Javier and Mariah
Pretty Doll: Alejandro and Solimar
Bonus:

BUY HERE
https://books2read.com/u/bprv29

NEW DARK ROMANCE

LITTLE LIES
BUY HERE: https://books2read.com/little-lies

I AM DARKNESS.
I AM SIN.
I AM YOURS.

A truth imprinted onto my skin—its sharp vines digging into my flesh as our bond strengthens with each shallow intake of breath my love takes. Her life is intertwined with the devil, a man who hungers for depravity and death, and yet, I bend my knee for her.

Only her. Always her.

She is mine and I will kill to protect. Kill to own her.

BEAUTIFUL SINNER SERIES

BEAUTIFUL SINNER SERIES
Each book is a standalone.
Now Live!

SIN (#1)
COVET (#2)
MINE (#3)
YOURS (#4)
RISQUE #5
OWN #6
Beautiful Sinner Spin-Off
CORRUPT
MY SINFUL VALENTINE
SAVAGE KISS

ABOUT THE AUTHOR

Elena M. Reyes is the epitome of a Floridian and if she could live in her beloved flip-flops, she would.

As a small child, she was always intrigued by all forms of art: whether it was dancing to island rhythms, or painting with any medium she could get her hands on. Her passion for reading over the years has amassed her with hours of pleasure, but it wasn't until she stumbled upon fanfiction that her thirst to write overtook her world.

She's a short and sassy Latina with an adorable pup, a kiddo that keeps her on her toes, and a husband who claims she'll cause him to go bald prematurely. Lol

Elena's Marked Girls.
Come join the naughty fun on Facebook.
Link: https://www.facebook.com/groups/1710869452526025/

NEWSLETTER SIGNUP:
http://bit.ly/2nHJxTI

Email: Reyes139ff@gmail.com

- facebook.com/ElenaMReyesAuthor
- x.com/ElenaMReyes
- instagram.com/elenar139
- bookbub.com/authors/elena-m-reyes
- amazon.com/Elena-M-Reyes/e/B00E3E26X8/ref=dp_byline_cont_pop_ebooks_1
- tiktok.com/@authorelenamreyes

ALSO, BY ELENA M. REYES

FATE'S BITE SERIES

LITTLE LIES

LITTLE MATE

HALF TRUTHS DUET

HALF TRUTHS: THEN

HALF TRUTHS: NOW

OMISSION PART 1 & 2

COME TO ME (2024)

THE HUNT (2024)

TERO (TBD)

BEAUTIFUL SINNER SERIES

Each book is a standalone.

Now Live!

SIN (#1)

COVET (#2)

MINE (#3)

YOURS (#4)

RISQUE #5

OWN #6

Beautiful Sinner Spin-Off

CORRUPT

MY SINFUL VALENTINE

SAVAGE KISS

ONE RULE

(BOOK #2 LIONEL TBD)

(Marked Series)

<u>Marking Her #1</u>

<u>Marking Him #2</u>

Scars #2.5

Marked #3

(I Saw You)

<u>I Saw You</u>

<u>I Love You #1.5</u>

Teasing Hands Duet

<u>Teasing Hands #1</u>

<u>Taunting Lips #2</u>

SAFE ROMANCE:

<u>Taste Of You</u>

<u>Doctor's Orders</u>

<u>Back To You</u>

STANDALONES:

Craving Sugar

<u>Stolen Kisses</u>